WHIT FRASER

COLD EDGE OF HEAVEN

A story of love and murder in Canada's Arctic

BOULDER
BOOKS

Dedicated to my mother,
Louise: a fiddler, a storyteller, and a Grant.

Library and Archives Canada Cataloguing in Publication
Title: Cold edge of heaven : a story of love and murder in Canada's Arctic / Whit Fraser.
Names: Fraser, Whit, author.
Identifiers: Canadiana 20220235600 | ISBN 9781989417454 (softcover)
Classification: LCC PS8611.R3875 C65 2022 | DDC C813/.6—dc23

© 2022 Whit Fraser

Published by Boulder Books
Portugal Cove-St. Philip's, Newfoundland and Labrador
www.boulderbooks.ca

Design and layout: Tanya Montini
Editor: Stephanie Porter
Copy editor: Iona Bulgin

Printed in Canada

We acknowledge the financial support of the Government of Newfoundland and
Labrador through the Department of Tourism, Culture, Arts and Recreation.

Funded by the   Financé par le
Government   gouvernement
of Canada   du Canada

CHAPTER 1

STORMS—MIND AND SEA

The three constables looked sharp in their uniforms, brown leather riding boots polished and spirits high after two weeks of training and briefings in Ottawa. Will Grant, Erik Zalapski, and Vincent Villeneuve had just stepped off the train in Quebec City and were dockside at the St. Lawrence River.

Their superiors were emphatic: the sworn duty of the three Mounties—to assert Canada's claim and sovereignty over the Arctic—was a national priority. The Arctic was described by many in Ottawa as a vast, uncivilized, unpopulated, frozen land of ice and snow. The Mounties had accepted the mission with a combined sense of adventure, duty, and optimism. Not to mention the money they would save during two years in near isolation in the Arctic, setting them up for future comfort.

All three men had survived the battlefields of a world war. They believed that the horrors and dangers in their young lives were finally behind them. In front of them, the CGS *Arctic* was rigged and ready to set sail the next morning, July 18, 1924. The men approached the gangplank.

Will Grant, from Nova Scotia, was comfortable around ships of all sizes. He sounded a note of caution. "Good Christ, boys. She's so low in the water, I doubt if we'll even get to the middle of the river. Forget crossing the Arctic Circle."

All three shook their heads as they considered the mastery required to stack and secure lumber, crates, and hundreds of 100-pound bags of coal so high on the deck that it made the bridge nearly indistinguishable.

"I hope the skipper knows what he's doing—"

"I assure you, Constable Grant, that there is no captain better or more knowledgeable on Arctic waters than Joseph Bernier."

The trio halted, snapped their heels together, and saluted Inspector Ransom O'Halloran, their commanding officer.

"Sir, I meant no disrespect." Will was mildly embarrassed.

"Well, Grant, I'll be interested to hear your views on the captain after you've met him and he drops you and your cargo on Devon Island." O'Halloran allowed several awkward seconds of silence to pass. "Now, chaps, come aboard, let me show you your quarters, and if you think the deck is cramped, be prepared."

The three would have roommates for the 3,000-mile Arctic odyssey: five other Mounties, bound for the settlements of Arctic Bay, Pond Inlet, and the first sovereignty post established at Craig Harbour a few years earlier.

The eight shared a long, cramped cabin just beneath the main deck, with bunks, a table, and benches where they ate, played cards, and whiled away the hours. Some tried to read, but the light was poor, whether it was a kerosene lamp or from the weak dynamo that laboured to produce electricity.

After 10 minutes in their cabin, everyone had the same idea:

spend as much time as possible on the open deck facing the wind. An unbearable stench filled the ship, a combination of rotten fish, dead rats, fuel, and God knows what else. Will gagged with the first breath.

The ship's crew and deckhands suffered even more than the Mounties; they were one deck below. The lower one went in the ship, the worse the stench became.

O'Halloran was in the forward cabins, with a contingent of government agents that included John Craig, a senior official of the Department of the Interior. Craig's wife, as well as various assistants, a photographer, a doctor, two surveyors, scientists, and an artist, was also on board.

During a pleasant afternoon briefing on the deck two days after leaving port, O'Halloran explained the pecking order.

"Together, we are the Annual Canadian Eastern Arctic Patrol, tasked with asserting Canada's sovereignty. Craig is in charge. He determines everything that happens on land. Bernier is the captain of the ship. He determines what happens on the water. In the past, they have clashed.

"Bernier has said for years that Canada needs to become more aggressive in asserting sovereignty. He's written Prime Minister Meighan and made speeches to politicians and business interests, especially mining companies, about our lack of sovereignty. The captain thinks we could lose the Eastern Arctic just as easily as we lost Alaska to the Americans."

O'Halloran paused. "I'm not sure how much of this they told you in the briefings, but the fact is, Joseph Bernier is probably Canada's greatest and least recognized explorer. He staked about one-third of this country. Every one of the high Arctic islands in the archipelago was claimed by Bernier in the name of Canada."

"We didn't get that from the Department of the Interior," Zalapski offered.

"Makes sense. There's a lot of petty political jealousy."

It was a pleasant afternoon, and the Mounties shared a growing sense of purpose and camaraderie. They were considered Canada's finest—men of mettle, strong, courageous, true, and, above all, proven.

The Great War and Ypres, Passchendaele, the Somme, hills known by numbers 60 and 70, and Vimy Ridge were imprinted on every Canadian mind. The war bound the Arctic mission rank and file together. Grant, Villeneuve, Zalapski, and Inspector O'Halloran had all served.

O'Halloran called the three constables on deck the following day. The day was as pleasant as the one before, as the ship headed northward toward the Strait of Belle Isle, now out of sight of all land.

"You all accepted the posting without question. Just like I expected you would. Nothing was said at the training session, but I think you should know why you were picked, and why you three are together," O'Halloran began. "For this post, I needed strong and loyal men, but also those with different skills.

"What you have in common is that none of you are city boys like me. I was raised in Winnipeg; my father is in the fur business. I know all about grading and buying fur, but I've never skinned an animal, let alone snared one. But you three know what it's like to endure the cold and storms."

Villeneuve, who was from northern Ontario, had experienced cold, snow, and hardship. So had Zalapski, a strong and dedicated prairie Ukrainian homesteader's son.

"And Grant has already reminded us of his Nova Scotia seafaring spirit. That's why you were picked, Grant, not for your sharp blue eyes and curly hair."

Their laughter felt genuine. O'Halloran was signalling that they could joke with one another.

The inspector and the constables had enlisted in the police force at nearly the same time, in 1920, when the former Northwest Mounted Police expanded into a national police force, with a new name, Royal Canadian Mounted Police.

O'Halloran had a distinguished military record. As a second lieutenant, he commanded an infantry platoon at the Somme on the Western Front and knew the trench horrors experienced by Villeneuve and Zalapski. For the latter part of the war, he had been transferred to counter-espionage and provost detachments, which brought him into police work.

Erik Zalapski was a stable and competent man, with good morals. He was also physically strong, and true to Saskatchewan's rural roots, not afraid of nature's elements and challenges. Unlike most policemen, he didn't complain about paperwork. His reports were meticulous; his investigations, organized and exact.

Vincent Villeneuve had been appointed senior constable for this posting because of his perceived natural leadership qualities. Physically, he was strong, forceful but measured, and focused in any crisis. He was a decorated hero from the infantry, and his background, working in mines and cutting timber in the northern Ontario bush, prepared him for the rigours of the High Arctic. He stood over 6 feet tall, with thick arms and chest. He shaved every morning, but by the evening, rather than a 5 o'clock shadow Villeneuve had thick black whiskers.

O'Halloran had more in common with Villeneuve and Zalapski than with Grant. They had served in different regiments and fought on different battlefields but had endured similar horrors in the trenches of France and Belgium. In every sense, they had faced their firing line, steeled in the rigours of combat, and overcome mud, rats, the stench of death, and constant shelling, and returned home as heroes.

When the war ended, they struggled to put it all behind and get on with the rest of their still-young lives.

Erik Zalapski worried about his family. He wanted to earn enough money to send home to his parents to help the suffering of their other son, whose mind had been damaged by the war. Vincent Villeneuve was a solitary man. The Force allowed him to live in his closed world, control his surroundings, and protect himself from the secret dreams and war demons that haunted him nightly. Will Grant knew that he didn't want to be a fisherman. He had been shopping around for a life and future when he answered the RCMP's call.

They were the kind of men Canada and its emerging national police force needed.

Will also had an impeccable war record. He had been a rigger in the Royal Flying Corps. Airplanes needed dry fields that lay well behind the front lines. As a fine craftsman, he repaired and replaced the bullet-torn fabric and fractured struts on Sopwith Camels and other biplanes, damaged by German pilots, and got them back in the air, sometimes within hours.

Will had run to meet crippled and shot-up airplanes as soon as they landed. Sometimes their propellers were still turning as he helped young comrades feel the ground under their feet.

Some laughed, some cried, some threw up, and others shook uncontrollably. Some immediately got drunk; others sought seclusion. Either way, within hours or days, they climbed back into the open cockpit, took off, and disappeared into the skies.

From the trenches, Zalapski and Villeneuve sometimes witnessed the aerial dog fights.

Despite their intense experiences, the constables talked little about the war. The few times they did, Zalapski and Villeneuve teased Will about being "a gentleman of the Air Corps."

The war now behind them, they were heading for a different front line—the High Arctic of North America. In diplomatic and political circles across much of Europe and the US, it was also no man's land.

The Canadian government embarked on its policy of Arctic sovereignty using the Eastern Arctic Patrols by the national police force. It fell to the RCMP to assert Canada's political and diplomatic position: occupy and defend.

The 165-foot-long, overloaded *Arctic* could barely reach 7 knots an hour. Most times, when winds were unfavourable, and steam and smoke belched from the single stack, Bernier could only do 3 or 4 knots.

A vicious storm slammed the *Arctic* a week out of Quebec City, at the midpoint of the Strait of Belle Isle, a treacherous body of water separating Newfoundland from Labrador. Winds reached 70 miles an hour and churned seas into 50-foot swells. As frightening as the wind was the torrential rain.

Only Captain Bernier and his crew had ever experienced anything like it.

Will turned to the others after they had all been thrown to the floor in the crowded cabin. "We could all die right here tonight, chaps." No one argued and no one panicked.

O'Halloran burst into the cabin. "Everyone on deck. Half the deck cargo has let go. We need to help."

He turned, scrambled up the ladder, and shouted as others came on deck, grabbing one another and any close object to hang on to.

"Some lines let go and 100-pound coal bags are washing around the deck, plugging the scuppers."

The eight Mounties fought their way forward. Some attached a lifeline but discovered that they couldn't move quickly enough to dodge the rain-soaked sacks of coal were careening around like 100-pound cannonballs. They had to depend on the rail to keep them from going overboard in the waves that crashed over the deck.

Will could see that the skipper had gotten all the sails furled; the wind and rain lashing his face told him that the ship had been turned straight into the gale. Ice-cold water almost paralyzed his hands. He clutched whoever he was close to, often not able to see a face, and felt them grab him for support.

Instinctively, the Mounties went with the flow and roll. As the ship listed or lurched fore or aft, port or starboard, it sucked the load violently in the same direction.

Suddenly everything seemed to stop still, as though the storm gods were deciding where to attack next.

A few seconds reprieve—precious seconds to grab one or two bags and heave them over the side. Then brace for the next pitch, plunge, and pause. On it went for hours. Will could see Villeneuve almost smiling, sometimes grabbing a bag in each hand, groaning, and shouting in French. He used his powerful legs and knees to propel the bags over the rail.

Heavy lumber and square beams were shooting about, awkward but easier to get between the rails and off the deck than bags of coal.

For three hours, the Mounties fought the cargo and the storm.

O'Halloran brought more news. "The engine room is flooded. There's no power and they're pumping by hand."

The Mounties worked even harder to throw the cargo overboard. The *Arctic* was sinking, an inch at a time. Berner had had precious little freeboard when they left Quebec City.

Will washed up against Zalapski.

"How are you doing?"

"Exhausted. I haven't got much left."

"Me either. Just hang in there and hang on."

By now, most of the coal bags had been tossed over the side, and waves that were washing over the foredecks escaped through the scuppers.

The wind subsided before the rain and, finally, daylight came, not with a sunrise but with deep grey rising clouds that announced that the worst was over. Swells would roll for days. The *Arctic* was still afloat, but now 6 inches lower in the water than when they had left port.

Bernier came on deck after daylight to thank all hands and provide an update. "The boilers are out and badly damaged. And the engine room is awash with a foot of water. We have no power. This ship needs to be hand pumped. It could take a week."

O'Halloran didn't hesitate. "We're here to serve, Captain."

Within minutes, eight Mounties began the tedious job of

hand pumping a badly damaged and flooded ship.

Ten hours a day, back and forth, push and pull, on a long wooden handle. Each stroke spitting about a half-gallon of dark water over the side. As predicted, the task took nearly a week.

Bernier, his engineer, and boiler crew waded and worked knee-deep in the slop, patching pipes, and finally getting a fire burning in the damp boilers. Word spread quickly. It would take two days before there was steam.

With a little wind and sails, they passed the whaling station of Killinik, at the end of Labrador, then headed slightly northeast into the Labrador Sea.

Bernier knew, as did all mariners, that the fastest way to the top of Baffin Island was by sailing across the Davis Strait, to the southwest coast of Greenland, and picking up the southerly Gulf Stream. A thousand miles beyond, north of the 70th parallel, winds and currents shift to favour a westward heading into the Northwest Passage, between Baffin and Ellesmere Islands.

Two days into the Labrador Sea, when he was confident that everything was under control, Bernier came back on deck to speak with the Mounties.

"Merci beaucoup. Thank you. I and the Eastern Arctic Patrol are in your debt." He turned to O'Halloran. "Inspector, I watched your men fight that storm. They may have saved the ship and all hands. You can be proud that you picked the right men for this important mission for Canada's future."

He poured drinks for everyone and proposed a toast to sovereignty. "Those damned Americans need to get the message: the North and the Northwest Passage is Canada's territory. To the Arctic! Our Arctic, Canada's Arctic."

"Yes, sir, Canada's Arctic."

Everyone shouted and drank.

Will looked at Zalapski and Villeneuve, convinced that they were invincible. That they would walk together forever.

CHAPTER 2

COLD WORLD, WARM HEART

Will sat on the foredeck, away from the stench. The seas were calm. He was writing a letter, which would be mailed when the *Arctic* returned to its homeport, in two months.

"Dear Brother Ed." Will knew that it would be shared with everyone, particularly his beloved niece, Louise, and nephew, Francis, both in their mid-teens. "When you receive this, I'll be in a land I know nothing about. I don't know when I'll hear or see any of you again. Two weeks ago, in a violent blow in the Strait of Belle Isle, I thought I might never see you again. More than once Pop MacKay's weathered face flashed through my mind."

The letter described the storm and the events that had brought him to the ship. Will felt connected with his grandfather, Will MacKay, who had sailed these same waters. Will was named after him, and, in his heyday, Will MacKay had shipped out of Canso, on the most easterly tip of mainland Nova Scotia.

His grandfather had a reputation all around the big bay, especially in Canso and the courthouse at Guysborough. More than 30 years ago, before Will was born, MacKay had been charged with mutiny. Will once heard the story in a folk song. A drunken captain ordered full sails in another "violent blow and raging seas."

MacKay, the first mate, knew that the move would take them to the bottom faster than to port. He confronted the drunken captain, who pulled a pistol. They fought on the rolling deck and MacKay came up the winner, with the pistol in his hand, and took command, locked the captain in a cabin, trimmed the sails, and got all hands to port safely.

A mutiny charge was laid, then dropped, by the grateful shipowners.

Will looked out over the rolling waves. His eyes watered as he returned to the letter.

"Ed, tell Pop that I admire what he did all those years ago. He had guts. He did the right thing. I hope I have his courage and good judgment."

The *Arctic* sailed into the Greenland port of Godhavn on Disko Island—a safe harbour above the Arctic Circle at 69 degrees north—on August 5, 22 days after leaving Quebec City.

Godhavn's history as a whaling and shipping centre went back almost two centuries, to when it first came under Danish rule.

Captain Bernier had been to Godhavn many times. He took on fresh water and additional staples and secured enough coal to replace the precious cargo that had gone over the side, plus what the ship had burned since leaving Quebec City. He was satisfied that they could adequately supply the northern posts and have sufficient fuel for the return voyage.

Will, Zalapski, and Villeneuve wanted to plant their feet on dry ground.

"Terra firma," said Zalapski, when they came down the gangplank.

Above the narrow streets and one- and two-storey buildings lay Greenland's magnificent scenery. Sweeping volcanic mountains and patches of ice and snow in deep ravines made long V-shaped gravel beds accumulated from millions of years of rock slides and, below that, gently sloping green meadows. The constables caught a glimpse of the landscape that would surround them for the next three years.

They walked first through the village, then up a slope. Their legs were wobbly. The town seemed to be moving.

They stopped to regain their bearings and balance. Zalapski sat on a rock and lit his pipe. Will joined him. Villeneuve remained standing. All looked out to sea toward the southwest in the general direction from where the *Arctic* had sailed only hours earlier. They had become used to seeing the icebergs hugging the Greenland coast. They had counted close to 50 in the bay. About a half-mile beyond the harbour entrance stood two huge white floating ice columns, seemingly stationary in the flow of the Gulf Stream. Will remembered passing them.

"Perhaps they're grounded," he said. Zalapski nodded. Villeneuve didn't seem interested. To Will, they stood like sentries, marking and protecting Denmark's sovereignty. He studied them and their contrast against the clear blue sky and water.

"You fellas enjoy the view." Villeneuve broke the silence. "I'm going to keep walking. I feel like being alone for a bit."

Will and Zalapski watched as he strode back toward the town, with careful shaky steps on the rocky trail. He looked bowlegged.

"He's going to find a whorehouse."

Will was shocked. His Christian upbringing dictated his response. "Judge not, lest ye be judged."

"I'm not judging, Will. He's headed to a whorehouse."

They enjoyed the sweeping view of the harbour and icebergs.

After several minutes, Zalapski offered an observation that Will could not take exception to. "Will, there's no smell. We've left behind that godawful stench. I can breathe and I can swallow."

Will nodded. "Enjoy the moment—it's waiting for us."

Bernier wasted no time in port. Within 36 hours, he had confirmed his coal resupply and taken on fresh water and other provisions. He checked and rechecked the busy port for vessels he knew well.

The 72-year-old captain, who for years had agonized over Canada's weaknesses and frequent laissez-faire attitude in the matter of Arctic sovereignty, knew that no place was as strategically important as Godhavn. He invited O'Halloran to the bridge and pointed out two American vessels that would soon be sailing into the Northwest Passage in search of fish, fur, or minerals.

Will and Zalapski bought wine and hard liquor to replenish their ration and stock up for the long months ahead. They returned to the ship just before the evening meal. Villeneuve came aboard two hours later in a quiet mood, carrying his heavy pack. His breath revealed that he had at least found a saloon.

Will, Villeneuve, and Zalapski spent the days in port walking the deck, playing card games, making small talk, and engaging in the never-ending, futile mission of searching for the source of the terrible stench, while at the same time trying to find a spot to avoid it.

Finally, one evening, about 10:30 p.m., as the sun briefly found its spot barely below the western horizon, Bernier rode the tide out of the harbour, between the stately icebergs, steering a northwest course across the Davis Strait to Baffin Island, a week away.

A map on the galley wall tracked the voyage. One pin marked the last port, Godhavn, and every morning, at 6 a.m., a second pin marked the location and progress of the *Arctic*.

In four days, the prevailing south winds and Gulf Stream currents pushed them 500 miles northwest into the Davis Strait. Day after day, Greenland's high mountains, fjords, and glaciers were visible from the starboard rail.

It was a rare day when the constables did not spot whales, often swimming in pods. Humpbacks were the most common, but the giant whales—the fins and blues, once prized by whaling ships for their blubber, baleen, and oil—were also plentiful.

Will's reflection was loudly interrupted by the sound of broken ice scraping the *Arctic*'s wooden bow, sides, and bottom. They had gone from clear sailing to near paralysis. A massive icefield lay ahead, blocking Baffin Island and Pond Inlet, 200 miles and two days away.

Bernier steered a northwesterly course, attempting to get around the pack. For several hours, they made headway. Then, they were stuck. Bernier waited overnight for a wind change or a miracle. Anything to dislodge some of the ice, give the vessel a few yards to manoeuvre.

In the morning, Bernier decided they'd blast their way out. Crew members went over the side with kegs of explosives. The charges were set on port and starboard sides. When the explosions rocked the boat, everyone felt it settle back in the water. Bernier nudged the *Arctic* fore and aft, creeping her bow forward until, at last, she was free. In an hour, he found looser ice and could steer a new course eastward, slowly and cautiously.

Bernier found the eastern edge of the icefield, followed a lead northwesterly, hoping to swing back toward Baffin Island, find open water, or at least manageable ice off the north coast of Baffin. The ice was fast to the shore. He couldn't afford to wait. It could be that way for weeks. He figured the north side of Baffin Bay would have far better conditions.

Bernier told Craig and O'Halloran that they needed to adjust and sail for Craig Harbour, and then Devon Island. Perhaps Pond Inlet and north Baffin would be clear on the return voyage in early September.

The first part of the hunch paid off. As the *Arctic* sailed toward Ellesmere Island, the ice loosened and almost disappeared. Four days and nights after being locked in pack ice, everyone was on deck. Land was in sight and high above the three white buildings on the hillside, whitewashed rocks spelled out *RCMP Craig Harbour*.

The Mounties were in a group by themselves. Will, Zalapski, and Villeneuve would set up a new post on Devon Island. Four others would replace their fellow human flagpoles in Pond Inlet and Craig Harbour.

O'Halloran stood in the middle, knowing that he had a serious problem. The Eskimo guides that had been hired for Devon Island were stranded in Pond Inlet. The mission would depend on his finding suitable replacements in Craig Harbour. The chances were slim, as there were no more than a dozen guides there at any given time. He needed excellent hunters, and he needed an interpreter.

Someone commented on the rocky reefs, uncomfortably close to the sides of the overloaded vessel.

"Don't worry, lads. There's not a man alive who has spent more time in these waters than our captain," said O'Halloran reassuringly.

O'Halloran looked toward the bridge. Bernier was looking straight ahead, silent as usual.

"He's made a lot of history and is still making it. Some day, someone will write about it. You can be sure that he's one of the main reasons all of us are here. Them too." O'Halloran pointed to the cluster of other passengers on the port side, including expedition leader and senior government man John Craig. The men in both groups had become acquainted in the past month. None had become close and there was no reason to do so.

If any in either group were surprised at the scene that lay before them on the shore of Craig Harbour, it would be because there was so little to see. The white buildings on the gravel beach made up the RCMP detachment.

Suddenly Will heard the anchor going down. Three motorboats followed. Every man on the shore had been waiting for this moment for a full year. The excitement was contagious.

The captain had a ritual and his crew knew it by heart. The first to go ashore were those that had business there. O'Halloran, the replacement officers, Craig, Craig's wife, the doctor, and the scientists were in the first boat.

Everyone pitched in. They worked the tides. The cargo was off-loaded from the *Arctic* on a rising tide. These 24-foot open motorboats, with deep throaty Acadian engines, hit the beach as the tide reached full height. As it retreated, the boats were high and dry and everyone, including a dozen Eskimos, hauled crates, barrels, boxes, bundles, and bales up the beach.

For the second time, Will, Zalapski, and O'Halloran were struck by Villeneuve's brute strength. When a lift or a pull was too much for mortal men, Villeneuve charged at it, bull-like, to get it off the gravel onto a skid, or simply over his back, where he carried it up the beach.

After four high tides and off-loading for two days, the *Arctic* sat considerably higher in the water.

O'Halloran's luck was better than Bernier's. He found highly recommended hunters and guides, one with a wife to sew Arctic clothing and boots. They had only half a day to gather their belongings, including dogs, sleds or qamutiks, kayaks, tents— everything they owned.

Will stood at the ship's rail, gawking at the bustle onshore.

Two men, two small children, and one woman caught his eye. *Our guides? Will the woman be coming with us?*

The two men loaded bundles into the motorboats, checking each carefully to ensure that nothing was missing, forgotten, or lost. Then they walked up the beach and dragged huskies by the scruff to the shore. Not natural swimmers, the dogs protested at the water's edge. They were yanked over the gunwales of two of the boats and tethered on a short rope. It was quick and noisy work.

The first boat pulled alongside the *Arctic* and the taller of the two men climbed the ladder to the deck. He reached down toward the little boy, who had scampered up the rope ladder. It was clear that it was his father who scooped him up by his arms for the last few feet and over the rail onto the deck.

The woman was next. Will was puzzled—he had counted two children on the shore and there was only one in the boat. He looked at the woman as she clutched the ropes and set her feet on the ladder. Her back was large and moving. Her oversized hood held a small child. He would learn that the parka with the large hood for carrying a baby or child was called an amauti.

The other man was in the bow of the second boat, along with more of their bundles and a dozen dogs. A third motorboat appeared from the stern with more dogs tethered across the aft deck. Finally, the last guide climbed the ladder, carrying a large bag holding dog harnesses and ropes. The last items to be taken on board were the kayaks.

O'Halloran, who had arranged for their hire only yesterday, stepped forward.

He offered his hand. "Welcome." He shook hands with each, turned, and gestured. "Vill-en-euve," he introduced, as the big Mountie shook hands all around. O'Halloran grabbed Zalapski's forearm and had him step forward. "Za-lap-ski." Zalapski shook hands.

Will didn't know why, but he was relieved when O'Halloran simply introduced him as Will. He shook hands first with the men, then the woman, who blushed and turned her face slightly away, and finally with the little boy who was standing by her side. Will liked the way the boy grabbed his hand and gave one firm pump.

The older of the three, the dog boss from the third boat, stepped forward.

"I am Pudlu. This is Teemotee. Naudla." He tapped Naudla's bulging back. "Piapik." And he touched the boy on the back of his head. "And Kootoo."

Everyone shook hands again, the constables saying their name first and then acknowledging the name of their new mates: Pudlu, Teemotee, Naudla.

The small group again checked their belongings, making sure that nothing would go over the side. The captain gave a long pull on the whistle. Steam and smoke belched out of the stack, and they were under way.

The men on shore waved. They knew as those on the ship knew that this would be their last contact with the outside world for at least a year—depending on the ever-unpredictable ice. From the deck, every hand waved back and every English-speaking voice offered three customary "hip, hip, hooray" cheers.

It was early evening. Their next destination lay two days' travel southward, across Jones Sound, into Baffin Bay, and around the east side of Devon Island at the entrance to Lancaster Sound.

O'Halloran spoke to Pudlu. "Come, we have a place for all of you."

Pudlu, Teemotee, Naudla, and Kootoo followed O'Halloran down about six steps toward the cabins. Will was sure that the first sound came from the little boy. "Arrrggh, Arraggh!"

No one needed an interpretation. Gagging has a universal sound. The little boy shot up the stairs. The others followed.

"We camp here." Pudlu pointed to the space below the bridge where coal, crates, and lumber had been stacked only two days earlier. O'Halloran nodded. They pitched their tent on the deck. Will had noticed that the tents at Pond Inlet were secured to the ground with large rocks. He was not surprised when Pudlu and Teemotee pulled bags of coal out of a bundle for the same purpose.

The captain watched from the bridge, amused.

Will woke early the next morning and left the cabin as quickly as possible. He wondered, did he—did all of them—stink also? Had they become oblivious to the stench clinging to themselves?

He had noticed several times when he woke during the night that the ship seemed still. On deck now with a mug of hot coffee in his hand, he was amazed at the stillness of the waters of Baffin Bay.

It was also quiet. The dogs were sleeping in the sun.

On the port side, Pudlu sat on a stool. These were familiar surroundings for him. In his hand was a small black book. Will approached him. Pudlu looked up.

"Good morning."

Pudlu smiled. "Ullaakuut. Good morning."

Will repeated deliberately, "Oo-laa-kuut."

"Eee." Pudlu nodded. "Yes."

Will gestured toward Pudlu's book. He passed it over.

Will studied symbols that resembled shorthand. Among the brief training and familiarization sessions the Mounties had been given were presentations from Catholic and Anglican clergy who had carried out missionary work across the Arctic. He knew that in recent years an Anglican missionary, Edmund James Peck, had adapted a written word for the Eskimos from a syllabics system developed years earlier in Manitoba for the Cree language by another missionary, James Evans.

Eastern Arctic Inuit had quickly accepted Peck's language system. It was easy to learn and teach, as each symbol represented a distinctive sound. Parents could teach it to children and often children taught each other.

Pudlu had moved to the Pangnirtung station during his teen years, hunting, trapping, guiding, and whaling. As he was one of Peck's first converts and students, it was natural that he be given a bible. He learned enough English to become a trusted and sought-after translator.

Will held Pudlu's bible, thumbing the pages. Will reached into his pocket and brought out his own, similar in size and shape, also showing signs of wear.

The two smiled at one another. Will found a place to sit nearby. Both men spoke to God in their own tongues and voice. On the bridge above, Captain Bernier watched them.

In time, Will started toward the cramped quarters, and Bernier met him near the rail, midship.

"Mr. Grant, I saw you making friends with Pudlu. May I give you some unsolicited advice?"

"Of course."

"I know Pudlu. He's sailed with me and worked for me. He's a fine man, the kind you want to stay close to and trust. In my experience, people who work closely with their local guides are those best able to cope in this tough place."

"Thank you, sir. I'll remember that."

CHAPTER 3

SEASONS CHANGE, PEOPLE CHANGE

For two days, Will felt seasick on a deadly calm, frozen ocean. They were still in ice, but it was broken and navigable.

The swirling in his gut began the moment they sailed from Craig Harbour. This was not because of the sea or the stench, but rather an old-fashioned mix of fear, apprehension, excitement, and the knowledge that one's life is about to change forever.

He could neither eat nor sleep. Villeneuve and Zalapski were equally distracted. Alone, Will paced the foredeck. An hour earlier, O'Halloran had confirmed that they would reach Dundas Harbour early the next day, Tuesday, August 19. Will stayed on deck to watch the sunset.

He retreated to the shared cabin and put the last of his travelling clothes in his duffle and footlocker. He dozed briefly, then returned to the deck. The sun was on the eastern horizon. Ten or 15 miles in the distance, reaching high above the horizon, he could see the sheer rock cliffs, mountaintops, and the ice cap of Devon Island.

Only hours away, the crew prepared for landing and off-loading.

As at Craig Harbour, there was a system and a tight deadline. Bernier knew that he would be there for 10 to 12 days. The Mounties needed to unload and build a post.

O'Halloran summoned the Devon Island patrol on deck. Craig was with him. The ship was a mile offshore, still steaming. A vast rocky beach stretched before them.

It's not really a harbour at all. To Will, it was more like a sweeping cove, slightly sheltered on the east and west sides by sloping, rocky points.

Directly up from the beach, a wide mountain valley stretched as far inland as one could see. A stiff breeze was blowing. The sun had given way to overcast skies. Breakers were crashing on the shore. His upbringing on Chedabucto Bay had taught him about wind and water. "I expect it's going to get rough beaching a boat in that."

"You're right," said Craig. "But that's not the plan. That's to be the post, not the landing site. We will land and off-load in a little cove beyond that westerly point."

Half an hour later, the anchor dropped and, within minutes, two motorboats were lowered and bobbed in the water, motors chugging and sputtering, a sound Will found comforting.

Will, Villeneuve, Zalapski, O'Halloran, and four other Mounties were in the first boat; Pudlu and Teemotee in the second, surrounded by the first load of huskies. They came ashore at almost the same time.

The cove was sheltered and safe. Pudlu and Teemotee led the chained dogs up the hill to the base of a 60-foot rock wall. There they staked out long, secure tethers and tied the dogs, with several feet of chain to allow movement but no contact.

The Mounties quickly had the first load of crates out of the launch and moved them well above the high-water mark. The motorboat with three Mounties went back for the second load. Will was among those remaining onshore.

Pudlu, about 150 yards farther up the grade, motioned for Will to join him. "Look. Real old Inuit camp. A long, long time ago."

Pudlu pointed to rock circles in the gravel on the flattened mossy soil. The outline of tent rings showed where, long ago, someone had placed rocks in a circle to secure a skin tent. Many boulders were partially covered with decades or even centuries of mosses and blowing topsoil. "Look at the mountain. Do you see the woman's face and tattooed chin? We call this place Talluruti." It took Will a few moments to trace the rock shapes and shadows, but then the face became as clear as though it had been sketched.

"Incredible." People had been here eons ago. No Englishman discovered Dundas Harbour. Just as Columbus had not discovered America.

"In our old stories, we tell of the times we believed we were the only people in the world." Pudlu looked at the mountain's tattooed face.

Will promised himself that he would take Bernier's advice but, more than that, he would start a journal to note Pudlu's observations. The Arctic people who had learned to survive in these harsh conditions sought shelter from the elements, but Will's government bosses were doing the opposite by challenging the elements. Survival was secondary. Being visible was paramount.

The Dundas Harbour detachment wouldn't be visible to those plying the Northwest Passage if it was set up in a sheltered cove. But on exposed beach, it would be difficult to miss, especially with Canada's Red Ensign flapping in the stiff Arctic winds and the name spelled out high on the hillside with big whitewashed rocks as he had witnessed at Craig Harbour.

With the Mounties bound for Pond Inlet, the government men, and the ship's crew, the off-loading went faster than O'Halloran and the others, including Will, had expected.

Cooks brought hearty noon meals ashore for everyone. Evening and morning meals were eaten on board the *Arctic*. Most of the Arctic cargo consisted of building supplies and lumber to build the detachment. The walls and floors for the main detachment building and storehouse had been prefabricated in Quebec of 12- and 8-foot panels that were heavy and awkward to handle but saved precious weeks in the construction process.

On the second day, the wind shifted offshore. The beach was quiet. About half of the panels could be dropped directly in front of the location of the detachment and hauled 150 yards to the building site rather than over the ridge from the cove, saving more time.

It was Will's turn, with Villeneuve and Zalapski, to work in the landing boat. Panels came out of the hold of the ship and deckhands with pulleys and lifts lowered and placed them lengthways across the gunwales, where they were tied down. Suddenly, someone was shouting on the deck.

"Eureka, we found it. Eureka, we found it!"

In one of the holds, somewhere, somehow, this year or last, someone had left sacks of fish that had rotted. Making matters worse, it was in a hold closest to the boilers.

Will smiled at Zalapski. "We knew how bad it was, but it did give us something to talk and joke about, and remember."

The main off-loading was placed on hold. Men with faces

wrapped in heavy cloths frantically shovelled the rotten fish into barrels and dumped the whole damn lot over the windward side as quickly as possible. In the landing boat, an enthusiastic "Hip, hip, hooray" went up. The captain wore a broad smile.

By the third day, everything for the detachment was off the *Arctic*. Both beaches were lined with panels, lumber, crates, and barrels. The Mounties worked as men possessed.

Pudlu and Teemotee relocated their tents to a sandy, smooth knoll just above the main beach on the east side of the mile-long gravel shoreline. A small stream from the mountainside was close by. This was Naudla's territory. Her camp and tent were secure. She cooked, chased the two kids, and picked ripe blackberries that grew on tiny vines that clung to the soil.

Down the gravel slope from her, four- and six-man crews struggled with the panels: one at each corner, two in the middle on the bigger ones. Some had shoulder straps and laboured over rough terrain with each section. Others hauled boards, roofing material, barrels of nails, flour, sugar, gasoline, kerosene, gunpowder, ammunition, and more wood. Everything needed to build a detachment and then survive for three years had to be hauled and stored.

The storehouse was about a quarter-mile from the detachment to keep marauding bears at bay and give the Mounties and their guides a chance to defend themselves from any four-legged intruders.

Naudla watched four Mounties lay large flat stones for the cornerstone and foundation for the storehouse. Another three men followed with packs on their backs. Behind them, four more with another prefabricated wall section.

WHIT FRASER

Will carried a 100-pound barrel of flour on his back. His legs were throbbing. This was his fourth trip across the esker, and it was still early afternoon, with many hours and trips to go before bedtime. The fact that it was flour made the load a little easier. He enjoyed baking and thought of freshly baked bread and bannock. The bannock that northern people ate was the same recipe he had grown up with in St. Francis Harbour.

The rifle shot startled him back to reality, causing him to lose his balance. He looked around. Everyone had dropped their burdens. They were looking in every direction, startled. *Where had it come from? Had someone been shot?*

Will knew that sound: it was a high-powered rifle and it was very close.

A second shot echoed across the landscape.

Since Bernier had dropped anchor, the west to east moderate winds continued pushing broken ice pans eastward. Two polar bears, unnoticed, had moved from the ice onto the beach.

Will's eyes swept across the beach where the foundation crew stood, bewildered. Then he looked beyond them toward the beach and saw, about 100 yards from where they were standing, a polar bear slumping forward. Its front legs slowly spread forward and outward. Its hind legs and quarters collapsed backward, leaving it spreadeagled and belly down, dead.

Will and the others looked beyond the first bear closer to the shore and watched a second bear stagger and then make a feeble attempt to run, but its heart was draining of blood. Its legs folded and it dropped.

On the little knoll up the beach eastward, Naudla got to her feet. She had been lying on her belly over a bundle of furs and canvas. When she stood and turned to Piapik and Kootoo, Will could see a high-powered rifle in her hand. She set it aside and hugged the kids.

Along the beach stood more than a dozen shocked and grateful strong-armed men.

Pudlu and Teemotee moved quickly. Each ran to a downed bear. They stopped 10 feet away to observe, then moved closer. Will watched Teemotee move a front leg with his foot and saw blood coming from the chest. He and Pudlu quickly confirmed that both bears were dead, both shot clean through the heart. They walked up the slope to join and congratulate Naudla.

O'Halloran was the first of the Qallunaat, or white men, to respond. When he reached Teemotee and Naudla's tent, he offered her his hand and his gratitude. Pudlu translated.

"You saved someone's life. We are all very grateful."

In a moment, all the others on shore joined him, including Craig and his senior clerk. They too offered a hand in appreciation and admiration. Will, Zalapski, and Villeneuve joined the growing circle.

Will saw a strength of character he had never witnessed in anyone. She was calm and confident. She needed neither praise nor attention. The bears were a threat. There was no time to look for help.

O'Halloran wasted no time in getting down to business. Desperate to show gratitude, he said to Naudla, through Pudlu, "I want to buy the skins and pay you to make clothing for the detachment. A month's pay for each skin and a month for sewing."

That meant about $30 in total. He thought it fair, given that Pudlu and Teemotee earned 50 cents a day.

Pudlu translated. Naudla smiled and raised her eyebrows, a gesture meaning "Yes."

Will watched Teemotee, who stood close to his wife. The kids were at his thigh. He was looking at her proudly, with unconditional love and respect. Will felt a pang of envy.

He waited a few more minutes until the brass backed off. Then, left with Villeneuve and Zalapski, he simply offered his hand and said one of the first words he had learned. "*Nakurmiik.* Thank you."

She smiled back, raised her eyes, and looked into his.

It didn't last a second, but the glance jolted Will's heart.

Will turned to Pudlu, gave him a friendly elbow in the ribs, and smiled. "I thought you were the best hunter."

Pudlu enjoyed the joke. He laughed and poked his chest. "Pudlu is the best hunter. Naudla best shot."

They all laughed.

The cue to get back to work came from Naudla, Pudlu, and Teemotee. She took the kids and went back to the small berry patch. Her husband and his brother-in-law opened a canvas bag and took out knives and sharpening stones. They went back down the slope toward the bears.

As they skinned and butchered over the next few hours, everyone else stepped in for a closer look. Will paced the distance to where the second bear was shot. He had long ago mastered a 3-foot stride to gauge distance. He counted 310 yards to the first, and then paced another 35 yards to the second.

Will lingered with Pudlu as he skinned and butchered the larger bear. Pudlu's knife skills impressed Will, particularly his precision in removing the claws from the massive paws. Each cut was clean, bloodless, the skin unbroken. He was like a surgeon.

Will used his tried-and-true one-step-equals-3-feet measure and estimated the animal's height to be well over 10 feet. He examined the paws and claws, spreading them apart. He spread his own fingers wide on each hand and joined them together at the tips of each thumb. The spread would be over a foot wide; his extended hands, finger, and thumbs together barely matched one massive paw.

Pudlu and Teemotee cut and filled tin tubs and buckets with chunks of meat, most of which would become dog food. This would come in handy, considering that the dogs devoured about 30 pounds of meat a day—more than that when they were working. Close to 2 tons of meat piled up on the beach. Neither dogs nor people would go hungry this winter.

The ship's cook, always in search of fresh meat, filled two large pails with chunks to boil up for the next day's evening meal.

In the days ahead, Naudla's marksmanship became part of daily conversations among the three Mounties. Zalapski naturally put it in the context of their months in the trenches. "What do you say, Vee-Vee, almost 400 yards? She could have been a sniper."

Silence. Villeneuve looked back, blank, then snapped, "Don't talk about snipers."

Will and Zalapski locked eyes just long enough to ask each other, silently, what's that about?

Bernier was pacing the deck. He had heard the shots and had the full story, but his concern was on the increasing ice floe. That night he told O'Halloran, Craig, and the others that they needed to leave soon. If the ice thickened, if it jammed up at the easterly mouth of the Baffin Bay between Devon and Baffin Islands, he would risk being overwintered.

The next morning at daybreak, the pace picked up. Everyone had been working as hard as they could, but worked harder, took fewer and shorter breaks, carried heavier loads. The captain assigned more men to shore detail to get the detachment—where the Mounties would live and work from—erected and closed in. Supplies such as coal, gasoline, and lumber could remain at the landing areas and be transported later by dog teams and qamutiks.

After 10 days, on the last day of August 1924, Bernier weighed anchor and blew the *Arctic*'s whistle. From the deck, crew and passengers shouted traditional cheers of farewell. Will wondered if the cheer was a goodbye or an expression of joy, realizing that they were at least on board and moving south, and not on land or ice-locked—at least not yet.

On the shore, six adults and two children lined up to wave goodbye. An official photograph, requested by O'Halloran, was taken for the record.

The image burned in Will's mind the instant the shutter clicked. On his right, Constables Vincent Villeneuve and Erik Zalapski, and from his far left, Pudlu, Teemotee, and, beside him, Naudla. The children were in front of their mother and father. Will pledged to himself that in the years ahead, he would find a copy of that photo, because he was next to Naudla. He couldn't yet admit his growing attraction to Naudla—not even to himself.

The group watched the ship for several more minutes as it disappeared behind the easterly cape of Dundas Harbour.

In the drawer of O'Halloran's small writing desk were a half-dozen letters that Will and the others had written. Their families would know of the adventure that had brought them to this forsaken coastline, but they would not hear another word for a very long time.

Villeneuve gave his first direct order. "We need to get back to work."

"Where do we even start?" Zalapski looked at the array of partially finished buildings, scattered supplies, and barking dogs.

"The buildings, including the shithouses."

Teemotee and Pudlu had laid the floor for their small cabin. They began raising the walls. Villeneuve and Zalapski moved inside the detachment and uncrated and assembled a large cast-iron stove. They cut holes in the ceiling and roof for the stovepipe, covered the inner walls with a thick burlap-like material designed to stop drafts and provide dead air space for insulation. In this environment, the insulation fell into that oft-used better-than-nothing category.

They had been warned not to install the burlap near the stove. Two years earlier, Mounties at Craig Harbour had barely escaped their detachment alive with essential equipment when the burlap caught fire. Their water extinguisher was frozen. That crew spent several months living in a small blubber shack.

Will took on the second priority and proclaimed himself a shithouse architect. He carefully chose locations, just behind the detachment, with a clear view of the sunrise over the bay and ice.

With pick and shovel, he began digging the first hole. Barely a foot down, he discovered frozen ground. He chipped with a pick and chisels. It was slow and tedious work. Finally, he decided that 3 feet would have to do—maybe daily warm deposits would melt it a little deeper. The shithouses were fine structures: cozy, 3 feet by 3 feet with comfortable seating, a spectacular view, and no apparent concern about overflow.

The next morning, as he put the finishing touches on privy number two, Pudlu stopped by with a coil of half-inch rope and sage advice. The structures needed to be anchored firmly at all four corners lest they scatter across the icy ocean or tundra. Hundred-pound rocks made perfect anchors.

The daily routine came naturally. The chemistry between the three Mounties was good. The relationship with their hired guides was equally convivial. There was much work to do. No one had time to be bored or think about the world outside. Their world had shrunk to eight people, including two happy kids. September slipped by in a flash.

By October, the number of daylight hours diminished significantly. The temperature dropped well below freezing at night. And, as though on schedule, on the first day of the month, it snowed. Ice had already formed along the shore.

Will opened the detachment door to look at the ever-changing landscape. Six months of winter had set in.

"Think Bernier made it back to Pond and the south?"

It was a rhetorical question. Their isolation went far beyond eight people alone on Canada's fifth-largest Arctic island. It was not knowing, and having no way of knowing, what was happening with anyone else anywhere in the world. They were the same as the ancient people in Pudlu's legends.

There was no one else in the world—just them.

Will wondered about his family in Nova Scotia and how the Toronto Maple Leafs were doing. Villeneuve wondered if the war was still over and if the Germans were defeated. Zalapski's concerns focused on his brother Charles, who suffered from the horrors of the battlefield. Was he recovering or had he lost his mind completely?

Their guides, on the other hand, showed no interest in anything beyond the shoreline.

Will remembered the barrage of questions from the Mounties at Craig Harbour when they had stepped ashore. "Did the Leafs or the Canadiens win the Stanley Cup?" And hundreds more questions, which required short, clear answers. "The Canadians won. Yes, Mackenzie King was still prime minister and prohibition had ended in Alberta." And above all, "Yes, the war is still over."

A routine was established, and Villeneuve was uncompromising. The constables rose at 6 a.m. and worked until 6 p.m. Chores were divided and assigned. They shared cooking duties, although Will was the baker.

They washed and shaved daily, and cut each other's hair at least once a month. They heated buckets of water and did weekly laundry. All agreed that cleanliness was paramount in the detachment. The other buildings and surroundings, and equipment that their lives depended upon, had to be maintained, well stored, and protected.

As senior constable, Villeneuve was the administrator. He accounted for every staple that was consumed, the volume, and when. When Pudlu wanted a half-pound tin of tobacco, Villeneuve deducted $1.19 from his daily pay of 50 cents.

A sense of satisfaction pervaded the group as October waned. They were adjusting to their new routines.

The number of hours of daylight had decreased to a few hours a day, but the detachment was shipshape and early patrols were being planned. They'd do short trips of 8 to 15 miles, close to shore, opportunities to exercise the dogs and give the Mounties experience in handling, harnessing, and managing the sometimes uncooperative huskies. Pudlu and Teemotee were fine teachers, with the simplest rules for maintaining control.

"Show him who's boss," Pudlu advised, as he whacked a stubborn or snarling husky across the head or hind with the handle of his long hide whip.

In the evening, Will and Erik talked, played cards, or read. Each had brought a bundle of books, and the force had supplied a library.

Villeneuve was not a reader and had lost all interest in playing cards. He often sat silently on his bunk or in a chair close to the fire. If the drafts were open, he stared at the flames and burning coals as though he saw something in their embers.

The first Arctic blizzard came with Halloween.

Zalapski was the first to comment as the wind shook the building. "It's even too damn wild for Halloween ghosts."

The wind increased by the minute. Windows and doors rattled. The downdrafts rumbled in the stovepipe like mini thunderclaps. Will opened the door and peered out. The driving snow lashed his face. He could not identify a single landmark or even see as far as the shithouse.

The burlap was no match for an Arctic gale. The wind seemed to rip through the walls and under the door. This was their blizzard baptism. As whiteouts go, it was not a severe gale, but the barometer against which they would measure all future storms.

Undeterred, they loaded more coal into the stove and felt relatively secure.

"Are either of you worried about the boats?"

"They're well lashed down and tied to heavy rocks," Villeneuve replied.

Zalapski added, "Pudlu and Teemotee put bigger rocks on top."

Outside, the wind raged and howled, but, inside, Will and Erik Zalapski sensed the silent darkening clouds gather and build in Vincent Villeneuve.

All night, Villeneuve thrashed in his bunk. Once his scream scared Will.

Zalapski heard it too. "Jesus, what is that? Are you okay, Vee-Vee?"

No response, just stirring.

A few minutes later, the big man got up and banged about in the darkness.

Will listened. They had all seen death and destruction—the war might have been over for six years, but with every passing month, lingering shell shock became more evident among many who had served.

Will feared that, in time, the storms inside their shared living space would be more dangerous and unpredictable than the gale-force winds and whiteouts outside.

Several more times that night, Villeneuve got up and banged about in total darkness.

Will rose as usual at 6 a.m. and lit the oil lamp hanging over his bunk. He was surprised to see Villeneuve sitting on his bunk. He was wearing his parka, arms folded and his hands tucked under his armpits.

"Are you okay, Vee-Vee?"

There was no immediate response. Will asked again.

"I'm fine. The wind kept me awake."

Zalapski poked the coals in the stove, stuffing in more coal and kindling to bring the room to life again. He had lit the second lamp. Villeneuve still didn't move, and wouldn't for some time. Finally, Villeneuve fell back in his bunk and curled up, arms folded, in a fetal position. He seemed to have fallen asleep.

Will and Zalapski looked at one another. They would talk about this moment, alone. Zalapski's eyes said that he hadn't slept either and he shared Will's worry.

The congeniality and expertise of the guides hastily recruited by their inspector at Craig Harbour allayed the Mounties' private fears, at least partially.

The true leader was the translator, Pudlu. He was multi-talented: the best hunter, sailor, guide, craftsman, mechanic, and, to everyone's delight, musician. Neither Teemotee and Naudla and their children, Kootoo, about five years old, and Piapik, about two years younger, spoke English.

Within days of arrival, the kids didn't have one uncle, but four. The Mounties adored the kids, made little boats to sail in the puddles along the barren and rocky shoreline, and skipped stones or kicked the rubber ball that Will had instinctively tucked into his duffle just before they embarked Montreal.

Truth is, the Mounties were less intimidated by an unfamiliar language around the kids. They could talk to them in English, see a bird and ask, "what's that?," listen to the reply, and in this new and difficult language repeat it slowly and try and remember. It was far less embarrassing to ask Kootoo how to count to 10 than a highly recognized camp leader, hunter, and guide such as Pudlu.

Early after they had arrived at Dundas Harbour, Will visited Pudlu's tent, where he was carving small ivory and soapstone figures for a chess set. The 32 pieces were magnificent, unlike anything Will had ever seen or held in his hand. Sixteen were snow-white ivory, carved from the tusk of a walrus or narwhal. Sixteen more were jet-black serpentine soapstone, common in the Cumberland Sound area of eastern Baffin Island.

The pawns were seal pups. Polar bears served as rooks. The knights stood out with their tusk armour and fierce walrus faces. The head of a breaching whale was the bishop and a man and woman were king and queen.

Will casually asked, "What do you call the pawns in Eskimo? Can you teach me some words?"

"Good idea, Will. The first word you have to learn is *Inuit*. It means the people. In-nu-eat."

"In-new-eat."

"Close. We've never called ourselves Eskimos. That's someone else's word for us."

Will tried a second time. "In-nu-eet."

"Much better. We're Inuit, and as one man, I'm an Inuk. I hope that someday all people will know us for who we are—Inuit."

CHAPTER 4

INTO THE UNKNOWN

The logbook on November 2, 1924, underlined the start of a new phase at the detachment. *The sun set today and will not rise for another 10 weeks!*

It wasn't the black of 24-hour darkness that surprised Will and the others, as much as the mystic light.

The sun stayed below the horizon, but on days when the sky was at its clearest, which was usually the coldest days, dusk and dawn extended their arms, joined hands, and embraced Devon Island and the Far North with a magnificent glowing Arctic twilight.

After the storm subsided, the three Mounties marvelled at how it had changed and reshaped the landscape. Between the main building and their neighbours, a new hill was crafted from a long, massive snowdrift. Kootoo and Piapik were enjoying sliding together on a handmade sled. Near their cabin, Pudlu and Teemotee cut snow blocks from another snowdrift.

Will was surprised by the extent to which the wind had driven and packed the snow. His foot did not sink. He left barely a trace of a footprint.

The sled stopped near him. He took the rope from Kootoo and ran with the kids up the drift and hill—all three of them laughed the whole way. He turned them and with a gentle push sent the sled southbound toward the beach.

"Oo-laa-koot," said Will, somewhat pleased with himself.

"Ullaakuut" was the friendly simultaneous response from Pudlu and Teemotee.

Will could see that the snow blocks were being placed around their cabin for insulation. He said that he and the others would do the same.

Back home, he and his brothers had been tasked with the same chore, placing blocks around the drafty 100-year-old home built by their settler ancestors. There, they filled a slab-wood box frame with seaweed. He liked snow blocks better. At least they wouldn't have to be hauled away in the spring.

"Good time to go hunting for umimmak." Pudlu pointed to the vast mountain valley behind them.

Will looked puzzled.

"Muskox," said Teemotee, pleased with his venture in a new language.

"I'll talk to Villeneuve."

Will started back downhill, impulsively racing the kids down the sloping drift to the bottom. He wondered if he would ever have a family of his own.

Villeneuve and Zalapski were outside, also looking skyward and toward the horizon, their eyes adjusting to the new conditions. Will told them about the possibility of hunting. Villeneuve nodded and gave him the familiar okay sign, making a circle with his thumb and index finger.

"For us, it will also be a sovereignty patrol."

"Okay, I'll arrange it," affirmed Will, thinking that he was rapidly becoming the emissary, messenger, and social conduit between two camps and two tiny worlds.

"First, we should also bank our living quarters," Will suggested.

They walked to the storehouse to search their supplies for the snow knives that they had been issued. These had big blades, 15 inches long, with sturdy wooden handles. The blade tapered from about 3 inches at the tip to 1.5 inches at the narrow wooden handle. The knives had become staples in all trading posts, replacing the traditional snow knife made from bone.

Will unwrapped one from waxed paper. "I bet the East India Company sells these in the tropics as machetes." He offered his habitual small talk.

Each Mountie wielded a knife in his hand, feeling the balance and weight.

"My God, this is quite a weapon," added Villeneuve.

Will and Zalapski smiled, both silently acknowledging that it was the first time in three days that Villeneuve had said more than one word.

The two junior Mounties were becoming closer. They could talk, joke, play cards, and find comfort in each other's silence. Neither had been able to develop any bond with Villeneuve. If anything, he grew more distant as the hours of daylight decreased.

The steel knives cut through the hard-packed snow as if it were butter. The three carved out blocks about 2 feet long, 1.5 feet high, and 8 inches wide. They stacked the blocks against the outer wall, one on top of the other, until they reached the window bottoms. They cut and carried blocks for most of the day, each hour becoming more familiar with the changing light conditions.

As they worked, Will considered the increasingly uncomfortable relationship with Villeneuve. He was one of the few men that Will had ever met that intimidated and, sometimes, even scared him.

It went beyond Villeneuve's physical strength. His deep-set dark eyes, set off by his thick jet-black eyebrows, held mystery. There were no lines of laughter or glints of brightness that came with joy. The range of emotion they held varied between dark, sullen, depressed, and—the most powerful—black fire. The mystery and origins of the sleepless stormy night lingered.

Will frequently reminded himself that Villeneuve was the elder, his boss, and had shown himself to be solid in a crisis. Looking to give him the benefit of the doubt, Will acknowledged that anyone could have a bad night, and he tried to quiet his thoughts on the matter. He noted in his journal: *Villeneuve. War and peace. He seems more at ease with the former than the latter.*

Pudlu stopped by a few times to check their progress, and smiled approvingly, satisfied that at least he had a few Qallunaat who could cut a decent snow block when iglu-building time came.

Three days after the storm, two 10-dog teams were harnessed. The dogs spread out in a wide fanlike hitch, barking, jumping, waiting for the anchor to be pulled from the packed snow; waiting for Atee-Atee—the let's-go signal—and the crack of the whip; waiting to run and pull, exactly as they were born to do.

The qamutiks were loaded, but not overladen. They would be gone only a few days. More than 100 pounds of dog food, mostly polar-bear meat, was the heaviest item. The Mounties packed one big canvas tent for emergencies, small Primus oil stoves and lamps, bags of hardtack, bannock, canned beans, stew, tea, and sugar. They were used to boiled polar-bear meat. Running out of food was the last thing they worried about.

Naudla and the children would remain at the post. Instinctively, Will was about to ask if they would be all right. The flash of two dead polar bears raced through his mind, checking his chivalry and chauvinism.

Finally, the logbook would record an official activity: the first Dundas Harbour sovereignty patrol. The team would assert Canada's ownership by building cairns on high points of land and leaving written records of who placed them in sealed canisters.

This wasn't the police work Will envisioned when he had joined the RCMP four years earlier. He had been surprised when he received a letter from Inspector O'Halloran telling him that he had been chosen for this assignment. It was important work; he was told that Canada's future was at stake. The $1.50 a day, with the chance to bank all of it, was also attractive.

Teemotee and Pudlu were shouting at the dogs, pushing them on. The qamutiks were side by side, with Will, Villeneuve, and Pudlu on the right and Teemotee and Zalapski on the left.

Both Teemotee and Pudlu were sitting toward the front of the qamutik, just behind the dogs. Each held a long whip at the ready. It trailed across the snow and ice, parallel to the 8-inch-high solid wood runners. An instant and expert snap of the whip, delivered inches from the side of the head of the lead dog, would turn the team, or if needed, bring it back in line. The snap was the warning shot. The dogs knew from experience that the next one would sting.

Will and Villeneuve were on Pudlu's qamutik, sitting high on bundles of fur and canvas bags lashed to the runners. The Mounties watched every move. They had attended training sessions on dog handling and soon would be driving teams themselves.

The qamutiks had no nails. Sturdy cross boards about 2 feet long and 4 inches wide, spread about 2 inches apart, were lashed to the runners with strips of rope crafted from walrus hide. It was built to bend to the drifts and contours of the frozen tundra. This was the tried, true, and traditional mode of Arctic travel.

Will's eyes were adjusting. Thankfully, the snow reflected what little light there was. Although recognizing details in the distance was difficult, this dawn-dusk period of the working day was manageable.

After the first hour, the dogs had slowed to a trot. By the second hour, a break was called.

The men softened hardtack in hot, freshly steeped, strong tea. Pudlu and Zalapski lit their pipes. Will and Teemotee each rolled a cigarette. Villeneuve didn't smoke.

Will realized just how cold one's hands can get. In the time it took to roll a cigarette, his fingers had become almost numb—and this was a good day, -25°F, with only a slight breeze.

The group stopped once more before making camp for the evening, having travelled just short of six hours that day. Pudlu estimated a distance of about 20 miles. He had left about an hour of twilight for him and Teemotee, with help from the Mounties, to build two iglus.

The work went quickly. The experienced hunters began in a deep drift, cutting out rectangular blocks about 2 feet long, 16 inches high, and 6 inches thick. They motioned to the Mounties to do the same. Soon, it was a smooth assembly line, with Villeneuve passing the blocks to the builders. The walls went up in a spiral formation. Each block was shaved at a slight angle to fit snugly at the sides and top of the piece below. The domed lodge quickly took shape.

Teemotee, the taller of the two builders, shaped the final piece into a near triangle. He lifted it through the last hole, manoeuvred it, balancing it with one hand, and shaved the sides with the other until it dropped perfectly in place, locking and compressing all the other blocks. Will knew that he had just witnessed the genius of dome construction.

The exhausted dogs were tied and fed and fell almost instantly asleep.

Will, Zalapski, and Teemotee were together in one iglu. The Mounties were surprised by the warmth of the iglu. The small oil lamp provided heat. They ate more hardtack and boiled seal meat and heated two cans of red beans, which the three of them shared.

"At least we can all share the blame later for the stink that's bound to follow," Will said laughing. "Erik, I remember that last time we had this."

Zalapski laughed. "I heard Villeneuve all night. I don't know whether it was snoring or whether he shit his bed."

"Pudlu has to put up with him tonight, so we can laugh at them both."

Teemotee looked puzzled.

There was little room to move around in the iglu. Each took a turn arranging his bed, laying out furs on the elevated snow ledge, then spreading the eiderdown sleeping bag on the fur mattress and shedding his outer clothing.

Will was warm. He was comfortable and wide awake and thinking about Teemotee's wife. He remembered her beautiful smile as she waved goodbye. Teemotee fell asleep instantly and moments later was snoring loudly.

How strange is this? Will liked Teemotee and felt comfortable in his presence. He admired him for the way he carried himself and his tenderness toward his wife and children. Will did not have an ounce of resentment toward his travelling companion— but, God, how he envied him.

Will considered the contradictions, the clearly stated warnings in the training sessions about touching Inuit women. Not that different from Reverend Kingsbury's Sunday sermons back home about coveting one's neighbour's wife.

Nothing had prepared him for his own reality. Love and lust for Naudla, and respect and admiration for Teemotee, sleeping 2 feet away.

They were up and moving at what Zalapski called "the crack of twilight." Pudlu and Teemotee hitched the dogs. The Mounties repacked the bedding and gear and lashed it to the qamutiks. Pudlu re-checked everything, subtly, without ever appearing to do so. In a half-hour, they were back on the qamutiks and energized. Watching Villeneuve and Pudlu interact reminded Will of Captain Bernier and the government man Craig, and their ability to accept who was the captain and who was the expedition leader.

Still, Will wondered, out here, which is which?

"Atee-Atee," Pudlu shouted from the front of the qamutik. The dogs were a little slower than they were yesterday. It had been months since they had a vigorous run. Will wondered if they felt stiff and sore the way an athlete does after the first game of the season or had aches and pains similar to his own.

An hour out, Pudlu reined in his dogs. Teemotee followed the cue. They set the anchor in the packed snow. Pudlu unwrapped his tarnished and scarred brass telescope. Will and the others peered to the west—10 o'clock is the way Will set it in his mind. He could see rocklike formations against patches of snow and windswept tundra.

Pudlu passed the telescope to Villeneuve, looking at him. "Umimmak. Umimmak." Villeneuve could discern the outlines of the big animals looking in their direction but not moving. Without a sound or look, he passed the telescope to Will, who looked and passed it to Zalapski. Three large shaggy animals stood, shoulder to shoulder. Their profiles were now clear, but to the naked eye, especially the untrained eye, they faded into the landscape.

The Mounties took their cues from Pudlu and Teemotee by kneeling behind the qamutiks, themselves trying to blend in with the terrain. Teemotee produced two white sheets of camouflage fastened to thin wooden strips, part of the Inuit hunting kit, as Pudlu quickly untied their rifles from canvas scabbards, lashed firmly atop the bundles.

They crouched and crept slowly toward the muskoxen. The Mounties kept their position and passed the telescope back and forth. Each had binoculars in their pack but knew enough not to make unnecessary moves.

The dogs were quiet, resting.

Without the telescope, it was difficult to identify either the hunters or the hunted.

Will was holding the telescope when two rifle shots cracked the Arctic stillness. The muskoxen on the left and right folded and fell. The one in the middle stood, dumbfounded, for three seconds, until a third shot brought him down. In unison, the hunters and their observers-turned-students moved to the downed muskoxen.

Will and the others all had the same thought: *This is sure to taste better than that damned polar bear and seal meat.*

Will had considerable experience as a skinner and butcher. His father and brother Ed bartered their services around St. Francis Harbour, Hadleyville, and Sheep Creek. They could skin and dissect a cow, pig, or sheep as well as anyone and, similarly, a moose or deer. Will had been their assistant many times.

He welcomed the opportunity to prove his worth here with Pudlu and Teemotee and show Zalapski and Villeneuve what an Air Corps guy could do. Umimmak, Umimmak. Will was absentmindedly repeating the word out loud so that he would not forget it.

Will gestured to Zalapski and Villeneuve and turned to Pudlu. "We'll do this one."

He didn't realize how much work was ahead of them.

Skinning an animal requires smooth movement with a keen eye, steady hand, and sharp knife, splitting the skin from nose to asshole and then at right angles inside all four legs and cutting to the bone just above the hoofs. Then it is a matter of short back-and-forth cuts, separating fat and muscle and rolling and peeling the hide from the carcass.

Skinning an umimmak was more difficult than skinning moose, deer, or cattle. Under the belly, the long flowing muskox hair was coarse and tangled. Will cut it away bit by bit, finally finding the exposed skin under which to slip the razor-sharp point of the knife.

Periodically, each skinner stopped, honed his blade on a steel sharpener, and passed the tool to one of the others.

Will was not as fast as the others. But he didn't embarrass himself. Villeneuve had had his own experience butchering animals in the wilds of northern Ontario. Zalapski did too, being a country boy. The fact that each was able to hold the animal on its back and spread the front and hind legs wide apart made Will's job easier. Pudlu and Teemotee straddled between the front and back legs and used their bodies as leverage as they worked silently and efficiently.

Finally, Will's muskox looked like the others. Naked, pink and white, and thankfully for Will's ego, not bloody or hacked. He reached high into the chest cavity, cut away the esophagus, separated the lungs from the ribs, pulled out the intestines and organs, and laid them intact on the snow. He harvested the heart, liver, and kidneys, the same as he would have done with an animal back home, and the same as Pudlu and Teemotee were doing beside him.

Pudlu and Teemotee nodded approval. Will was proud that he had been able to show that people from the south, especially Nova Scotians, could fend for themselves.

Teemotee and Pudlu were already enjoying their first taste of fresh muskox. Pudlu cut off small pieces of raw liver and savoured it. He motioned to the Mounties to try. At first, they resisted. Will said, "Why not?" Will felt the warm liver slip around in his mouth. He chewed, swallowed, and took a second, and then to his surprise, a third piece.

After hesitating for a moment, Villeneuve and Zalapski followed. All three experienced a boost of energy from the warm liver.

The three muskoxen were systematically dissected and quartered: the hind rumps, front shoulders, neck, backbone, ribs, and shanks. Will carved away the tenderloin strips from both sides of the backbone. Pudlu and Teemotee did the same. *For all our culture, language, and geographical differences, we all know where the best cut is.*

"We are going to eat well tonight, lads." Will was sure that he heard the dogs respond.

Eat well they did, roasting strips of loin over an open flame. The meat was deep red, like beef, but the taste was a full, meaty flavour, and with little hint of the strong woody aftertaste so characteristic of moose and venison. From his prairie experience, Zalapski offered, "It's a bit like bison."

They slept as well as they ate.

When they awoke on the third morning, Villeneuve was all business and determined to push as far up the valley as possible. They broke camp, and travelled some 20 miles. Mountains stretched above them on all sides. They were now in a canyon about a half-mile long and a half-mile wide.

"Tomorrow we will put a cairn there." Villeneuve pointed to a ledge at the end of the valley that was several hundred feet high but appeared accessible. "Can we camp here, Pudlu?"

Pudlu nodded. Walking in a big circle, measuring snow depth with a long pole, he stuck the snow knife in a drift. Within 90 minutes, the dogs were fed and the men were warm and comfortable inside the iglu, their fresh muskox in pots on two small stoves.

In the morning, the group re-examined the north face of the valley: it offered the best location for a cairn. The east and west walls were sheer cliffs, and above them sat mountainous, rounded snowdrifts like crowns set against the darkened sky and morning stars. Villeneuve wanted to push as far as possible up the slope. Pudlu and Teemotee harnessed the teams. They mushed upward until they hit patches of windswept bare gravel.

The Mounties continued on foot, armed with small picks

in their hands and Canada's sovereignty declarations in the canvas packs on their backs. In an hour, they were at the top, gathering and stacking rocks for their first cairn. They all signed the proclamation that claimed the land "in the right of Canada, on November 7, 1924." It was a good feeling. They shook hands, and stood for a moment, as though on parade. Villeneuve quickly wrote a description of the location and then shoved his cold, stinging hand back into the mitt he held under his armpit. He would make the detailed entries in the logbook back at the detachment.

Pudlu and Teemotee were with the dogs, watching this peculiar performance silently, amused. It was not unusual in summer for white men to do the strangest things on the land. Pudlu laughed, muttered to Teemotee, and translated, for his own enjoyment. "Inukshuk pointing nowhere."

Pudlu had watched others gather and place little rocks and weathered bones into wooden boxes and carry them back to the ship. No one ever told him what they were doing, and he didn't ask. It was better to observe; someday he would share the spectacle with other Inuit in a big iglu and join everyone laughing uproariously at the crazy Qallunaat.

The Mounties solemnly began their descent. Zalapski suddenly asked, "Why walk when we can slide?" He pointed 50 yards eastward to their left, where the sweep of drifted snow filled a summertime gorge and mountain stream.

Three strapping constables became, for the moment, little boys, racing to the slope. Villeneuve's mood was buoyant, and he laughed as he slipped on the icy overflow from the stream. Pulling his pack off his back and holding it to his chest between his arms, he dropped to his ass, then rolled backward, turning his parka into a smooth sled. He reached forward, grabbed the back hem of the parka and held it up in his fur mittens, thrust his heels in the snow, and propelled himself downward.

Will and Zalapski shouted, "Go, Vee-Vee, go." They quickly lost sight of him in the dim light on the shadowed slope.

Zalapski turned to Will. "Watch this, pardner." He used the same technique but had a much faster and smoother start. He was a snow rocket!

Will stuffed the few small articles in his pack inside his parka. He ran, building up his head of steam, and then, in one quick motion that he had learned as a playful boy, swung his pack behind his ass, dropped to the ice, and lifted both feet high in the air.

Instantly, he was speeding down the slope. Always the competitor, he decided on a few moves of his own. He twisted his hips, hands, and the pack in a counter-clockwise motion, and easily did a complete turn.

Devon Island and the RCMP Arctic Patrol with all its pressures and discipline had robbed them all of any sense of fun and freedom, until these exhilarating moments.

Will yelled the "Yes, yes, yahoo!" of a carefree child, and began another spin. He hoped that the others could see him, see how fun is done Nova Scotia-style.

The valley exploded in a thunderous crack. The sound echoed from every direction. A massive snowdrift overhanging the easterly mountaintop lost to nature's hold. That snow mountain may have been there for decades, accumulating in the winter gales, melting and freezing again in the summer months until the weight became one pound too heavy.

Or was the sound of their joy, shouts, and laughter the impetus? They would never know.

Will heard the deafening sound of certain death charging at him down a mountainside. Helpless and terrified, he did not even have time to think of God or pray. He could only watch the enormous white cloud explode on the slope and change into a massive avalanche, engulfing everything in its path.

It hit him again and again. He was propelled into the air, slammed into the snow, picked up again, thrown down, and rolled over a half-dozen times, then thrown airborne again. He lost consciousness.

In the dim light, Pudlu and Teemotee had been watching, laughing, and applauding the finally carefree police-ee. The fun turned to horror for everyone in the same instant.

All four spectators heard the explosion and watched it unfold. It lasted no more than 30 seconds. To the veteran soldiers standing helplessly, all the cannons from the battlefields of Europe couldn't compare with that sound.

About 150 yards lay between Pudlu and Teemotee and where Villeneuve and Zalapski were observing Will's gold-medal run. Another 100 yards separated them from Will.

Two Inuit hunters and two hardened Mounties saw Nature's deadly force sweep in front of them. Their faces stung and they were blinded as immeasurable tons of snow crashed down the mountainside. The next few minutes felt like an eternity. Then, stillness and silence.

Pudlu shouted an order to Teemotee and ran toward the Mounties. They saw him coming.

Teemotee untied one of the dog teams. Whether they would

help in this frantic and panicked search, he didn't know, but he knew that, let loose, they would sniff to find something. He grabbed a cargo box that protected two oil lamps that he now pumped, primed, and lit. He passed a lamp to Pudlu, the closest person to him. They fanned out, Teemotee on the downslope, Villeneuve on his right. Pudlu was a few yards to Villeneuve's right, Zalapski at the end link. They all shared the light from the two lamps.

There was nothing to say. They fanned out and raced into the destructive avalanche path. The snow was broken, uneven, and deep. Often one or all slipped to their knees.

They knew approximately where Will had been when the snow wall slammed him. Logic dictated that he had to be downslope from that. But how far and how deep down?

The avalanche's path was perhaps 100 yards wide. No one knew how long it took to cover it. It seemed like an eternity, but each man was worried that he was going too fast. What if they walked over him? It was easy to determine where the path of the slide ended by the hard, unscarred snow or patches of bare gravel beneath their feet.

Their panic intensified as they turned and spread out in a new grid, the same formation, but lower on the slope. The dogs were all over the place with their heads and noses down, at least adding some hope.

Over and over again, the men shouted, "Will! Will!" Each time stopping, listening, hoping, and then shouting again, and moving forward a few more paces.

"If it just wasn't so goddamned dark," Zalapski kept muttering, even with the lantern reflecting light from his left. "He could be 10 feet away, and we might not see him."

It was even darker under the snow. Will tried to open his eyes and grasp where he was and what had happened. He couldn't move. It was so silent.

He was alive. *Am I alone? Have the others been hit?*

If not, will they find me? Will needed to focus.

His hands and face were so cold, buried in the snow. He tried moving. It was difficult. He was pressure-packed and buried alive. How deep was he? Was his head skyward, sideways, or deep down? There was no way to tell. He hurt everywhere, especially in his chest and hands. He tried moving his hands and arms, aware that his left hand and arm were pinned behind his back and his right arm was against his chest. He couldn't move either. He was helpless.

Either his mitts were full of snow or he had lost them. All he felt was cold. He forced his right arm toward his face and found a bit of movement, perhaps half an inch. He pushed outward with as much strength as he could muster and moved another half-inch. Over and over, he repeated the motion, push up, push out, wiggling his fingers after each to move aside the snow.

Finally, his fingers touched his face and he realized that he had lost his mitts. His hands would surely freeze. He kept moving them back forth, only a few inches in either direction, but at last, a small pocket was carved and breathing seemed a little easier.

Where were his feet? He tried moving his legs. It was as though his right leg was paralyzed. He could feel weight all around it but couldn't move it, not even a fraction of an inch. He sensed possible movement in his left ankle, although his upper left leg, like the right limb, felt as though it was set in cement. He tried moving his left ankle again. Was it above the snow or in a pocket? If only his head was where his ankle was.

He was sure that he would die. But slowly the terror faded, replaced by dizziness and a slow, warm feeling creeping through his body. He was cocooned, as though he'd returned to the womb. The snow became soft and silky, like the pure white lining of a coffin. He tried moving his left leg one more time and again drifted from reality.

The frantic searchers crept forward. Villeneuve shook his head and blinked his eyes to bring them in focus. He saw something protruding 10 feet in front of him, between him and Teemotee. He shouted and, like a panther, bolted toward it.

The polar-bear-skin-clad foot and ankle could only belong to Will. The boots they all found so warm and comfortable, boots made by Naudla that required no spit and polish, were familiar.

Villeneuve grabbed with both hands. It was the left foot, an ankle, and half a calf. He tried pulling it, but it didn't move.

The others appeared beside him and eight hands, two of them with small picks from the packs, dug. They found the second leg, freed it up to the lower thigh, and then with one leg under each arm, Villeneuve on his knees tried backing up and lifting at the same time. He and the others didn't know if Will was dead or alive, but it was certain that he wasn't moving. When there is no air, how many seconds separate life and death?

Villeneuve changed his position. Facing away, with Will's feet still wedged between his powerful arms and chest, he squatted and tried a step forward, but the dead weight didn't budge.

The others were back on their knees, frantically digging with their hands. Suddenly, Will's legs were free to the upper thighs, then one hip. Villeneuve pulled harder.

"Thank Christ," he shouted.

The snow released its grip. One more big step forward and Will was free. A lantern sat on either side, just above where his head had been buried almost straight down. He was face down, with snow packed into his curly hair.

Villeneuve released one leg, caught the other under the thigh, and rolled Will over. The others cradled his head and shoulders, and in one motion he was on his back.

Will's face was bloodied, and snow packed his eye sockets, ears, and inside his parka. Zalapski tried to find a pulse from behind Will's chin. Zalapski could not feel anything, but he also knew that he was too cold, with too much adrenaline pumping in his veins, to be certain. He needed to overcome the uncertainty and respond with what he hoped for rather than what he knew to be true. "I think he's alive."

The race against time and deadly cold was just beginning. Zalapski and Pudlu worked feverishly, clearing the snow from Will's face. They opened his parka, swept away more snow and then cleared his parka hood. Will's fur-lined hat, that Mountie trademark, had been ripped from his head, probably in the first impact. They pulled the hood tightly around his face, covering his ears, and tied it snugly.

Teemotee, seeing Will's bare hands, stripped away his own bearskin mitts and put them on Will, ensuring that they were pulled high over the parka. He pulled his own exposed hands inside each sleeve of his parka and pushed both hands and arms into his pockets. There were extra mitts on the qamutik.

"Help me," Villeneuve said, as he lifted Will under his arms. The others brought him forward enough so that Villeneuve could lift him onto his shoulders.

Villeneuve had done this before with a wounded soldier and friend on a faraway battlefield in another time and world. The soldier had died on his back that day and in Villeneuve's mind every day since. Villeneuve would never forget the force of the bullet that ripped through his comrade's skull as he ran, almost knocking him off his powerful legs.

He took long strides, sinking deep into the broken snow, just as he had done in the muddy battlefield, but without ever stumbling and never yielding to the heavy load. He laid Will as best he could on the qamutik.

The others were behind him, all with the same three-point plan for what lay ahead.

Make Will as comfortable as possible.

Protect him from the cold.

Get him back to the detachment quickly.

Villeneuve and Zalapski rearranged the load and made a bed for Will with the canvas tent and skins. Teemotee and Pudlu rounded up the dogs by throwing chunks of meat around the harnesses. As the dogs gulped the meat, they slipped them into their traces. They decided to travel as light and as quickly as possible.

Pudlu covered Will with one of the recently skinned muskox hides. He and Villeneuve folded a second one, rolled Will on his side, and slipped the hide under him.

Together, they lashed him to the sled.

"How long back to the post?" asked Villeneuve.

"Maybe 10 hours. Little faster downhill." Pudlu took control, his hand at a slight angle pointing downhill. "Everyone travel light. Teemotee and Erik should make food caches. They can catch up."

"Yes, we can't waste any time," agreed Villeneuve. "You got that, Erik?"

"Understood, Skipper." He and Teemotee had already begun unloading the few hundred pounds of muskox meat, most of the dog food, and some equipment. "We'll catch up."

Villeneuve and Pudlu started. They would run for four hours, take a short break, feed the dogs and themselves, and continue. If Will should wake up, they would stop then as well, but not a moment would be wasted.

Zalapski and Teemotee hollowed out a snow cave to store the meat and other gear. Zalapski marked the spot with a flag that he had taken out of a petrol canister. This time he didn't salute. He estimated that they were about 30 minutes behind the others.

It was 5 p.m. Only one hour before, they had been at the top, raising another flag where he did salute, genuinely.

Zalapski and Teemotee cut chunks of raw frozen muskox meat and chewed it as they got on their qamutik.

Villeneuve and Pudlu had done the same and they also had a few pieces of hardtack in their mitts. Villeneuve kept his eyes on Will's face. It was now nighttime dark, but he could trace an outline of Will's jaw and eyes.

Finally, a groan. Will shifted slightly but did not wake. Every few minutes, more agonizing groans—beautiful sounds indicating that he was alive.

At 9 p.m., under a half-moon, which helped light and point their way, Pudlu pulled the dogs in. "Rest time." He worked quickly and efficiently, priming the stove and handing the kettle to Villeneuve to fill it with snow. The dogs collapsed, panting, their faces frosted. He scooped a small heap of tea into his hand

and dumped it into the boiling water. The hot tea was magnificent on their lips and in their stomachs. Three minutes later, it was merely warm tea. The temperature was -30°F or colder.

Villeneuve tried to pour tea between Will's lips. There was no indication that he swallowed.

Just as they repacked the kettle and stove, they heard more dogs. Zalapski and Teemotee had caught up. They, too, needed a short break.

Villeneuve said, "Zalapski, if you can get ahead of us, do so, try and get the fires lit and that place warm. He's going to need care."

Pudlu didn't need to be told to translate to Teemotee who responded, "Eee."

Two hours later, they heard the second dog team again. It was hard to see in the dark. They simply went on, maintaining a strong pace. It was almost 11 p.m. Villeneuve estimated that they were more than halfway there. He could see no distinguishable landmarks but did sense the downslope terrain.

Several times in the next two hours, he heard more and more groans from Will. Each time, he stirred or thrashed under the heavy hide.

They stopped one more time. Lit a lantern to go with the stove and ate hardtack soaked and softened with hot tea. Pudlu threw chunks of frozen meat to the voracious dogs.

Villeneuve stood close to the lamp, reached under his heavy parka, and found his watch. It was 2 a.m. They had been on the trail for nearly eight hours. They had probably covered 30 miles.

Suddenly, a groan turned recognizable. "Where am I? Where am I?"

Villeneuve and Pudlu rushed to him.

"You're okay, Will. You're okay. You're with Vee-Vee and Pudlu on his qamutik, and we are getting you back to the post. Lie still."

"I'm so tired. My hands are burning."

"Just stay quiet. Here, take a sip." Villeneuve held the warm tea to his lips. Will sucked in two or three small sips and fell back to sleep.

Pudlu lifted the snow anchor, shouted the familiar Atee-Atee command, but the tired dogs turned mule. They wouldn't move. He laid out a few cracks of the whip, a few stirred, but the lead would not budge. Two more cracks, one on the hindquarter and one behind the ear persuaded him that he still had energy. The others, hearing the yelp and cracks, followed.

The final two hours went by more quickly. Toward the end, a half-hour out, the dogs, sensing that home was near, picked up the pace.

It was still too dark for Villeneuve to make out much more than clouds around the half-moon. In other clear spots were distant clouds. Then he saw the flicker of a small light in the distance—the oil lamps from the detachment.

Pudlu brought the dogs up to the door, where they dropped, exhausted.

Zalapski and Teemotee were waiting. Naudla had joined them. The four men used the muskox hide as a stretcher, carried Will into the cabin, and laid him on a bunk.

"Thank you, lads," Will responded.

Villeneuve asked, "Are you awake?"

"I have been for a little while."

"Don't talk now. You have to get into your bunk."

Will was able to move enough to make it easier for the others to get him out of the snow-laced, half-frozen clothing, and into a dry warm bunk.

Naudla washed his bloody face. He had several cuts and gashes and swollen eyes. Her tender touch was soothing, and he began to breathe softly, and relaxed.

His fingers were white. Some appeared frozen. Everyone understood frostbite, none more than Pudlu, Teemotee, and Naudla. There would be trouble ahead, but they also knew that he would live. So did Will, who looked at Naudla, and went back to sleep.

Only hours away, the crew prepared for landing and off-loading.

CHAPTER 5

NUKARA—BROTHER

Will Grant, Erik Zalapski, and Vincent Villeneuve had been together for almost six months, beginning with their familiarization training and preparation in Ottawa in June 1924.

Despite all that they had endured—hardship, dangers, and isolation—they were unable to seal a deep three-way bond of brothers. Erik and Will were close, but Villeneuve was always the outsider.

This shared crisis, the realization that one life was at stake, brought them closer, and each recognized that. But no one realized that it was only temporary or how far apart cold, geography, and circumstances would eventually isolate them from each other, every bit as much as they were isolated from the rest of the world.

By the time Villeneuve and Pudlu arrived at the detachment with Will, Zalapski had done more than light the fires. True to his meticulous nature, he had also laid out bandages and bedding. A big pot of stew extracted from half a dozen tins was hot on the stove. Baked bread had been thawed and warmed in the oven, and the kettle held a gallon of boiling tea.

Stacked on the table were the emergency medical books, and Zalapski, who shuddered at the thought of being thrust into the role of field doctor, had already begun to read them—or at least identify the passages that dealt with severe cuts, broken bones, and frostbite. They had already addressed step one in all three books: *Ensure that the patient is warm and comfortable.*

Pudlu, Teemotee, and Naudla left quietly.

"I'll sit with him for a while, Skipper," Zalapski said, "and see what I can learn from these." He tapped the manuals. "You should try and sleep."

"Thanks, Erik." Villeneuve's voice seemed softer.

Villeneuve peeled off his sealskin boots, called kamiks. "Never thought these things could be so warm and comfortable."

"And light," added Zalapski.

Villeneuve removed the polar-bear pants that Naudla had finished sewing only a few days earlier. She had scraped, cleaned, and dried the hides, then cut them precisely to shape. She painstakingly sewed intricate stitches that would repel the fiercest wind and water. After making three pairs of pants, there was enough hide left for three pairs of mitts.

Villeneuve allowed himself to think out loud. "You know, if it weren't for these pants and boots, Grant would have been a helluva lot worse off. His legs could have frozen."

Zalapski realized that it was the closest he had felt to Villeneuve. He was surprised at the positive comments toward the Inuit, Will's word to identify them.

"We'll need to wait a few hours to see if Will's hands and fingers will come back. This book says that it depends on whether they are frozen solid—which is the worst, or just down past the second layer of skin, which means that he may heal. I suspect it will be a bit of both."

"We'll know better tomorrow," said Villeneuve, now lying under his blanket, eyes closed.

Zalapski was doing his best to concentrate. He had been awake for almost 24 hours and was physically and emotionally exhausted. He slumped back in the chair, asleep.

The cold woke him. The fire was down, and outside the wind was blowing. Zalapski could see his own breath and Will's, faintly. At least with the big stove and lots of coal, the cabin would heat almost as fast as it had cooled.

Zalapski boiled water, shook a few cups of oatmeal into the pot, and made some hearty porridge.

He checked on Will. "You awake, pardner?"

"Hard to breathe. Can't move my hands."

Villeneuve was up, pulling on his woollen issue heavy-duty trousers, tucking them into his kamiks. "Let me see you."

He pulled the lamp closer, folded back the muskox hide and blanket, and removed the mitts. "Christ."

Will looked at his hands. So did Zalapski.

The left hand was worse than the right. Two fingers were a deep purple, and big red blisters had already formed or were forming over the backs and palms of the hand. The right hand did not appear as damaged—it was blistered, but not as badly— except one finger. The right hand's little finger was black.

"How's the pain?" Zalapski asked.

"Awful." The word trailed off into a groan.

Villeneuve stood up straight. "I'll give you a shot of morphine from the medical kit." Villeneuve's only experience with needles was practicing on a dummy at the training centre. But he wasn't going to admit that now. He tried to sound in control.

"What else do you feel—or don't feel?"

"My right side is very sore. I think my ribs are broken."

Villeneuve and Zalapski took turns gently probing his rib cage. Directly under his armpit was badly bruised and swollen. Will could barely stand them touching it.

The medical books were more detailed than Zalapski remembered or expected. How to set broken legs, arms, and shoulders. The section on broken ribs said that they generally heal in six weeks. A punctured or collapsed lung was the danger.

Will's breathing appeared normal but painful. He was not spitting up blood or other discoloured fluid. That much was in his favour.

Villeneuve and Zalapski followed the instructions and put a towel over the swollen area and wrapped it firmly with a wide cotton strip, with several overlapping twists around his chest. They would monitor and adjust the bandage every few hours, depending on the swelling.

Will said that it felt better already.

"I think you need to eat and drink something," Zalapski insisted. He pulled his chair closer with a big bowl of porridge with brown sugar and thick evaporated milk.

Will could not feed himself. Zalapski soaked hardtack in hot tea, softening them, and Will ate two. He was feeling better and complimented Zalapski on his bedside manner and nursing skills, as Zalapski alternated between delivering spoonfuls of porridge, bites of hardtack, and sips of tea.

Suddenly Will had the panicked realization that this

WHIT FRASER

pampering may have a limit. He had to piss and no one was going to hold and aim his dick.

"Help me up. I got to take a piss."

"You're staying here, and you can piss here," ordered Villeneuve.

"Don't worry," added Zalapski. "Our supply guys thought of everything. Look what I found when I unpacked the medical supplies last night."

He produced a powder blue bedpan. A low-slung design that slipped right under the ass, with a little dip and slide for any reasonably sized pecker.

Will allowed Zalapski to pull down his heavy underwear and slide the pan under him. He manoeuvred himself into place, using the tip of the middle finger on the right hand.

"Christ, Erik, what a relief."

Trying to hide his embarrassment, he also confessed. "My dick is the only part of me not throbbing."

Zalapski slid the pan away and dumped it in the honey bucket.

Villeneuve and Zalapski brought the lamp closer to Will's hands, now folded on his chest. Their colour had changed. No longer stark white, they had reddened as though they had been scalded rather than frostbitten. Large water blisters were forming, particularly around the knuckles. The medical manuals indicated that these were second- and third-degree frostbite.

Three fingers set off alarm bells. The little finger on Will's right hand, and the ring and little finger on his left were blackened down to the knuckle. They didn't need a doctor to tell them that the fingers would likely never recover.

From the forests, prairies, and the Arctic of Canadian winters, all had witnessed frostbite and severed fingers and toes.

From the trenches and field hospitals, the Mounties also knew about gangrene—how quickly it can set in and its infectious and deadly consequences.

They checked Will's arms for discoloration or sign of spreading infection, and were relieved not to see any, at least not yet.

Villeneuve was direct. "I don't think we can wait very long."

"Maybe we can wait a few hours to see if his fingers change colour," Zalapski suggested.

Will looked at the black fingers and the red boils and blisters.

"Give me a little time. I want to think. Can I have another shot of morphine?"

Villeneuve seemed relieved. He also needed to prepare himself for what lay ahead. As a senior officer, he could not delegate this responsibility.

He prepared a needle, withdrawing the prescribed amount, estimated about 20 per cent additional to compensate for the fact that it had been frozen, and then punched it into Will's hip.

Will went back to sleep. Villeneuve and Zalapski took stock: they had bandages, sutures and needles, scalpels, forceps, and sharp pliers that would easily sever a finger bone. They had everything—except a doctor.

Teemotee, Pudlu, and Naudla came by and looked at Will's face and hands. No one spoke, but their eyes said it all. They, too, knew the perils of frostbite and the symptoms when flesh is frozen beyond recovery.

When Will woke four hours later, Villeneuve and Zalapski gave him their assessment.

Villeneuve laid it out. "Those three black fingers are getting worse. You can see the black pus building. I think they have to come off, or you risk losing your life with gangrene."

Will looked at them. "Have you ever cut off someone's fingers before?"

Zalapski spoke first. "You know damn well we haven't, and we're as scared as you, but what choice do we have?"

"I want you to get Pudlu. I'll ask him to do the cutting."

"Are you fucking crazy?" Villeneuve's temper flared. "I won't let a goddamned ignorant nomad operate on one of my men."

Will tried reasoning, reminding Villeneuve how deftly Pudlu had skinned the polar bears, leaving even the claws, and his precision in gutting the muskox.

"Those were animals, for Christ's sake." Villeneuve seethed. "I can't agree. I won't agree. It's unheard of."

Zalapski was as surprised as Villeneuve about Will's choice. He considered Will's practical assessment and the risks.

"You know, Vee-Vee, we're all in a bad spot here and we need all the help we can find. Why don't you handle the ether? I'll follow the books and guide you, and we'll see if Pudlu can do the cutting. Who knows? Maybe he's done this before."

Villeneuve stared at Zalapski, anger burning in his eyes. Will broke the silence.

"Please go get him, Erik, and let me talk to him."

Zalapski put on his parka. "That book says that you shouldn't eat or drink anything before an operation. I'll be right back."

Villeneuve remained silent, and Will tried again.

"Vee-Vee, I'm right about this. I'd guess there are people in hospitals cutting people open with half of Pudlu's hand and eye skill and precision."

"It's unheard of—a nomad—a goddamned Eskimo savage."

Will was infuriated. Even with bandages, he was ready to fight for his friends. Will's voice lowered and became more controlled. His eyes burned into Villeneuve's. Anger overrode intimidation. The words came, slowly, clearly, and clipped. "This is my choice. My hands. My life. I know what I have seen and I know what I want. I know who's best here to cut and sew me."

Zalapski returned in minutes. Teemotee, Naudla, and the children were with him. Teemotee put the children on Zalapski's bunk and warned them not to move or speak.

Zalapski wisely hadn't broken the news about Will's decision. Everyone felt the conflict. Tension speaks a universal language; silence can make such an angry sound.

Will was relieved to see Teemotee and Naudla. Her presence was his only comfort.

Villeneuve knew that he was cornered. "Okay, Grant, it's your show."

All three Inuit had seen the swollen hands and blackening fingers—realities of the rigours of Arctic life. They exchanged a few words, easily and correctly interpreted as "It looks bad—really bad."

Will spoke directly.

"Pudlu, I want you to cut them off. You have the best hands and eyes. We have all the tools." He pointed his head toward the table with the surgical instrument spread out. "Vee-Vee has the stuff to knock me out. I want you to cut the black parts off the fingers and sew me up. Will you do that?"

Pudlu looked Will directly in the eye, offered a faint smile, raised his eyebrows, nodded in the affirmative. "Eee."

He removed his parka and outer layer of clothing.

Will and the others were shocked. They had known Pudlu

by his deep, dark brown, leathered face and hands. Now, he was standing before them, his torso bare, displaying magnificent muscular arms and perfectly sculpted white shoulders.

Villeneuve snapped out of his funk. "There's a lot to do. We'll use the table. Everything needs to be sterilized."

Zalapski cleared off the table and brought clean bedding and blankets.

Pudlu turned to Will. He moved a lamp closer to Will's hands and studied them carefully. He didn't touch them but traced imaginary lines around the lower parts of the three fingers, about halfway from the knuckle to the first joint. It was clear that he was drawing a plan in his mind.

Pudlu spoke to Teemotee, who left and quickly returned with two more surgical instruments. One was a small carving tool that Will had seen Pudlu use for carving rounded ivory chess figures. The other was a small ulu, a traditional crescent-shaped knife from Naudla's collection. These went into the boiling water with needles, thread, knives, and scalpels.

Pudlu had witnessed more than one surgery. Only two years earlier, he had seen Dr. Livingstone remove a man's leg on the galley table of Bernier's ship. And not many years before that, he had watched the same doctor sew a man who had been ripped apart by a polar bear. "I watched a man lose a leg. Everything needs to be very clean." He began scrubbing his hands, instructing Naudla to do the same.

Villeneuve stayed silent but took up a position above Will's face that afforded him the appearance of control and followed Zalapski's instructions from the medical books, drawing the correct doses of morphine and ether from bottles.

Zalapski and Naudla had also scrubbed their hands and were threading several needles. Teemotee stood back, silent and observant.

The four men approached Will. They lifted him onto the table, using the sheet as a stretcher.

Pudlu put his hands on Will's shoulders and looked at the others. "First we pray." He closed his eyes. "Attata," he began, reciting a prayer in his language. "Please, God, help Will be strong." Everyone chimed in with a soft "Amen."

Villeneuve covered Will's face with a cloth and applied drops of ether, listening carefully as Zalapski read the instructions.

Will went rapidly into the other world. Pudlu moved to the table and began with the left hand. He tied a sinew tourniquet just above the knuckle; the sinew was also wrapped around a pencil that he used to tighten and cut off the blood flow. With the scalpel, he made a 360-degree cut around the bone of the little finger, then two parallel cuts on the inside and outside of the finger. He used his carving tool to peel the underside of the little finger back about half an inch—like skinning a banana—and tucked it against Will's palm. He placed a clean towel under Will's blackened and dead finger, held the tip securely, took the sharp crescent ulu in his right hand, and with one short rolling motion, severed the finger, quickly and cleanly.

He loosened the tourniquet, allowing blood to flow for several seconds and drain accumulated pus, and then retightened it. He folded the loose tissue over the severed bone and nodded toward Naudla. She stepped forward, pointed Will's hand upward, motioned to Pudlu to steady it, and made three quick stitches, cut and tied them, then stitched the outside and inside incisions on the short nub of the finger. Pudlu and Naudla repeated the procedure on the ring finger, and then moved to the opposite side of the table to remove the right-hand little finger.

The combined procedures did not take 15 minutes. Villeneuve and Zalapski were astonished. It was left to them to apply bandages, and as they did so, they noted how little blood oozed from the stitched stumps.

The four men moved Will back to his bunk, where he slept for three more hours. Villeneuve and Zalapski were there when he woke up.

"What happened?"

Zalapski spoke. "It's all done, Will. I think the worst is over. You made a good choice. But it's going to be a while before the blisters heal and you can use your hands."

Villeneuve stood silently, unwilling to acknowledge the primitive but skilful operation he had just witnessed.

Will looked at the bandages. "Get me the piss-pot, please." He wasn't able to get the job done without help from Zalapski.

Stating that he had to check on the storehouse, Villeneuve dressed, took his rifle, lit a lamp, and vanished into the darkness.

Zalapski fed Will more porridge, bread, and tea, while giving him the play-by-play of how it had all gone down, beginning with Villeneuve's finding him and carrying him to the qamutik and ending with his administering the ether.

Will responded, "He still seems so distant. He's hard to read, for sure."

After hearing the details of Pudlu's and Naudla's surgical work, Will asked Zalapski to invite them to visit.

Zalapski pulled on his parka.

In minutes, Pudlu and Naudla entered the room.

Will looked at Pudlu and smiled. "Ullaakuut, Doctor." He said the last word slowly, clearly, and reverently.

"Ullaakuut, Will."

Pudlu came closer. Will tried touching him with his bandaged arm. "Brother."

Pudlu was pleased. He placed a hand on Will's shoulder. "Nukara. Brother."

Will looked toward Naudla and smiled. "Nakurmiik."

The four sat in silence.

Pudlu and Naudla sat on the wooden footlockers at the end of each bunk, trunks containing a constable's worldly goods.

In a vain attempt at privacy, the bunks faced opposite walls in such a way that it separated their snoring by about 16 feet. Zalapski's bunk was on the west wall, at a right angle to Vee-Vee's, on the north, and Will's on the south.

Will dozed off. He didn't tell them that the pain was returning. The throbbing in his remaining fingers pained far worse than the amputations. When he awoke, he was alone with Villeneuve. "Erik told me what you did, Vee-Vee. I am very grateful. Without you, I might not be alive. You saved my life."

Villeneuve smiled faintly, nodded. "I was lucky to spot you when I did." But he offered no more, leaving Will to wonder if he resented the fact that Will had insisted on Pudlu's doing the cutting. He sensed long and tense weeks ahead.

Will looked at the bandages. Three fingers were gone. How would this change his life? Would he be able to do the things that make him who he was at heart, a craftsman?

Will remained in his bunk one more day, staring at the

rough ceiling. A thousand thoughts ran through his mind—good and bad, from happy days fishing with his father and brothers to the lost love of his life who had found the war too long to wait and had married someone else. Probably for the best. He looked ahead, and even after being at the detachment for almost three months, he was still unable to imagine what lay ahead of him.

Villeneuve spent most of his days working outside in the storehouse. He had discovered boards that had been pried away and loosened, likely the work of a polar bear. Perhaps the dogs had scared him away. He reinforced the corners with additional boards, nails pointing outward every few inches to discourage another bear from trying to rip away the boards.

Zalapski had become nurse and cook. He also fed Will and carried out piss-pot duties.

Will decided that he needed to try his legs. He lifted the blankets and muskox hide back with his elbows, wiggled himself upright, and swung his legs over the side of the bunk.

Zalapski came into the room carrying a bag of coal. "Let me help you." He provided an arm for Will to lift himself to his feet. Will's ribs hurt, but the pain was tolerable. The morphine tablets Villeneuve had been giving him decreased the pain but made him feel tired and confused.

Will stood for a few moments, took a few steps forward and backward, and sat back down. "It feels okay. Maybe I can sit in the chair by the stove for a few minutes."

He got up a second time and Zalapski stayed with him, offering support as Will eased himself onto the chair.

"Are you ready to look at the progress?" Zalapski pointed to the bandaged hands.

"I think we should. The pain is not as bad, or maybe it's the pills." He watched Zalapski wash his hands and undo the gauze. *They must have used a yard on each hand.* Zalapski used warm water to soften the bloody bandages and then lifted them. Both men were pleased that bleeding was minimal. Naudla's stitches had closed the incisions tightly, and they were confident that the healing process was progressing.

Every part of Will still hurt, including the three missing fingers. "How long has it been now, Erik? I've lost track."

"About 72 hours. I'd say you're over the worst of it."

"I have to accept that I must make the best of it. Erik, I will not allow myself to become the camp cripple. Remind me of that if you catch me feeling sorry for myself."

Zalapski kept the mood upbeat. "I think the blisters are going down. The books advise that we not break them and that in a few days they will go away."

The door opened and Pudlu stepped in.

"Ullaakuut, Doctor." Will smiled. "Making rounds, are you?" He had hoped Naudla was with him but hid the disappointment.

"Good to see you awake." Pudlu looked at Will's hands, also pleased. He raised his eyes and eyebrows for an emphatic though silent affirmation.

Zalapski covered the incisions with a new bandage and rewrapped the longer bandages.

When he had finished, Will asked to try holding a mug of tea.

The hard upper part of Will's palm just below the wrist was not blistered and had some feeling. He discovered that he could hold the mug steady between his upper palms. He could at least do this one thing for himself, and he savoured the warm drink.

It was much the same ritual for the next two weeks, but with longer and longer periods in the chair. Gradually, Will's ribs began to feel better, and daily, Zalapski adjusted them as the swelling decreased.

Pudlu stopped in every morning; Naudla, Teemotee, and the kids in the afternoon, never staying more than a few minutes. Occasionally, Zalapski would wait for Naudla's visit so that she could see the progress and examine her fine handiwork. Sometimes she lightly touched Will's hand and the healing stubs, a gesture tender and electric at the same time.

In two weeks, the bandages had been reduced to wraps between his thumbs and the stubs of the missing fingers. Zalapski snipped the stitches and used tweezers to pull the threads free with quick jerks, with only a few drops of blood from each.

Will regretted not asking Naudla if she wanted the honour of finishing her work.

Will was developing some use in his fingers. Although the tips were sensitive and tender, at least he could now get his fly open and no longer needed help on the honey bucket. He was certain that Zalapski was more relieved than he.

Finger freedom, as he dubbed it, meant that he could begin feeding himself and rolling his own cigarettes, although Zalapski and Pudlu always ensured that there were half a dozen for him on the table near the ashtray.

Will and Zalapski played cards and talked, mostly about the skipper, who was spending more and more time by himself.

"What is he doing?" was Will's opening and predictable morning question. Zalapski didn't have a direct answer, knowing that none was expected.

"He's out there. What he does is beyond me, but he's out there, and in here it's easier."

On a fine clear day, Villeneuve would go either east or west along the shoreline carrying out "a foot patrol." He had also developed, with some help from Teemotee, a short trapline for white foxes and had even caught a few.

About five days after the avalanche, he'd joined Teemotee for the journey up the valley to retrieve the food cache and discarded gear. Teemotee began his trapline on that same trip, and Kootoo came with them.

Will looked forward to the day when he could get outside. He became focused on setting up his trapline for a semblance of recreation. A few white pelts would bring a tidy sum at one of the trading posts or at the big auction house in Montreal.

"Gin," said Zalapski, laying out a spread and marking the scorecard.

In the afternoons, Pudlu came to see Will for at least an hour, his second daily round, and they played chess.

Will lived for the few moments that Naudla came for a visit, and then wondered why he was afraid to properly welcome her.

Will knew that his mind was wandering all over the place. One moment he was glad to see Teemotee, then wondered if he was suspicious. Did he catch one of Will's sneaky stares at Naudla?

When Will was alone, the avalanche went over and over in his mind. Had he caused it with his silly antics?

So many questions, no answers.

His friendship with Zalapski solidified but the O'Halloran hand-selected trio of constables were anything but cohesive. The fragile connections forged in the early days of the mission increasingly splintered. Will was especially troubled by the widening gulf between Zalapski and the skipper.

On December 21 twilight lasted only a few hours, but the next day was the New Year, as far as Will was concerned, because every day after this, the sun would move closer to the horizon. After five weeks of confinement, there was no better time to take his first steps outside.

He dressed. His hands were tender and pinkish. Girly hands. He was determined not to feel sorry for himself, but the simplest tasks were challenges, making him feel like less than a fully strong man.

He found strength from his war experience. He reminded himself that he had come home alive and in one piece. *How many bodies did you see in graves? How many hundreds of men on that homebound ship had left behind arms, hands, and legs on a muddy battlefield?* He remembered a saying from his Nova Scotia home: *what doesn't kill you makes you stronger.*

There had been several days of clear skies and light winds. The air felt good when he stepped outside. He was determined to again pull his weight.

Villeneuve, Zalapski, and the Inuit—as Will now referred to their guides—were cutting and hauling ice blocks from a small freshwater lake. The ice at the top was more than 2 feet thick. They cut the blocks 6 inches wide and 1 foot or longer to make them easy to handle. A good whack with the 10-pound sledgehammer produced a bucket of ice chunks to melt on the back of the stove for fresh drinking and bathing water.

Dozens of bags of coal were stacked outside the door and they always kept a high stack of scrap wood for kindling.

The blizzard that engulfed them for two days was unlike anything they had imagined. They would soon learn that even Pudlu and Teemotee had only rarely seen anything like it.

The gales obliterated Christmas. For five days, 80-mile-an-hour winds blew first from the northwest, then turned and came back from the northeast, so strong and so blinding that they couldn't see but a few feet in front of the detachment.

Will and Zalapski read or played cards. The only real conversation centred on whether the roof would stay on and what they might do if it didn't.

Villeneuve talked little. Sometimes he paced. Sometimes he made notes in the official logbook, maintaining the inventory of goods used. This included the tins of tobacco that he sold to Pudlu, Zalapski, and Will.

On December 31, the silence woke them. The wind had stopped and the roof was still over their heads.

"Finally," shouted Villeneuve, jumping out of his bunk and taking thumping strides to the stoves to stoke the fires. The men ventured out. The area behind the detachment was almost totally covered by a massive drift. Some stacks of barrels and lumber were covered. But it was the sea ice that caught Will's eye, a beautiful blue with a clear smooth cover. The driving winds and snows had polished the ice to a glassy finish.

An old expression shot through Will's mind: *It's an ill wind that blows no good.* It was as though the storm had wiped away Villeneuve's inner dark clouds. Like the winds, his mood had shifted 180 degrees.

Villeneuve was laughing. "We didn't blow away, boys. We'd better feed our dogs. They must be starving." The three donned their outer parkas and pants and walked to the dog lines.

He was right. The animals were ready to devour each other. For anyone to try and feed them in the grip of that whiteout gale would have been life-threatening.

It was at that moment that the smiling Villeneuve suggested that they make up for their lost Christmas with a New Year's party. "We'll call it the First Annual Devon Island New Year's Ball," he proclaimed.

Surprisingly, he walked up the hill to deliver the invitation to the others. Will's and Zalapski's spirits rose.

It was as if Will was getting ready for a big date. He melted ice, heated water, and took a bath in the folding rubber tub. He cut his curly, reddish brown hair and examined his muscular 5-foot, 11-inch, 200-pound frame. He had lost weight during his ordeal, but suddenly, the idea of a gathering, with Naudla present, made him feel healthy and happy.

Villeneuve returned, still buoyant. "Tonight, we are not lonely human flagpoles. Tonight, we are part of high society and we will celebrate." With that, he dug into his footlocker and produced a 40-ounce bottle of rum.

Each of them had brought their own "liquor cabinet," no more than a half-dozen bottles each, and rationed it to his tastes. Vee-Vee splashed a sociable 2 ounces into mugs for Will and Zalapski and generously half-filled his own.

As the evening progressed, Villeneuve made several trips to the cupboard to refill his mug.

Zalapski opened a bottle of scotch and shared two modest drinks with Will.

Will's contribution sat on the table: a bottle of champagne

that he had bought especially for New Year's and a bottle of red wine. He had stored them in his footlocker to keep them from freezing.

About 10 p.m., the honoured guests arrived.

Naudla was radiant. She removed sealskin mitts and shook Will's hand tenderly, looking at the healing fingers and stubs. She released her gentle grip slowly, and then, in a single fluid motion, grabbed the shoulders of her amauti. With one swift move, she slipped it over her head. Glancing around the room, she dropped it on Will's bunk.

Will wanted to believe that that small gesture was intentional. Naudla's laying her parka across his tidy bunk gave him an unexpected jolt of pleasure.

Kootoo and Piapik bounded into the cabin with a burst of cold air, greeting the Mounties as though they hadn't seen them in weeks, rather than mere hours.

Naudla helped Piapik with her parka, took Kootoo's from his hands, and placed them on Will's bunk on top of hers.

Pudlu and Teemotee dropped theirs over a small wooden crate.

Naudla wore a heavy knit sweater and a tartan wool dress; on her feet, handcrafted sealskin kamiks, halfway up her lower legs to the hem of her dress. Her hair was brushed and glistening with reflecting light from the hanging lamp. It flowed back and over her shoulders, midway to her slender waist. Her hair framed every inch of her smiling face, more angular than round, a characteristic of the north Baffin people. Naudla's complexion was deep brown, her skin soft, with striking deep-set eyes. Will imagined that, generations ago, there may have been a Viking influence in her bloodline.

He had never seen anyone so beautiful. He caught himself staring. Did anyone else?

Vee-Vee poured small drinks for the guests. According to the rules, he was not allowed to give them any alcohol. The Mounties knew that if crimes were committed in the Arctic, alcohol would be a factor. No exception.

Will had set a slightly cramped table for eight, improvising a tablecloth from a bedsheet. They had a stock of candles and just enough dinnerware. What they lacked in trimmings they made up for with a spirit of celebration.

The bottles were placed in front of Vee-Vee and he guarded them as though he were guarding a prisoner. He again poured small amounts for Pudlu, Teemotee, and Naudla, twice that amount for Will and Erik, and more still for himself.

The champagne maintained its sparkle and pop. They ate, toasted, and shouted "Happy New Year." Teemotee and Naudla took extra joy in saying "Happy New Year" slowly and clearly, laughing loudly at their success.

Pudlu said grace in his language. He paused. The Mounties, sensing the moment, offered "Amen" in unison.

Pudlu did his best to translate but table talk became difficult. Languages and cultures clashed. A shared sense of occasion became lost in strained silence.

"Look at us! We're trying to be part of the real world. For all we know, the real world may have ceased to exist with new fashions, fast cars, weird dances, and movies." Maybe the last toast had gotten to him. Will never was much of a drinker.

Vee-Vee and Erik looked puzzled.

Pudlu didn't try to translate. Why would he? The fads of the

Roaring Twenties meant nothing to him. He knew only one world and, for the moment, he, Teemotee, and Naudla had stepped outside it.

They ate and celebrated mostly in silence. Plates were again filled and the helpings devoured.

Pudlu sat on a short stool, an accordion on his knees, feet apart. The uppers of his below-the-knee sealskin boots were flecked with dried seal, polar bear, or walrus blood, the footwear of the hunter. The kids were dressed for a special occasion, in new hand-sewn clothes, likely Christmas presents, and new kamiks, beautifully patterned from harp-seal skins.

Will's arm was locked at the elbow with Naudla's, as they whirled and twirled to Pudlu's music. It was surreal. A five-person square set with one beautiful woman and four strapping men, one of them her husband. Will's three swings lasted only a few bars in Pudlu's reel.

Adding to Will's joy were the Scottish and Irish jigs and reels that comprised Pudlu's repertoire. How many times had he shouted to brother Ed on his violin at a good old-fashioned kitchen ceilidh to play the same tunes? "Red Wing," "Cock o' the North," and the energetic "High-Level Hornpipe."

As the note and tempo changed, Will released his arm, watching Naudla's hair and skirt flowing as she locked arms with her husband.

Will whirled with Vee-Vee, then Zalapski, and then he and Teemotee were hooked together, both laughing.

Will had liked Teemotee from their first meeting. Even though they couldn't communicate directly, they had hunted together and worked together building the cabins. Will was mastering basic dog-handling skills from observing Teemotee's every move.

With another high note Teemotee was gone from his right side and Naudla was swinging toward his left.

Will and Naudla locked eyes and twin shocks of longing shot deep into his stomach and loins.

Nothing that had come before matched the way Will felt at that moment.

With every tune, Naudla seemed to have more fun. The kids had fallen asleep while the adults moved from swing sets to simply dancing solo in a circle, stepping, clapping hands, laughing.

Will watched Teemotee, maybe as a distraction from lusting for his wife. Teemotee was watching Villeneuve, whose stares at Naudla were much less subtle. Will could see the senior constable crossing over to the drunk side of the happy line. Zalapski had pulled out of the dance set and was smoking his pipe. Pudlu watched everyone, and played, his expression unchanged.

They counted down to midnight on the Baby Ben alarm clock, shouted Happy New Year, and cheered.

Pudlu knew the occasion and the tune to go with it. He struck the first notes of "Auld Lang Syne." The Mounties bellowed out the words, surprised that their guests were singing along but in their own language. A century or more of contact with whalers and traders ran deeper than jigs, reels, and accordions. Consistent with tradition, they sang the first two verses. The music finished and Pudlu laid the accordion across his knee.

As tradition dictated, the handshakes began. Will's and Pudlu's grip confirmed a growing and trusting friendship. Zalapski grabbed Will's elbow as they shook hands, and looked him straight in the eye. "Happy New Year, Will. Let's wish for good days."

"Thank you, Erik," said Will, as he turned toward Teemotee. Villeneuve hadn't moved, and did nothing to welcome the first magic moment of 1925. He was staring, wide-eyed, slightly swaying. If he moved, it would have been a stagger.

Will was holding Teemotee's greeting hand, appreciating his efforts to say Happy New Year in English, when Villeneuve's voice boomed. "Happy New Year, beautiful Naudla. Give me my New Year's kiss!" He lunged forward and grabbed her waist. Naudla pulled away and turned in the same motion. Teemotee ripped his hand from Will's, turning it into a clenched fist.

With a police officer's instinct and training, Zalapski blocked Teemotee's path.

The Mounties had all heard sailor's tales that Inuit men shared their wives. That may have happened in some place, some time, but not here and not now.

Pudlu let the pipe he was lighting drop and he thrust the expanded accordion inwards. Its loud belching sound filled the room. Everyone stopped.

"Taima." It's over. The end, no more—finished.

The real leader in the room had spoken.

Villeneuve immediately backed off. So did Teemotee.

Naudla was shaken and embarrassed.

"Too late—everybody tired," said Pudlu.

"Atee-Atee," he snapped toward Teemotee and Naudla.

In an instant, they had dropped their heavy parkas over their heads. Teemotee scooped up the sleeping Piapik and dropped her into the hood of Naudla's amauti. He spoke to her softly in words

WHIT FRASER

no one except Pudlu and Nudla could understand. He bundled Kootoo in his powerful arms, and they left.

Every ounce of warmth, good tidings, and Happy New Year went out the door with the family.

The detachment was never as cold, nor as silent.

Villeneuve was sitting at the table, plates and cold food scattered. He had poured himself another drink, perhaps draining the bottle. After several minutes, Zalapski spoke. "Do you know what you've just done, Villeneuve?"

"I've done nothing and don't talk to me, you sick fruit."

Villeneuve turned away, gestured with the back of his hand as though to sweep Zalapski aside. In the other hand was his mug half full of straight whisky. Villeneuve drank half of it.

"I'm not talking to either one of you fags. You can go to hell."

Will had learned a long time ago not to argue or pick a fight with a drunk, especially not a mean one. Will knew that he wouldn't be able to keep his temper if he engaged. He needed to wait and hold it all in, for the safety of all. He stared at Villeneuve for another moment and then, in a voice colder and calmer than he recognized, added, "We'll deal with it tomorrow, but you're wrong, Villeneuve, dead wrong on just about everything."

Villeneuve gestured him aside with the sweep of his hand. "The brass should not have let either of you pansies come on this patrol."

Will looked at Zalapski, who was unmoved by the insult—or had decided to keep the fight for another time and place.

Villeneuve remained in a black mood. He paced and stomped. He drank the last of his rum. Pissed in the bucket rather than go outside. Finally, fully clothed, he flopped on his bunk.

Finally, Zalapski and Villeneuve were snoring. Will remained wide awake, still feeling Naudla's warmth and his hand on the small of her back as they danced. The brief brushes from her hips and thighs as they twirled had him half hard all night, thankfully hidden by two layers of wool trousers.

He rolled to his side, closed his eyes. The bunk felt warmed by her garments. In his mind, and not for the first time, he was stroking Naudla, slowly and softly.

Thou shalt not covet thy neighbour's wife was God's ninth commandment and, like all others, lay at the core of Will's values. He was a Christian, raised in a small Anglican church. The deep voice and dark piercing eyes of Reverend Kingsbury from the Sunday pulpit was burned in his memory and conscience.

CHAPTER 6

WALKING ON EGGSHELLS

D undas Harbour detachment log, Thursday, January 1, 1925. *Clear cold conditions outside, north wind, 35 below—spirits good!*

Those two last words were a bald-faced lie. In truth, New Year's Day, 1925, began with fear and remorse. The party that could have solidified friendships between colleagues and cultures turned into a drunken fiasco. All three Mounties knew that, but the perpetrator refused to admit it.

The cabin was freezing. Yet, no one moved from their bunk. To Will's surprise, Zalapski, generally the timid one, broke the icy silence. For Zalapski, good order and discipline extended beyond personal fears.

"You made a mess of things, Skipper, and you've got to fix it."

Will had been searching for his own words, perhaps a little less direct, and certainly less confrontational. But it was hard to argue with Zalapski's assessment. The evening had been a disaster. A drunk and obnoxious Villeneuve had made unwanted advances toward Naudla and then denied any responsibility.

"There's nothing for me to fix—except this goddamned stove." And Villeneuve was on his feet, a long, steel poker in one hand, a bucket of coal in the other, with more blaze in his eyes than in the stove.

Will tried to reason. "Let's just go up and say, 'Sorry, too much joy juice. We all got carried away.'"

"That'll be the goddamn day that I apologize to a bunch of snow gypsies after treating them as best I could."

Then he turned and faced Will, still holding the poker. "You've been wanting to get between those long legs since August. Maybe it's you who doesn't want to share."

"Skipper, you are so wrong, so very wrong. It's pitiful." But he felt exposed. Since August, he tried never to show his longing for Naudla, and he believed that he was fooling everyone.

"Do you think for a minute that when O'Halloran hired them last year, he didn't think that from time to time we would all have a whack at her? Why do you think she's here?"

"She's here, Villeneuve, because her husband and her brother would not come without her." There was a firm tone in Zalapski's voice that neither Will nor Villeneuve recognized.

Will had often asked himself a similar question. Why were he and Naudla here? Was this a strange and twisted destiny?

Villeneuve swore loudly in French and flung the poker against the back wall. He dressed in snow pants, kamiks, and parka, took his rifle from the rack, checked it, put some food in a pack, and left. It was dark, but he had established a well-worn trail close to the shoreline.

Zalapski looked out the window until the skipper vanished into the morning darkness. "Do you think we can fix things, Will?"

"I'll go up in a little while, Erik, and talk with Pudlu. But I'd say the biggest problem is how much booze Villeneuve drank and how quickly he can become one miserable drunk."

"Believe me, Will, he can be miserable when he's not drinking too. Last night was not the first time he's called me a fruit or a pansy. How many personalities does the bastard have?"

Will took a few steps toward Zalapski, who was sitting at the table.

"I don't believe it."

"Don't believe what? That I'm a fruit or that he thinks that I am?"

"I don't believe you're that way, and I need to be clear in saying that I'm shocked that he would think that and say that to you."

"There are no fast answers here, Will. We just have to figure it out a day at a time."

They looked at the kitchen, another aftermath that needed attention, but one that could be more quickly cleaned up. The water was hot, and they busily washed dishes, pots, and pans.

The uphill walk was longer and slower than usual for Will, made more so by the message than the biting wind and cold. He had been keeping track. This was only the second time that he'd been out since the accident. He was surprised to see that a rather large iglu had been built, close to the cabin with a rope stretched out between the two. The gales and blinding whiteout conditions from the past week told him that it was a lifeline.

It was mid-morning when Will opened the door to the cabin without knocking. He was still adjusting to this northern custom of simply walking into someone's home.

"Ullaakuut, everyone, and Happy New Year."

"Ayii," was the response from the three adults. The two kids hugged his leg.

"Pudlu, I know you will translate, but I need to tell all of you how sorry I am for the way things ended last night. That was not right. I'm sorry, Naudla."

Pudlu's interpretation was brief. Teemotee and Naudla both nodded but said nothing. "You did nothing wrong, Will. It just ended badly. We will try to forget." He paused, took a long draw on his pipe, and looked at Will again. "Will, I think you need to be careful. I think the boss is a troubled man, full of bad spirits."

Naudla offered him a mug of tea, which he took.

They sat in silence, but for the first time, Will found it uncomfortable and strained. Do they think all white men are like Villeneuve?

He needed to break it.

"Are you living in the iglu, Pudlu?"

"Sleep there. More room and good for snoring." Will saw the hint of a smile.

"I need to be active again, get out more, and do some things. Can we go soon and set some traps?"

"Eee. Maybe tomorrow."

"Great. I'll be up early and ready."

A tense silence prevailed in the detachment for most of the day.

Will told Zalapski that he had tried apologizing, adding that the tension had not diminished overnight.

Villeneuve, who had been gone all day, returned. Wordlessly, he put his gear away, ate some of the boiled muskox, wrote the daily log entry, undressed, and went to sleep.

Will set out his gear for the next day, told Zalapski of his plans, read for an hour, and went to sleep.

In the morning, Will was the first up. He got the fire and porridge started, packed extra food, and, as soon as he heard the dogs barking and howling, he was ready to help Pudlu harness them.

They headed west along the sea ice. As soon as the detachment disappeared behind the point, Pudlu seemed relieved. He slipped off the qamutik and ran alongside, motioning to Will to move up to the front, then passed him the whip and jumped on board behind him.

Will laid out a few practice strokes on either side of the lead dog, at the same time looking over his shoulder to get a response from his teacher. Pudlu gestured with an extended right arm. "Not too far from the shoreline."

After an hour, Pudlu pointed to a small valley and riverbed stretching northward. Will tried a few cracks and shouted the command to "go" he'd heard many times: "Hai, Hai!" The fan of dogs began arcing toward the shore and along the frozen riverbed into the small valley. He told himself that he would spend some time practicing the whipping technique.

Pudlu shouted and reined in the dogs. He asked Will for the book that he knew Will carried in an inside pocket and sketched a little picture of the landmark, indicating the trap's location. Pudlu then cut a piece of cloth and secured it with rocks to make it easier to find. He swept away the snow around each trap to remove his scent.

Will had 20 traps to set, secure, and mark up and down the small valley. On future trips, Will would tend his own traps, the same as Zalapski and Villeneuve, and he would check them every week.

Mid-morning, they boiled tea. Pudlu was prepared for the inevitable question.

"Are you and the others still upset about New Year and Villeneuve?"

"It's not like being upset, or something we will forget. We don't trust him and we are afraid of him. If you want to learn Inuktitut, you have to learn the word *Ilira*."

Will responded, "Il-a-ra. Ilira."

Pudlu, nodding approval, explained this small word with a very big meaning. "Ilira means fear of the Qallunaat, like fear of the unknown. All Inuit feel it. We are not taught Ilira. We just feel it."

"Do you feel that way about everyone? Were you afraid of Reverend Peck when you first saw him?"

"Even Qallunaat fear Peck."

"Are you afraid of me?"

"Not anymore. We can talk. Most white people don't talk to us. They tell us what to do and think. The fear goes away when we see that sometimes we are the same. It's that way with you, and Peck, and Captain Bernier. We called him Kapitaikallak—stout little captain or leader."

Will listened. "I think in English we call that good chemistry."

"Eee, but with Villeneuve that Ilira is always there. We feel his bad spirits and troubled soul. We fear him and we fear most Qallunaat."

Will bared his soul. "Pudlu, nukara, sometimes Zalapski and I fear him too, but we can't show that. We know he's troubled, but we have to work with him until they come back for us. Why did you come? For the money?"

"Money not important. Can make better money trapping on Baffin Island near Arctic Bay. We wanted to see this country. Heard stories about the west of here. Never for the money. That's not Inuk way."

They sat in silence for a moment. Will decided that he should let Pudlu know what was troubling him most. "Sometimes I wonder if they will ever come for us. We don't even know if Bernier made it all the way south."

Pudlu touched Will's shoulder reassuringly. "Kapitaikallak always comes back, but he can't always land. Atee-Atee." They continued up the valley for a few more hours until the twilight faded into total darkness. They quickly carved out a small iglu, fed the dogs, and slept warm and peacefully.

The next morning, Pudlu reassured Will that the next trip would take only a day. They had spent most of their time wrestling heavy rocks to mark locations and anchor the traps. Night had fallen by the time they crossed the snow-packed ridge on the way home and saw the outline of the detachment. The smoke from the chimneys billowed and hung low, pretty in the rising moonlight.

For half an hour, Will and Pudlu watched a magnificent display of northern lights build in the distant sky, growing brighter by the minute, moving and sweeping in long waves of gold, reds, greens, and hues that only the most gifted poets, like Will's favourite, Robert Service, could properly describe. Directly above them, vast coloured columns stretched straight down toward them like heavenly floodlights. Will felt as though he could reach out and touch them.

He realized that sometimes this big land was getting into his mind and soul, and tonight he was content to go with the flow.

Sitting back on the qamutik, looking skyward, he marvelled and drew it all in. It was a rare moment, when he had not a care in the world. The dogs knew where they were, and they would take them home.

Both men were in sync with the Arctic's artistry. It mattered not how many times Pudlu had seen magic in the cosmos, it still moved him; it was a glimpse into ancient legends and spirits. "Barking dogs make the northern lights dance. They are the spirits of the dogs."

They watched the spectacle until the dogs brought them to the shore below the detachment. Will and Pudlu worked quickly to unharness and feed the team. Then, they untied their packs, agreeing that the rest of the gear could wait until tomorrow.

Will watched Pudlu disappear into the darkness as he walked toward his iglu up the slope that became higher and steeper with each storm. Will quietly savoured his two unforgettable days with a good friend. The Arctic light show that he watched for another full minute was its icing on the cake.

He opened the door of the detachment.

"Don't look at me, you sick fruit."

Villeneuve was in his bunk, anger blazing in his dark eyes. Zalapski stood a few feet away, near the stove, no longer dumbfounded by the unwarranted attacks and abuse. "I was not staring, and neither am I a fruit, or sick."

Villeneuve became more aggressive. "I know what you are. We locked up perverts like you in Regina."

"Back off, Vee-Vee. Leave him alone. No one deserves that. We're in this together, and we'll need to stay together. Erik is not sick, not a fruit, not a pervert."

Villeneuve began to get up as though to physically challenge Will, but slowly sat back down again and pulled a blanket around his shoulders.

"I know what he is." Then he fell mute and did not move for another hour. It stretched for an eternity in the now still and silent room.

Will was relieved that, weeks before, Zalapski had told him of the accusation and verbal abuse. Zalapski was no doubt relieved that he now had a witness. They would talk—but privately.

Weeks of tedium, days of tension, and hours of terror wondering or waiting for Villeneuve's next outburst marked the next six weeks until, finally, the sun showed its face, on February 6, although only for about an hour and barely over the horizon.

All eight residents of Dundas Harbour watched and let out a cheer. The Inuit watched from a big drift near Pudlu's iglu. The Mounties watched from the front of the detachment, where they raised the flag. In the absence of fireworks, Will fired both barrels from the 12-gauge shotgun.

They knew that the sun would stay up 45 minutes the next day, and the day after that, even longer. Spirits lifted, even Villeneuve's—he smiled that night when he recorded the event, including raising the flag, in the logbook.

It was like a different man speaking. "Pretty soon, gentlemen, we're going to have to start planning the first of the two long patrols we have to undertake each year."

"I hope it's soon," offered Zalapski.

The next morning, two hours before sunrise, Villeneuve set out on foot by himself, by now not an uncommon practice.

Not long after he disappeared over the drifts and beyond the point, Zalapski said, "That was a welcome change last night, but how long will it last?"

"I don't know, Erik, but can we go for years walking on eggshells, wondering what will set him off?"

"Will, I hear him scream in the middle of the night. These books tell us how to cut off your fingers but not how to deal with shell shock."

"Daylight will give us some relief—and he did seem excited about the first major patrol."

The next morning, Will was up early, harnessed his six dogs, and set out on his private excursion. He would also check Pudlu's closest traps. He was feeling good, confident, and independent, knowing that he could fend for himself in this hard, cold, and beautiful place.

His hands had healed well but were extremely sensitive to the cold. Will learned to adjust and wore an extra pair of mitts. His hands hurt in the time it took to roll a smoke outdoors, so he began rolling a stash in the cabin and carrying them in a tin.

The sky was a striking bright blue in the full sunshine. The reflection off the snow and ice gave it hue and depth, unlike anything he had ever seen. He wore the tinted glasses that had been issued, but every time he had to exert himself, the damn things frosted up. Snow blindness, he knew, was just as dangerous as frostbite.

The trip yielded two pelts, which he initially thought rather pitiful considering the time, distance, and effort. But Pudlu was grateful to have the traps and pelts retrieved, given that they wouldn't be back for six or eight weeks. He didn't like feeding valuable fox skins to scavengers.

Villeneuve was again communicating with Pudlu. He called him into the detachment and spread out a large map on the table detailing Baffin Bay, Devon Island, and Lancaster Sound.

Heavy dark dots marked the south coast of Ellesmere Island and the Craig Harbour Post, and toward the bottom middle, north Baffin Island, Pond Inlet, and Arctic Bay. In the middle of the map, Devon Island and Dundas Harbour were marked with a big black X.

Pudlu looked at the map carefully. Will knew that in his head Pudlu saw every natural and manmade landmark between every marked point. On their travels together, Pudlu often pointed out the traditional cairns, or Inukshuks, that were built on high points of land to show the way by both land and sea.

Villeneuve drew his pencil along the south coast of Devon, westward around the island, and up the west side. He pointed out Beechey Island, also bearing a dot: 200 miles away. The total journey would take them well beyond Beechey Island, perhaps 250 miles in all and another 250 miles back.

Pudlu studied it carefully. "Long trip, maybe six weeks, maybe two months, very long trip." He smiled. "When do you want to leave?"

"March 25? Two weeks."

"Eee. Two weeks. Eee. Lots to get ready."

Pudlu was excited, and it finally occurred to Will that he, Teemotee, and Naudla were probably also bored and stir-crazy in their cramped surroundings—if not suffering the degree of turmoil in the detachment and Villeneuve's mind.

"Christ, I hope he doesn't lose it again out there, Will." But Will scarcely heard Zalapski. His eyes were fixed on the map and the dot marked Beechey Island. What about that place gave him a strange feeling?

The Mounties had been told about Beechey Island in the Ottawa briefing and instructed to erect a cairn there in the name of Canada. They had also been given some of the island's history, and it was part of their tiny library. That night, Will read it again and felt even more uncomfortable.

Beechey Island was no more than a few square miles, hardly more than a gravel ridge at the southwest side of Devon Island, almost in the middle of Lancaster Sound. It was noted not for its size but rather for its sheltered bay and harbour that had been marked on maps by early explorers more than a century earlier and most notably used as a base in the search for John Franklin.

Franklin had sailed from England in 1845 with two ships, *Terror* and *Erebus*, and 134 men. His orders from the British Admiralty were to find the Northwest Passage. By September, he had sailed past what would become the Dundas Harbour Post. He then encountered impenetrable ice barricades, like those—at least in Will's mind—that had confronted the *Arctic* when Bernier tried to get them into Pond Inlet; like the frozen, floating barriers that Bernier feared he would face when he left them back in September.

Two days before the journey, preparations were finalized and qamutiks packed. The items they needed most were placed on the top: tea, sugar, food, guns, and bullets; those they used once a day—tents, sleeping apparel, and hides—on the bottom.

They could never carry enough food for eight people and more than 30 dogs for 40 or more days. But they needed enough kerosene, tea, sugar, flour, oatmeal, lard, cans of salt pork, beans, beef, and vegetables, hardtack, and that one cherished luxury—toilet paper.

The bright sunshine and the deep blue, cloudless skies were in marked contrast to the temperatures. The calendar spring,

March 21, had just passed, but at 10 a.m., when the heavily laden dog teams set out on a 500-mile return sovereignty odyssey, Villeneuve recorded the mercury at -35°F.

Yet no one complained, and, indeed, the sun that was now in the sky 12 hours, and staying longer every day, had a warming effect. Will could feel the warmth penetrating his heavy parka lined with duffle wool. All were dressed in bearskin pants, and the children wore matching boots and parkas.

The expedition would be long and unprecedented, but it did not have a schedule. No one expected at the beginning, nor anywhere along the frozen route, that there would be a need to set a frantic pace.

The dogs wanted to run and Pudlu, Teemotee, and Villeneuve, who was commanding the third team, let them go. After half an hour, the dogs slowed to their own pace. Will and the others often got off the qamutik and ran alongside to keep warm. The sun continued to beat at their faces, and the Mounties frequently cleared the frost off their goggles.

Pudlu, Teemotee, Naudla, and the children wore traditional snow goggles, thin bands of bone carved with tiny slits that cut the glare, allowing just enough space to see the land, the ice, and, in time, basking seals.

Will rode with Pudlu. Sometimes Kootoo would scoot from one qamutik to the other, jumping on his uncle's lap. Pudlu allowed him to hold the whip, letting it trail behind.

Pudlu handed Will a pair of his traditional goggles. At first, Will had trouble adjusting, but he soon learned to focus through the centre of the slits. They didn't fog up.

The next day, sitting on the qamutik, Pudlu carved a second

pair, offered them to Zalapski, who tried them immediately. The following day, he generously offered another new pair to Villeneuve, who accepted with apparent skepticism. He would put them on, wear them for a few minutes, return to the sunglasses, note the continued fogging, then return to the bone goggles. By the second day, and a dozen tries, Villeneuve was converted.

Naudla and Piapik rode with Teemotee, and Will consciously tried to avoid staring. The sun was shining on her face, which was framed by thick fur trim. She was radiant. Will looked at the fur brushing her cheek and forehead and smiled. He first believed that parka fur came from wolves until he saw Pudlu dispatch a dog that had been badly gutted in a fight and then casually remove the dog's hide. He knew that his RCMP issue parka was trimmed with wolverine, considered by all to be superior for its ability to shed breath frost and retain heat inside the parka hood.

They travelled on sea ice parallel to the cliffs of Devon Island that stretched skyward, in some places 500 to 600 feet, occasionally giving way to valleys and fjords.

Will recognized the river valley where he and Pudlu had set traps, and motioned. Pudlu smiled. "We'll go there on the way back. There's a lake with big char, but now they're down too deep and sleeping."

They had set a pace of about six hours a day—perhaps 18 miles. They would not travel on Sundays, resting themselves and the dogs, and doing chores, washing underclothes mostly by using snow, or inside a tent or iglu with lukewarm water from melted snow and ice. On Sundays, Pudlu and Will read their bibles and set up the chessboard that Will had been instructed to bring. Pudlu carved small seal pawns as he contemplated strategy and waited for Will to move. Most times, Pudlu won.

WHIT FRASER

The days quickly turned from adventure to routine. Four days out from the detachment, Teemotee saw a big square flipper seal on the sea ice. He reined in his dogs and the others followed his cue.

As with the muskox hunt months before, the others stayed silent while Teemotee took his rifle, camouflage shield, and—to the surprise of the constables—Kootoo. They crept side by side together to get 100 yards closer. The little boy watched his father's every move.

Everyone let out "Yeah!" when the rifle cracked and the seal's head snapped back and it dropped motionless on the ice.

As Teemotee skinned and butchered the seal, the others set up camp close to the shore for the night. Seal blubber and liver filled the plates at the evening meal.

On the fifteenth day, they glimpsed Beechey Island.

"How uninspiring" was Will's response.

Instinctively and instantly, he didn't like the place. His earlier unease when he saw it on the map and read scarce details of Franklin and his misfortunes still haunted him. More troubling, he didn't know why.

Villeneuve was determined to camp on the island, spend a few days there, and reclaim it once more for Canada with canisters, a written record, and flags placed solemnly in cairns erected by the British 75 years earlier.

The exercise was anticlimactic as Britain had ceded the Arctic islands to Canada in 1880. The Mounties, by their presence, were sealing the deal, Will supposed. He gazed along the snow, ice, and rocks that swept a mile or more in front of him, stretching to high cliffs and a rounded crown.

The sheltered bay, named after Franklin's ships *Erebus* and *Terror*, by a Franklin search party, separated Devon and Beechey Islands by no more than 2 miles. Beechey's distinguishable geographic feature was a massive rounded cape, flat on the top at its eastern extremity, pointing the way back to Britain. It sloped downward toward the west, like the back of a crouched multicoloured tabby cat, in shades of browns, blacks, and greys, and a long, stretching gravel tail, the isthmus of a peninsula that at its narrowest point connected to Devon Island.

As the Mounties walked the beach, they were drawn to the four wooden grave markers that they had learned about in briefings. No more than 45 inches high, the markers dominated the bleak landscape—solitary and stark against the winter snows and darkening skies.

Will, Villeneuve, and Zalapski stood before them and stared in silence.

The weathered markers were half covered with snow, which the men gently and reverently brushed aside, revealing the names of those who had perished there during Franklin's last expedition.

A fourth grave belonged to a sailor who died several years later, one of many casualties of the dozens of expeditions that spent a decade searching in vain for this most famous failed quest for the Northwest Passage.

Twenty years earlier, a member of Bernier's crew had repainted the names, ensuring that they would not be eroded by years and decades of vicious winter winds and driving snows. A lump formed in Will's throat as he read aloud: "John Torrington, age 20; John Hartnell, aged 25; William Braine, aged 30."

Villeneuve appeared to be shaking. Will and Zalapski looked

at him. Perhaps it was the cold, Will thought, considering that it was still -30°F and the wind was stiff. It never stopped blowing in this desolate, doomed place.

Villeneuve finally spoke. "Jesus, they are the ages of the boys we left on the fields in France." He paused. "Will, you should say a prayer for them."

They knelt, closed their eyes, and clasped their hands together.

Will's prayer was soft. Most of it was lost to the howling wind and muffled by fur caps and parka hoods covering their ears—except the final "We pray for their salvation."

Three solemn and shaky voices added, "Amen."

As Will rose to his feet and looked at the sweep of the most damned and desolate place he had ever set foot on, a severe emptiness gripped his gut.

He had just prayed for lost souls—and wondered if he had just lost his own. His mind raced. *Were prayers ever answered in this place? Is this truly God's forsaken land? Did those young men buried here in the frozen gravel, and the other 126, also pray as their misery, starvation, scurvy, madness, pain, cold, and suffering gripped them?* Their true story could never be told, because no one survived.

Will and Zalapski had read how Francis Leopold McClintock, a Franklin searcher, had discovered scattered bones and expedition members' personal belongings hundreds of miles south on King William Island.

The three Mounties walked westward, wind in their faces, the first day in 10 that the sun was not painting a blue sky. It was overcast, damp, and bitingly cold, as though the weather had changed to match the despair of this desolate High Arctic graveyard.

Walking was challenging. Ice- and snow-covered round rocks and coarse gravel had been whipped and pushed up the steep slope by centuries of wind and tides. The narrow terraces were barely wide enough for two people to walk abreast.

A half-hour later, and a mile from the graves, Will found the remnants of the yacht *Mary*. The sturdy little vessel had been towed across the North Atlantic up the Davis Strait and into Lancaster Sound by Sir John Ross in 1850, five years after Franklin had left England. Will had read the history at the detachment and hoped at least that some of the ships would still be here.

Ross had hung on to the faint hope that, after five years, somehow Franklin, or some of his crew, would find their way back there. And if by a miracle they did, the sound little sailing ship *Mary* would be there for them, rigged and ready for a return to England.

Ross had overwintered on Beechey. He had had no choice, but Will was impressed by his commitment. When Ross returned home, he had full knowledge of the hardships that Franklin and his crew had endured there.

The keel of the *Mary* was now buried in the gravel and ice, and most of her planks had been torn away by the years. Her mast, which once stood tall, a beacon of hope, now lay like driftwood in the gravel.

On the gravelled terrace behind Will and the Mounties stood a large, eight-sided wooden post with a round ball on top. "Originally, it had lead plates on each side with the names of all the men engraved who died looking for Franklin. It's a sort of cenotaph," said Will. A marble plaque commissioned by Lady Franklin had been cemented in front of it.

Will and Zalapski were keen to share the history they'd read on the eve of their departure with Villeneuve.

"In 1852, the Admiralty dispatched five more search ships, and they used Beechey as a base. One of the commanders W.J.S. Pullen, who had not given up hope either, built this storehouse," said Will, as he walked with Villeneuve around the skeletal remains of the building, "where they cached supplies and provisions in case Franklin made it back. He named it Northumberland House." The roof had long since caved in, and three of the four walls had collapsed. The structure had been constructed with substantial-sized hewn square timbers, most 6 by 6 inches. One half wall had been built by stacking flat stones.

The inside of the building, once filled with supplies, now had only scattered barrel staves, metal hoops, and empty cans. Seventy-plus years of marauding polar bears, the fierce weather, and the odd souvenir-hunting explorer had taken their toll. The constables stared at the ruins and destruction, each finding deeper meaning and lessons among the ruins.

All this had been left seven years after Franklin had disappeared. Will couldn't help but wonder—was that a statement of unwavering faith, or a complete loss of it? If Bernier hadn't made it home last year, would anyone do half this much for them?

CHAPTER 7

THE INEVITABLE

At their midday break, the two qamutiks sat parallel, no more than 6 feet apart: Teemotee, Naudla, and Pudlu on one; and Will, Villeneuve, and Zalapski on the other. The kids were playing tag. The sun was shining directly on the Mounties' faces. Pudlu laughed. He spoke to his sister and her husband, and they too joined the laughter.

"What's so funny?" asked Will.

"Look at your faces. You don't look like Qallunaat. You look like us." Pudlu was animated, pointing to everyone's faces, still laughing.

Will, Zalapski, and Villeneuve looked at one another. How could they have missed this? Three weeks in bright sunshine, up to 18 hours a day, with the reflection off the snow and the persistent wind had turned their faces a deep, dark brown. Except for their eyes and hair, hidden under fur hats and parka hoods, they were almost indistinguishable from their companions.

Will and Zalapski shared the laughter.

"Must be eating too much seal meat," added Zalapski.

Villeneuve smiled faintly. "My tan is French brown."

The group decided not to push their remarkable luck any further. They were on the ice of Wellington Channel, 30 miles north of Cape Spencer on the southwestern half of Devon Island.

On Saturday, April 11, Villeneuve recorded 250 miles travelled over 22 days. The weather: light winds, a temperature of -30°F, and bright sunshine. They had built their last cairn three days ago.

No one needed to be reminded of their good fortune: no inclement weather, no accidents, no disasters. Their provisions were holding up. They had been blessed with an abundance of seals on the ice to keep both themselves and the dogs stocked with fresh meat.

Will finished the tea that always cooled before he could drink it. "Never thought I would get homesick for our shack, but it will be good to get back to the warm stove, even if it takes a month."

As the words left his mouth, Will knew that he was not being completely honest. He sensed Villeneuve's agitation and was simply trying to change the subject without dismissing good humour and friendly banter.

He knew that Zalapski sensed it too. They had spoken about Villeneuve's moods several times. Would a return to the detachment mean a return to Villeneuve's anger, dark moods, and attacks on Zalapski?

The trip had been good for all three Mounties and Will was determined to enjoy the long ride home. They maintained the same pace of about six hours or 15 miles a day with rest on Sundays and did not challenge the weather.

The Mounties learned that two different conditions bear the term whiteout. The first is a blinding blizzard—which they had all experienced—when the wind drives the snow with such force that no one can see more than a few feet. The second is when there is no wind and a frozen fog rolls between an overcast sky and the ice. Snow and landmarks and open water all blend into one confining, confusing whiteness. The group had encountered two such days so far during this patrol and could expect even more on the way home, as the temperature rose gradually.

They travelled southward down Wellington Channel, which separates Devon and Cornwallis Islands, for three days before the ice fog began rolling off the floe edge from Lancaster Sound and the adjoining Parry Channel to the west. They could still see the cliffs on the southwest cape of Devon Island only a few miles away, when Pudlu suggested that they hunker down.

After three days in place, Will was relieved when the fog lifted and the skies cleared. They would travel westward beyond Beechey Island. No one wanted to go back there, including Pudlu.

Pudlu and Will had talked about it the day before, Sunday. They were sharing an iglu and Will was not surprised to see Pudlu take his tattered syllabics bible out of his pack and begin reading it. There had been many Sundays when they sat together, reading. For the first Sunday going back longer than he could remember, Will did not take out his bible.

Finally, he broke the silence.

"Pudlu, do you ever doubt that God hears us, or even exists? Did he ever hear the prayers of those poor bastards on Beechey Island, and wherever they went from there to suffer and die?"

Pudlu looked him squarely in the eye. He thought long before answering, maybe he was asking God to guide him.

"Will, nukara, how hard do you think it is for Inuit to believe?

We had beliefs and spirits, and Qallunaat told us we burn in hell. Reverend Peck talks about faith.

"God doesn't give us what we ask. The same as not giving children what they ask for. God take my wife and two babies, with the big Qallunaat sickness five years ago. But I believe."

Will was overwhelmed. "I'm sorry, Pudlu. I didn't know. I am so sorry."

"Will, it was my faith in your God, now my God, that helped me through. I came to believe that we are all part of his master plan, and we must have faith in his wisdom."

Pudlu paused. "In here," he pointed to his head, "I also have questions sometimes. But in here," his hand moved over his heart and down across his gut, "in here, I believe, and, in here, I know what I believe is right."

Will would be 30 in a few weeks. For as long as he could remember, he had been listening to Sunday sermons. None was more heartfelt than the words of this Inuk in an iglu in a land Will still considered godforsaken.

For the sake of friendship and brotherly love, Will let the matter lie, like the old bible in his pack.

Early Monday, they were back on the frozen trail. One more Sunday, two additional rest days, and three bad weather days all blended into one as the sun rose higher and higher in the sky, and the days grew longer, until April 28, when it did not set at all. With the long days came noticeably warmer temperatures, but still far below zero.

Sometimes, the only change in scenery was the dogs shifting places in the fan, until the hitch line became so tangled that the dogs seemed to be pulling one another rather than the load. Will often amused himself just watching them, wondering if this crisscrossing of traces was their own game, a way to break their boredom or even to get a break. Certainly, the dogs dictated the pace and timing for every occasion: a tea, a meal, a smoke, or a piss.

The teams travelled in single file, about 30 feet between the first and second, and similarly between the second and third.

Everyone took turns nodding off for short periods, weaving side to side with the gentle motion of the qamutik.

Will came out of a half-sleep to see, in the distance, the familiar rocky snout of the westerly cape that sheltered Dundas Harbour. Just ahead was the small river valley that he thought of as his trapline. He felt strangely at home.

Half a mile later, Pudlu kept a promise and turned the dogs up the valley.

They travelled for about three hours and Will was familiar with the terrain until the valley became narrower. They followed the river. In places, winds had swept the ice clean, and it was possible to look through the ice at the gravel bed below. The ice might have been 8 or 10 feet deep. The river flowed in a generally straight line, with one big bend toward the end where it opened into a small lake a mile long and half a mile wide. The valley and river extended beyond the lake, but how far into the interior of Devon was a mystery. Perhaps someday he would explore and find out.

Pudlu and Teemotee untied the ice chisels lashed to either side of their qamutiks. They had four: two with painted red handles that belonged to the Mounties, and two with rougher handles, carved from scrap wood. All had similar heads of heavy steel, weighing 3 pounds to provide a good punch against the ice. Standing face to face, Pudlu and Teemotee began chipping a hole,

6 to 8 inches in diameter. Villeneuve and Zalapski took the other two chisels and did the same.

They had never encountered 4-foot-thick ice before and agreed that cutting through it is not work for the feeble or frail. Although Will's hands were still tender, he could manage the long ladlelike strainer and scoop ice chips out of the way.

All four had been chipping for over an hour when Pudlu and Teemotee felt their chisels hit the soft and squishy spot just above the waterline. A few more punches created a small hole, into which water gushed, filling it. Will cleaned it out for the final time, then scooped a mugful. It was the purest, cleanest water he had ever tasted. The melt came from the million-year-old glacier that is the Devon Ice Cap. Everyone wanted to taste it.

Naudla had been watching with the kids, but she had their strong braided cotton lines ready.

Hooks were baited with a small chunk of seal fat. Naudla's line had barely found its full 8-foot depth when she screamed "Iqaluk, iqaluk!" Fish, fish! She laughed and pulled hand over hand on the line until a huge Arctic char flopped on the ice. It was over 2 feet long with a shiny black back, silver sides, and a snow-white belly.

Will had tasted char when at anchor in Craig Harbour. The cook had bought some from an Inuk. It was delicious and very close in taste, texture, and appearance to Atlantic salmon and the sea-run brook trout he had often caught back home—although the char here were much bigger and more plentiful.

Naudla's first fish must have been over 5 pounds. In a few minutes, she had another. Then Kootoo took a turn and, moments later, a fish about half his size also flopped on the ice. Even Piapik got a chance, although her mother did the heavy lifting of the big fish through the hole and onto the ice.

Will watched, and shouted to Zalapski and Villeneuve. "Look how beautiful and how magnificent these fish are."

These fish would have spawned in the area the previous year, and over the winter, their deep fiery red bellies changed to glistening white. Their sides were a beautiful silver grey. To Will's eye, their distinguishing feature was a black line running the length of the body from gill to tail.

Villeneuve and Zalapski were instantly invigorated to finish their hole. Pudlu and Teemotee were chopping a second opening, and Will resumed his scooping duties, shifting from one hole to the other.

He made it a point to stop and watch Naudla in between. She was still laughing. He had never seen her look so happy. Then she looked straight into his eyes. It was electric and, for the first time, she didn't look away. Their eyes lingered, and Naudla didn't stopped smiling. Will hadn't felt this alive since the dance. They both slowly looked away.

Six weeks ago, before leaving the detachment, Pudlu had told them to be prepared for this event, and their lines were ready as soon they finished the hole. They took turns. When Villeneuve hooked his first char, close to 10 pounds, his boisterous laughter echoed up and down the valley.

"Jesus, don't start another avalanche," Zalapski joked. He and Will had finally heard the big man laugh.

Zalapski hooked his first fish. Will took his turn. He copied Naudla's technique by laying on his stomach, face over the hole, watching the hook straight down in the clear water. Suddenly, from under the ice, a big char charged the hook, almost pulling the handle out of Will's hand.

Now Will was screaming and laughing with excitement.

As Pudlu and Teemotee worked on the second hole, the constables rotated between fishing, scooping, and laughing. Rarely would anyone's hook be in the water for more than a few minutes before a char would devour it.

Will considered the spectacle: hardened Mounties and war veterans, skilled Inuit hunters, one of them a beautiful woman, little children, all rolling around on the snow and ice, laughing, sharing the same joy. At this moment, there was no place he would rather be.

In an hour and a half, they had landed and stacked, like firewood, more than 60 big fish alongside a qamutik. Some had already frozen, others were nearly frozen.

Teemotee pumped and lit a Primus stove, filled a kettle with clear cold water, and boiled tea that kings and queens would envy.

Naudla filleted a char and cut the deep pink flesh into thick squares with her razor-sharp ulu. She served the bites on the flat blade, holding it out like a small platter.

Will was about to blurt "Any fingers on that thing?" recognizing the ulu as a surgical instrument.

"Hard to resist." He removed his mitt, grabbed two pieces, and popped them in his mouth.

"Mamaqtuq. Very good."

Will was pleased with himself for remembering the pronunciation from a Pudlu lesson. The raw fish tasted as pure as the waters it came from, with an aftertaste similar to that of a raw oyster. Neither Villeneuve nor Zalapski hesitated.

Zalapski made the predictable comparison. "I'll take this over raw liver any day."

They helped themselves to the dozen pieces Naudla had laid out on the snow.

Pudlu was a little disappointed. "Iqaluk is too far down. I wanted to use a spear." He was pumping his forearm in an up-and-down motion. "Bigger fun. Maybe we come back in a week."

If he was looking to Villeneuve for approval, he got it. "We look forward to it!"

They set up their last camp on day 43. If the weather held, they would be back at the detachment tomorrow. Will realized that he was losing track of the time of day, unlike the dark period when he was obsessed with time.

On that last night, the Mounties opted for the big tent, stoves, and fresh fish.

Will took his knife and cut two clean fillets, leaving only the head and backbone.

Pudlu watched. "Piuujuk. Pretty good."

Will smiled. "I hope so—the son of a fisherman, who was the son of a fisherman, who was the son of a fisherman." It was one more moment when he realized how much he could feel at home in this cold, bountiful land.

Before noon the next day, they had crossed the western cape of Dundas Harbour and turned toward shore and the detachment.

"Harmony Harbour," shouted Zalapski.

Forty-four days on the ice, 22 each way, more a coincidence than smart scheduling. They'd travelled nearly 500 miles. And because of the 200-plus pounds of char they'd lashed to the qamutiks the day before, the dog teams were still pulling heavy loads.

In all that time and miles, they had avoided a hundred potential mishaps: weather, open water, snow blindness, whiteouts, and avalanches. For 44 days, no one worried about their well-being or expressed concern about where they were or not finding their way back.

Will thought of Pop MacKay's favourite expression: *Safe as in God's pocket.* He wasn't free of doubts, but he did know that they were safe because of the skills and wisdom of Pudlu, Teemotee, and Naudla. Naudla was sitting on his right, upright on the load, her face directly in the sun, smiling. She caught Will looking at her, and smiled back.

The detachment had a homey feeling. The fires from two stoves felt good, the buckets of hot water in their collapsible bathtub even better. Clean bunks, clean clothes, clean everything.

Will laughed one more time at Pudlu's astute observation about the Mountie's skin colour when he saw Zalapski's pure white ass and shoulders slide into the tub, contrasting with his sunbaked face.

He laughed at himself too, when he looked into the mirror and shaved. He hadn't grown a beard on the trail but he did not have the luxury of a mirror on those occasions when he did shave.

Villeneuve had been the first in the tub. He dried himself, dressed, and went to check the storehouse and provisions, and returned with a sack of essentials: tea, flour, jam, and lard. He dug deep into his footlocker and produced the last bottle of rum, thumping it loudly on the table.

"Join me, chaps, and drink to a great patrol."

Will and Zalapski toasted without pause but worried as

Villeneuve poured himself another.

Villeneuve entered the events of May 1 and the final days of the patrol into the log, noted "mission accomplished," and poured three more fingers.

Will cooked char for dinner, tinned potatoes and vegetables, and fresh bannock—a fine and well-deserved meal. They ate mostly in silence. What conversation there was saluted the char and its freshness. Zalapski cleared and cleaned the dishes, while Will lay on his bunk, halfway between dozing and reading. Villeneuve stayed at the table.

Zalapski finished his chores and stretched out on his bunk, and jumped right back up. "Christ! It's all wet."

At that moment, from right over his head, Will heard a loud crack and creaking noise.

"I think we've got trouble overhead."

The three men scrambled up the steep, rough stairs to the cold loft used for storing lightweight provisions, including toilet paper, tea, rolls of duffel cloth, and extra clothing.

Against the northwest wall, over Zalapski's bunk, a small snowdrift, 2 feet high and 5 feet long, had formed from a small opening under the east gable.

"There's your leak," observed Villeneuve, as he raised a lantern, instantly revealing two roof rafters which had cracked and partially separated from the ridge beam.

"Hold this." He passed the lamp to Will and scrambled down the stairs. He returned in a minute with the two short planks they had used to bar the doors against bears when they were away. He wedged a plank vertically under each of the cracked rafters, kicking them into place with his heavy boot.

"I was worried about the drifts on top of the roof when we arrived today but thought it would be okay for another day. I bet that all the heat from the stoves has caused melting, and added weight." Villeneuve looked again at the rafters.

"You two get up there and clear it away. Take at least a few hundred pounds off this roof. Get Pudlu and Teemotee to help. I'll look after this."

As they came out of the detachment, they saw Pudlu and Teemotee, doing their chores and putting away the gear. They motioned to them. No one needed a ladder to get on the roof. They just walked up the long steep drift and began cutting blocks with steel shovels and snow knives.

Twenty minutes later, they watched Villeneuve returning from the storehouse with three 10-foot-long, 2-by-8 planks on his shoulder and a saw in his hand.

"You know, Erik, he's such a hard son of a bitch to read, but there's no one better in a crisis, and no one more difficult to read in good times. I don't understand."

"Neither do I, Will. I told you how he took control when you had your accident. I was proud to know him and serve with him."

Minutes later, they could hear Villeneuve hammering and cutting on the opposite side of the roof as they shovelled their way along the eve and up the roof, taking extreme care not to step on the damaged beams. Will lost track of time. It felt like 6 p.m., but actually it was an hour before midnight.

They met Villeneuve at the door as they walked into the detachment. He had shovelled the snow in the loft into empty coal bags and was dragging them outside.

"All cleaned up. Erik, you won't be wondering if you pissed

the bed." He was smiling. "Tomorrow, I'll add extra support, but I'm sure we're okay for tonight. It looks like you took a helluva lot of snow off."

They shared one final drink and turned in.

Will smiled, knowing he was not the only one oblivious to the time of day or night. He could hear the kids, running, playing tag, sliding, and, best of all, laughing.

May 24, Victoria Day—the queen's birthday was a favourite holiday in Will's Nova Scotia home. He and his three brothers and sisters were always outdoors. It was the big trout fishing week. Will smiled to himself: he thought those trout were large until he had seen Arctic char. But the trout were plentiful in the pools of the small stream that meandered through the meadow back of his century-old one-and-a-half-storey home. The house was small, three rooms upstairs—parents', boys', and girls' bedrooms—and three down—kitchen, living room, and dining room. The Grants, like everyone else in that part of Nova Scotia, were United Empire Loyalists. Easy living was not part of their history.

May 24 traditions were the same where Villeneuve and Zalapski were born. It was coincidence that Pudlu suggested that it might be a good time to try spearfishing up the little river valley.

They packed lightly, took only two dog teams, and planned to be gone only one night. Naudla and the children did not join them. Will wondered why, but he knew that it was not his place to ask. Perhaps she wanted some peace.

The pattern was the same as the last time: four men chipped away at the holes and Will bailed. He didn't think there could be more fish than the last time, but there were.

The kiviak, or spear, was a trident design: three prongs, with the two outer ones made from pliable bone to spring and clasp the sides of the fish. The centre prong was a steel-sharpened shaft, perhaps filed from a nail, with barbs to hold the fish in place. The kiviak Pudlu handed Will was much heavier and larger than those he had used back home for smelts.

The technique was simple: Keep the kiviak hidden in the hole, and dangle a shiny attraction in the water. When a char comes into sight across the hole, plunge downward hard and fast. All three Mounties missed on the first few tries, tending to scare the char away when drawing the spear upward as to cock the arm.

The char ranged from 2 to 10 pounds. And five grown men were having a marvellous time, pure joy on the ice. Between them, they caught over 60.

Naudla would dry and hang most of the char and make pitsiq. Will would do the same with his share; it was similar to the dried and salt cod that had been the mainstay of his family's diet back home.

On June 4, 1925, Will wrote in his journal:

June is surely the purest month. I can feel the warmth of the sun bouncing back from the walls of the giant cliffs, melting the snow into a hundred little brooks running seaward from the giant valley. It surely cleanses one's heart and mind.

Life became easier as the thermometer rose a few degrees above zero. Will realized the luxury of scooping clear, clean water instead of chopping ice and melting snow for cooking and washing.

The sky was alive with geese, ducks, and gulls, noisily flying overhead in search of nesting grounds. On the ice, the softer snow made travel easier. Seals and walruses basked in the sun. Teemotee and Pudlu had shot a few and cached enough meat for themselves and the dogs for the months ahead.

The three Mounties and Pudlu were standing close to the shore, watching a female polar bear and two cubs travelling across the ice. "She knows we're here," Pudlu said. "She can smell us and she's moving away from us."

Villeneuve remained in good spirits. He had quiet days when he spoke very little. Neither Will nor Zalapski had experienced his anger in weeks, nor did Zalapski endure personal attacks.

"I think we should do a short patrol, for a day and a night. Do a little hunting on our own. Perhaps we can spot muskox. Are you both in?"

"You betcha, Skipper," said Zalapski.

Will responded, "I'll make fresh bannock and get some grub ready. Are you thinking to leave tomorrow?"

"Tomorrow it is."

It was like a family picnic. They travelled across the ice and sucked up the sunshine and warmth. They stopped several times and walked inland, checking out the newly named Char River, and continued westward, exploring small valleys in the hopes of finding muskox.

All they found was fresh shit that Will said made thin soup.

At midnight, they set up a tent and slept on skins and sleeping bags.

During the return trip, Will signalled to Villeneuve to pull in the dogs. They were at the mouth of Char River where they had fished and set fox traps. He still had a dozen or so traps lying idle close to the cliffs between here and the detachment.

"I want to walk from here. I need to pick up some traps and maybe explore a bit." Will put bannock, hardtack, and jam in his pack, strapped the 12-gauge shotgun over his shoulder for bear protection, and set out on foot.

"I'm sure I'll be back by supper. I may even bring supper." He pointed to a flock of snow geese looking for a place to land.

Will walked toward the shore. The snow was soft. A few times, he sank to his knees. He could see the dog team and his colleagues disappear behind the point. It was good to be alone.

Within 10 minutes, he'd found his first trap, rolled the chain around it, and put it in the bottom of his pack. He picked up several more, stopped a few times for a smoke, and drank water which fell 200 feet straight down from a cliff into his cup. He could feel the sun's warmth reflecting off the cliff. He put his hands under the falls and washed his face. The water was cold but refreshing. He looked at his surroundings—a thousand miles of nothing in every direction, a warm sun, the falls, the ice, the lichen. He might never again experience a moment like this.

He stripped and walked naked into the cascade. His heart almost stopped. Instinctively, he gasped and held his balls. He stayed in the spray as long as he could. In truth, it was no more than a minute. With his last 10 seconds of stamina, he washed his face and hair, and stepped back with a shout that was lost in the ice-cold gush. "Yes. Yes. I'm alive—so alive!"

As he stepped sideways out of the spray, his bare ass met the smooth, warm cliff wall. Enjoying the warmth of the sun on his face, he dried himself, dressed, ate bannock and a biscuit, drank more water, and walked eastward.

All the traps were half an hour's walk from the detachment.

He saw something move along the cliff wall 100 or more yards in front and to his left. He walked closer. The figure moved again and emerged in the full sunlight. Will's heart skipped a beat. It was Naudla, but what was she doing?

She stood on a narrow ledge 10 feet from the ground, reaching up, on tiptoes. Will was close enough to know that whatever it was she was reaching for was in vain. He could see her hand 4 inches short of an invisible target.

Below her, beside a big rock, in the sun, were Kootoo and Piapik, fast asleep on a sealskin.

Naudla didn't see him and when he said "Ullaakuut," she jumped, startled. Then she smiled that warm beautiful smile that Will had spent nights dreaming about.

"Ullaakuut, Will." She stepped down from the ledge to greet him.

"What are you doing here?" Will gestured toward the ledge.

"Eggs." It was only one word, but it was like music. She pointed to a blanket close by nestled in small willows, holding about 15 eggs.

"Let's see if I can help." Will stepped up onto a series of smaller rocks below the ledge and extended his hand upward and along the narrow upper ridge as far as he could.

He was so overwhelmed with seeing Naudla that he had become oblivious to the squawking and swooping gulls overhead. A warm oval rolled under his fingers. He had found a gull nest, lifted out an egg, and gently passed it down to Naudla.

Her fingers lingered for a second on his as she took the egg.

He wanted the moment to last forever. He moved his other hand over the rock and found another, then another, and another. He picked each nest clean as he worked his way along the ledge.

Naudla lifted and held the hem of her outer woollen skirt in front of her, creating a basket. The creamy white eggs, twice as big as a hen's egg, floated in the fabric.

Satisfied that they had exhausted the yield, Naudla walked to the small blanket cradling her earlier harvest in the small willows. She was down on her knees, still holding the skirt basket gently.

Will knelt in front of her. Naudla picked up the eggs one and two at a time, and Will tenderly took them from her hands and placed them on the blanket.

They were face to face. He wanted to say something, anything, but couldn't because his throat was so dry. He took the last two eggs from her hand. Neither moved to get up.

They both looked at the children still asleep and then into each other's eyes.

Will had no fear. Was this destiny?

He touched her face more gently and softly than he had ever touched anything. She moved against his chest, her face buried in his neck, burrowing her lips and nose below his ear and neck, as Will kissed her ear and face, stroking her hair, and his arms went around her and he pulled her close.

Will lifted and turned her in one movement so that her back was to the sleeping children. He rolled over. She was on top of him. He rolled again, and he was on top of her, with the rock blocking the view of the sleeping children. Will now lifted both her skirts, and she was pulling his suspenders from his shoulders, and undoing the buttons on his britches.

He has known love and he had known lust, but never together.

He had been with women before, two were old lovers, a few mutual lust-laced encounters with no expectations, and others, especially in France, were pure economic transactions.

He could barely breathe; not even his crippled hands were distractions. She was holding them, rubbing them, directing them.

Nothing was ever like this. Naudla was a magnet. As naturally as their eyes had found and locked onto one another, she drew him deep inside her.

It had been so long since he had been with a woman, he knew that he would not last, and fear mingled with ecstasy. He looked at Naudla's face, into her eyes, listened to her sounds, watched and felt her movements, her hands on his face and her legs around his hips, and he knew he didn't have to hold back.

They laid side by side, still looking into each other's eyes, not knowing if they would or could ever be this way again.

Were those fleeting glances signals that this was what she had wanted?

She ran her fingers down her face and body, making gestures like tiny waves rolling over her. "Tussungniayuq."

Even though he had never heard the word before, Will knew what it meant. He wasn't sure if there was an English word that properly described that immense out-of-body feeling of well-being, that single moment that defines that once-in-a-lifetime moment.

"Tussungniayuq, Naudla. Eee. Tussungniayuq."

CHAPTER 8

THE WORST STORM

A drastically different Will Grant glanced over his shoulder one last time before crossing the gravel ridge. Naudla was lying beside her children and would stay with them until they awoke.

The guilt and anguish caused by his secret desires had vanished. Nothing in his life felt more right, more fulfilling, and more natural than those precious minutes with Naudla.

What had she been trying to tell him with those fleeting glances? What signals had he missed?

Will determined that he would no longer feel guilty about having lusted for her for months, or for making love with her today. Instead, he would live with that precious secret and accept facing each day and every long night, knowing that she would be only a few hundred yards away with her children and husband.

Society's rules, and the realities of duty and family, would keep them apart physically, but their spirits would, from this day on, be inseparable.

His mind was clear. Nothing—not the Mountie rule book, not his worn bible, nor Reverend Kingsbury's sermons—could ever convince him that what had just happened was wrong.

He looked at the small bundle in his right hand, smiled, and knew that for the rest of his life, every time he saw, touched, or tasted an egg, he would relive this day. Naudla had turned his shirt into a bundle basket for half of their eggs that now floated at his side as he walked.

Suddenly, a pair of nesting snow geese scrambled in front of him, the gander honking to distract attention from the nest.

Will placed his delicate bundle gently on the ground, lifted the strap of the double-barrelled shotgun from his shoulder, and aimed. He was confident that he could get both, and they would make the fine dinner he had half promised Zalapski and Villeneuve.

The female remained on the nest that she had scratched out of the fine gravel and small willows now lined with her soft, warm down, while the gander honked repeatedly, willing to sacrifice himself for her and their eggs.

He took his finger off the trigger, carefully uncocked the hammer, and lowered the gun. Snow geese mate for life. He couldn't end that—not on this day. Instead, he watched and wondered if another day would dawn when he and Naudla would be together as one. His hand lingered over the precious eggs, before picking them up by the carry knot she had tied from the sleeves and tails of his shirt.

He walked past the geese, gave the squawking gander a thumbs-up two-finger salute with his free hand, looked at the vastness before him, feeling again overwhelmed by the immenseness and beauty of it all.

A hundred little creeks bubbled down the gravel slopes from the melting drifts, driven into the rocky gorges at the foot of the massive cliffs that sometimes stretched a thousand feet above. In front of him, an infinite ocean of white, still frozen and impenetrable, set against a sky bluer and clearer than anything he could remember. He felt the need to capture in his mind every detail of this place and this day that would be the touchstone of his life.

As he crossed the western cape of Dundas Harbour, the geography changed. Suddenly, there was less gravel, shale, and sandstone, replaced by more vegetation, moss, small grasses, and Arctic tundra stretching northward into the big valley. Another magnificent landscape, now destroyed by the scattering of manmade structures: the storehouse, the detachment, the Inuit cabin, and two crooked shithouses.

He expected that Villeneuve and Zalapski would have arrived back a few hours before him and was still surprised to see Zalapski clearing snow from the pile of lumber near the storehouse.

Zalapski stopped when he saw Will approaching and waited until he got close before speaking or moving. "That storm we can never read or forecast is raging. I can't take much more of it, Will. I'm going to build my own shack."

"Back up, Erik. What happened?"

"Villeneuve's gone berserk. Pudlu met us at the dog pen when we got back, and when we told him that you were walking, he said maybe you'd see Naudla, who went gathering eggs. Then Villeneuve flew into one of his rages and told me to tend the dogs and stomped off and got heavy into the goddamn extract that's even more powerful than rum."

"How long ago did this happen, Erik?"

"About three hours. He went to the storeroom for an hour or

more, then came to the detachment and started raving. He's back to calling me a perverted fruit, and you're worse than me."

"Erik, we need a plan. This can't go on. You're the next senior constable, the second in command, and I think you're going to have to take over, but we need to figure out how."

Zalapski saw Will's bundled shirt in his hand.

Will raised it. "I did run into Naudla and the kids." He emphasized kids. "I helped her get some eggs off the higher ledges. We're going to have a treat—fresh eggs, and big ones at that." Will paused. "And you can count on my help if you want to build your shack. I was thinking, walking back, that we're going to be here for 15 more months. No one deserves the bullshit and abuse he's putting you through."

"Thanks, Will. I'll go in with you."

As soon as he stepped through the door, Will could see that Villeneuve was drunk, and his expression vile.

"So, you had a well-planned rendezvous with your little Naudla, didn't you? You sneaky bastard. Well, tell us, tell me, the fruit doesn't care, tell me, did you fuck her? I want to know."

Will wondered if Villeneuve could have seen him. He mentally calculated the hours, minutes, and distances: it would have been impossible for Villeneuve to have seen them and be back at the detachment for the past three hours.

Anger swelled in the pit of Will's stomach and raced through his body to the top of his head. He thought it would explode. He wanted to grab Villeneuve and choke him. The son of a bitch had just dirtied the most precious moments of his life.

Will took two steps. He stopped directly in front of Villeneuve, who had hardly moved but was now smirking, believing that he had the upper hand because of his superior physical strength.

"Enough, Villeneuve, enough. We're not going back to the bullshit you doled out before the long patrol, so shut it down." Will stood directly in front of him. In his initial rush of rage, he'd picked up a cast-iron frying pan off the table. Now he gripped the handle. He would use it if he had to.

Villeneuve switched his line of attack and abuse. "Does Will let you scrub his back, Zalapski? Does he still let you wipe his ass, you sick perverted bastard? Shut what down? I see you two. Maybe you liked him holding your dick and wiping your ass. He's a pervert. Maybe you are too, and I'm stuck here with both of you."

Will didn't realize he could move so fast. He slammed the heavy frying pan down on the table with all his force, inches from Villeneuve's elbow. Everything on the table flew 6 inches in the air, including Villeneuve's nearly empty pitcher of lemon and orange extract. The sound was like a shotgun, amplifying the silence that followed.

Will let the quiet prevail for several seconds, noting that Villeneuve had not moved or spoken.

"Get out. Get out now, Villeneuve, or I will take the side of your despicable face off with the next one. We will deal with the rest of this tomorrow, but for now, get out."

Several more seconds of stillness prevailed. Villeneuve slowly stood up, careful to move to his right to go around Will, who had not moved or let go of the frying pan.

"I'm tired of being here with you two perverts, anyway."

Will noted that Villeneuve scooped up the keys to the storehouse and the bottle of 80 per cent extract, and staggered out the door, carrying his coat, hat, and gloves.

They expected that he would go back to the storehouse and drink himself into oblivion.

Will set the frying pan on the stove and realized as he released it that his hands were shaking. Until this moment, he hadn't grasped the extent of his anger, just as a few hours earlier he had not appreciated the depth of his passion.

He felt a surge of panic. Where did Villeneuve go? Naudla was out on the land with the kids. He feared for her safety.

His instincts, coupled with the anger he and Zalapski had just witnessed, reinforced that Villeneuve could not be trusted.

He went outside. Villeneuve had not turned toward the storehouse as predicted. Will could see him along the shore, moving eastward, opposite from Naudla's path home. Still, for the next hour and a half, he kept watching until he saw three figures cross the ridge and walk safely into their cabin. The fact that she was safe diminished the anguish that came with the reality she was now with Teemotee.

Will fried eggs for himself and Zalapski. He marvelled at the colour of the so-called whites that weren't white at all but almost translucent. They both agreed that anything fresh was a treat, but these eggs were more than that. Two were quite filling with a few slices of tinned bully beef.

"So, what are we going to do?"

Will wondered why Zalapski didn't mention the rendezvous with Naudla. Was that a good thing? Was he keeping quiet because he was suspicious, or afraid of sounding suspicious? Will kept the focus on Villeneuve.

"Well, we know he's out of booze. But maybe the extract is worse. There's quite a bit of it there. Four or five cases. My brother always called it the sweet solution to prohibition."

"You know, Will, I don't think he knows what he's doing. As I said before, I think he's suffering shell shock or something. I've seen it before. So have you. Remember those poor souls isolated on the ships when we returned from Europe?"

"Erik, I know there's something wrong in his mind. What we must do is focus on how the hell we're all going to survive this for the next year and a half, or even longer?"

Zalapski thought for a moment before responding. "Has he told you to watch out for snipers?"

Will was puzzled. "What do you mean snipers?"

"When he's not calling me a fairy or a fruit, he's telling me we need to be on the watch for snipers. I've heard him say that's why he likes to go to that ridge of the easterly point—to look out for snipers."

"I don't recall hearing that specifically, but I'll look and listen for it. If he sobers, or half sobers up tomorrow, we'll confront him. As the next senior constable, are you prepared to take charge?"

"Yes, if I have to, but I'm hoping he'll snap out of it, somehow. Either way, I'm going to build my shack.

"You need to know," he continued, "I've been keeping a journal. I think we may need to have more than one record of what went on here. I have a hiding place, and I want you to know where it is, just in case."

Erik picked up a copy of F. Scott Fitzgerald's *The Beautiful and the Dammed*. "I found that New York high society is not my cup of tea. So great American prose became a wonderful Dundas Harbour fire starter. The covers, however, are spectacular camouflage. See how well my little journal fits right between them?"

Will laughed. "You're on to something, pardner. A book is the last place the bastard will look for anything." Will looked again at the title and smiled. *"The Beautiful and the Dammed. How fitting."*

Zalapski put it back in the bookshelf fashioned from crates. They had about 40 books in all: traditional classics, war journals, histories, and adventure novels. About half had been provided by the force, the rest were chosen by Will and Zalapski. Will liked lively poetry, Robert Service his favourite by far. Maritime-born Bliss Carman came second. Zalapski had a collection of eight Zane Grey westerns that he shared with Will.

Villeneuve owned none, touched none, and read none.

Will and Zalapski pulled the makeshift curtains to block out the midnight sun, a vain effort to maintain a semblance of day and night. Enough light crept in to make sleeping difficult and enough to see Villeneuve stagger in the door, kick off his boots, and fall, fully clothed, on his bunk and pass out.

In the morning, Will and Erik had more fried eggs and enjoyed the savoury flavours of the deep orange yolks. Villeneuve woke, went to the shithouse, returned, poured coffee, all the time not muttering a single word.

This had become his pattern—say nothing, as though nothing had ever happened, and let it blow over with enough time and silence.

Will, recognizing that silence is more dangerous than honesty, broke the quiet tension.

"Vincent." He surprised himself with the sound of Villeneuve's first name. He wasn't even sure that he had used it before, but it got his attention.

Villeneuve was sitting at the table. Will sat at the other end, Zalapski between them.

"From today on, there will be changes here. Drunkenness and abuse are against the rules. Zalapski is prepared to take command if he has to. But neither of us will allow one more day like we had yesterday." Villeneuve stared in stony silence. Will could see his big hands trembling. He knew that it was not fear, perhaps the alcohol, perhaps his fury—perhaps a combination of both. He did not move or speak for a full minute—neither did the others.

Will persisted. "Who is going to properly lead this patrol, you or Erik?"

"I am." Villeneuve paused. "I'm the only one who recognizes what's out there, who's out there."

Zalapski saw an opening. Villeneuve's twisted mind was shifting in a new direction, one that he could and would control.

"Tell us who's out there, Skipper."

"The Kraut snipers. German eyes are watching us here, just like they watched us in France and Belgium. Those bastards killed my buddy. He was in my arms. I had him on my shoulders, trying to get him to the medics, and they shot him through the head."

Will was dumbfounded. Zalapski sat, expressionless, expecting the answer that he had probed for. Villeneuve's eyes were wide, glazed, and darker than usual, as if looking deeply inward.

Will saw the truth. Villeneuve was shell-shocked. He hadn't seen it clearly until that moment. Seven years after the war's end, Vincent Villeneuve had become one of the walking wounded.

Should they try reasoning? Would they ever convince Villeneuve that his fears were unfounded?

"Have you seen them?" Will asked, tentatively. "We haven't

seen anyone or anything. How do you know that there are snipers?"

"You'll never see them. You'll just take the bullet."

Will decided not to probe further. He and Zalapski needed to talk. He tried to put their predicament in context. In all likelihood, they would not have any contact with the outside world for another 15 months, unless an unscheduled ship passed by this summer—but it would be folly to count on that.

They needed to accept that they would be here for more than a year, longer if ice conditions failed them in the summer of 1926. In that case, it would be 27 months before they would be picked up. Will fought off his nagging fear that Bernier had not made it south last year and no one would come for them, ever.

How, Will asked himself, could the isolation be the least of their concerns?

These last hours had made it crystal clear that he, Zalapski, and the Inuit had an ill leader, and none of them individually or collectively were equipped to understand the scope of his condition, let alone deal with it.

Will wondered if the best solution might be to lead from behind; for he and Zalapski to allow, even encourage Villeneuve to plan and direct patrols, the reason they were there. Over time, hopefully, they'd persuade him that the Germans had left, and that, indeed, the presence of the Mounties had driven them away.

Zalapski wanted an acknowledgment of what had happened.

"So, we'll put it all down to too much booze. Do you have any left?"

"No. I'm dry."

Villeneuve got up, picked up his coat, took his rifle from the rack, and walked out off the detachment eastward.

Will and Zalapski picked up the keys to the storehouse that he had left on the table and went to replenish some staples. They walked into a mess: empty cases and bottles on the floor, requisition pages scattered, ledgers incomplete.

Villeneuve had been raiding the vanilla, lemon, peppermint, and orange extract cases for some time: only a few 8-ounce bottles of vanilla and peppermint remained. Will and Zalapski inventoried, tidied up the mess, and took what they needed.

On the short walk back, Will congratulated himself for being so creative. The flour, sugar, and baking powder in his pack offered an opportunity to visit Naudla and the others. Especially Naudla.

Pudlu was in the cabin with Teemotee. Papik was in his arms. Will opened the door and instantly knew that Naudla was not there.

"Just checking to see if your supplies are okay—do you need flour or tea?"

"I think we're low on everything, but Naudla is gone looking for more eggs."

Will felt a panic in his gut. "Which way did she go?"

"East."

"When did she go, Pudlu?"

"Maybe two hours."

Will was sure that Villeneuve had watched her go. He was about to sound an alarm when Pudlu raised his fear.

"Teemotee is going to go for her. Piapik sick, very hot."

"I'll go with you. Zalapski too."

"Villeneuve is out there. I don't trust him."

Will then ran to the storehouse.

"Erik, hurry. I think that bastard is stalking Naudla. Take a rifle. Now."

They had to run to catch Teemotee. He knew the direct line that Naudla would be travelling, close to the cliffs and banks, looking for nests. Will thought at least Villeneuve went along the shore until after the first ridge.

Pudlu stayed with the children. Piapik had been fine when she awoke, but in the past two hours had become tearful and feverish. She wanted her mother.

They were spread out, a few yards between them. Half running, at a pace called double time in RCMP and military training. In 20 minutes, they had covered 2.5 miles.

Every few minutes, Will looked at Teemotee. They couldn't speak, but they both knew that as long as she was alone, as long as Villeneuve prowled the shoreline, she was in danger.

Just yesterday, he had made love to this man's wife. Right now, beside Teemotee, he felt neither guilt nor remorse but profound gratitude for those precious moments. He was no longer envious of Teemotee. He was concerned about the woman they both loved.

They crossed a steep point that jutted out from the cliffs and opened into a short valley stretching northward. Naudla was about 400 yards up the west side of the gorge, kneeling to gather eggs from a nest, while a pair of king eider ducks raised hell in protest.

Zalapski tapped Will and pointed straight ahead. Villeneuve was lying prone behind some rocks watching her. "Let's see what this does for the bastard's sniper paranoia."

A rifle shot echoed through the valley.

It startled both. Naudla had seen neither her protectors nor her pursuer. Will and Teemotee and Zalapski waved their hands

WHIT FRASER

frantically, motioning for her to come. Teemotee shouted "Atee-Atee!" at the top of his lungs.

Naudla gathered her bundle and rifle and moved toward them hastily. She stopped cold in her tracks when she saw Villeneuve emerge from behind the rocks, then picked up her pace into a partial run.

Teemotee ran forward to greet her. Will followed. He could hear the brief conversation, but only one word was familiar: "Piapik." Teemotee took Naudla's bundle and rifle. She looked past him, directly at Will. He saw the deep fear and panic in her dark eyes.

"Piapik is sick and we were worried about you." He pointed down the valley, confident that she understood.

The four of them maintained the steady and brisk pace back to the post. Will looked back over his shoulder. Villeneuve was following—but they did not wait for him.

They went directly to Naudla's cabin. Pudlu had his niece in his arms, rocking her. She was crying. Tears poured from Pudlu's eyes and his heart was filled with fear, as he remembered how his children, and then his wife, had died of a similar sickness. It had come on just as fast. They had burned with a fever and had trouble breathing, and no one had known what to do.

Piapik's crying subsided a little when Naudla took her in her arms. Zalapski put his hand on the child's forehead. She was burning up. Zalapski left to get tins of juice and the thermometer.

Illness was the great and deadly equalizer. Everyone—Will, Zalapski, and Villeneuve in their own way—had shared Pudlu's grief. Worldwide more people had died of the flu than had been killed in the war. And so many who died were children. They also knew that there was nothing in their emergency supplies to combat this. The constables wondered where the hell it had come from. Had they carried it with them in the supplies?

Villeneuve appeared. Naudla could not look his way. Before he had a chance to speak, Will interjected. "Piapik is very sick and everyone is afraid that it might be the deadly flu. We should go." He turned to Pudlu. "I wish we could help."

Will waited until they were back in the detachment to break the silence and godawful tension.

"You were following her, you son of bitch. You were going to attack her."

Villeneuve was suddenly calculating and coldly collected. "Be careful of accusing me of anything. I just happened to see her there. Maybe she found or followed me. You had your way with her yesterday. You are in no position to protect her virtue, if she has any."

Will was in a corner. He had to lie. He burned to tell this loathsome man, whom he now considered a degenerate, a stalker, and a potential rapist what Naudla meant to him—and how she had responded to him only yesterday.

"I wish I were worthy of her, but I'm not. But I'll tell you this, Villeneuve. I believe you were stalking her. I believe that you would have attacked her had we not come along. I believe that was your mission today. I believe that you saw her leave this morning and you scrambled to follow, pretending that you were going on your usual trek down the coast.

"There is one more thing. If you had attacked her, and we came along, Zalapski would have put that bullet through you. And if he didn't, I would have."

Just then Zalapski came through the door.

"Her temperature is 103.5. She's throwing up, crying, has diarrhea and a fever. Pudlu said that she aches all over. He's scared to death. He thinks it's the flu. I'm not so sure. I want to look something up in the medical books. I remember reading something about the dangers of eating uncooked walrus and polar bear meat. I told them to try and get her to drink as much as possible—my mother's remedy—but I'm very worried."

Neither Will nor Zalapski was sure that Villeneuve had heard the prognosis. He sat on the edge of his bunk, his steely, angry eyes fixed on Will.

"Screw you, Grant. I've done nothing, and you know it. You just want her for yourself. You've been panting like a dog in heat ever since the first day you saw her, and you think you're fooling the rest of us. No one here is stupid, not even Teemotee and Pudlu."

Will stared. Two can play the denial game. At the moment he was worried about the baby and thankful that they had found Naudla when they did. "You're not going to get away with that, Villeneuve. You're not going to deflect your ill-planned scheme to rape a woman by attacking me. We can't prove anything, but the truth and your intentions are clear. Now it's my turn to go for a walk."

Will picked up his pack, the 12-gauge shotgun, and his coat and walked westward to where he'd lain with Naudla just one day and one sweet lifetime ago.

He thought about the heated exchanges with Villeneuve concerning the booze and Naudla and told himself that he needed to be more careful. He had pushed him hard and if Zalapski had not walked in when he did, it could have become violent.

Will had been able to take care of himself growing up in Nova

Scotia and honoured the family nickname, "the fighting and fiddling Grants." He had long met the three criteria for a young man's survival and popularity around the big bay: he could dance, skate, and fight. But he was still no match for the powerful Frenchman. Will looked at his hands. In the words of the Grants of St. Francis, he considered the prospect of a physical confrontation "a wholehearted but half-fisted spectacle for sure." The Grants were poor but held to their proud Scots heritage and clan motto, *Stand Fast*.

Will had been pleased to see Zalapski willing to step in and told himself that he needed to hold back, be less assertive, and give Zalapski the chance to speak and lead.

Will lingered briefly, chewed on two stale hardtack biscuits, and worried about Piapik.

Naudla's cabin was silent when he approached the door. At least no child was crying. He tapped once and walked in. Pudlu was sitting with his sister and Teemotee.

"Any change?"

"Sleeping now, but crying a lot like she is in pain."

Naudla tried a faint smile. Teemotee nodded. Kootoo was asleep at the other end of the big family bed, stretched out on the floor covered with muskox and polar-bear hides and sealskins.

Will looked at this remarkable family, so close and so scared. *And they should be. And I am scared too.*

He didn't like the way Piapik and Kootoo looked, nor the way Teemotee coughed during their run to fetch Naudla, and again moments ago. "I will see you in the morning." Will took his leave. "If there is anything you need, Naudla, let us know."

Pudlu translated without being asked.

Will walked into a quiet detachment.

Zalapski and Villeneuve were in their bunks and Zalapski offered a warning: "Don't come too close, Will. I think I'm getting the baby's flu—if it is the flu. You're right, the book warns about eating raw or uncooked walrus and polar bear meat. It's called trichinosis, and it can be fatal. I'm not sure now about some of the meat we ate on the trail, especially when we were weathered in. Right now, I feel like shit. Every bone aches, and I have a temperature."

Will was barely in his bunk when he heard Zalapski scramble out the door. The thin walls of the detachment did little to diminish the sound of him puking his guts out.

Half an hour later, he was running again, this time for the shithouse. Within two hours, Villeneuve was up and down, in and out, barfing and coughing.

Will waited his turn. It didn't come. But he would never forget how sick he was with that flu five years ago, and the dozen or so people of all ages from around St. Francis who didn't survive, including a cousin and an aunt.

He also knew that he had eaten more tinned stew than walrus.

Will checked on Naudla and Piapik first thing the next morning.

Nothing had changed. She was still crying and vomiting and gasping for air. Teemotee and Kootoo were also sick. So far, Will, Pudlu, and Naudla were spared.

Healthy but helpless.

Will recalled the waiting game of the deadly Spanish flu.

After five or six days, people began to recover, if they were going to get better.

He felt sorry for Zalapski and tried to return the kindness Zalapski had shown during Will's recovery. At least Zalapski didn't need the bedpan or help with his dick.

Will didn't want Villeneuve to die, but he did take some solace in seeing him suffer. At least it made him quiet.

Will read the manual on trichinosis and concluded that it could be either food or the flu; either way, they had no choice but to let it run its course. He kept the cabin in order. Clean, cold drinking water was always at the ready, as were tins of juice, soup, and porridge in case the other Mounties could or would eat anything. Naudla and Pudlu did the same in their cabin.

The morning of the fifth day, Pudlu walked into the detachment.

"Piapik gone."

There were no words. Will's hands covered his face for a moment before wiping away a tear. A tiny innocent child that had so many times greeted him with a smile and a hug around his leg. In dreams about him and Naudla, conscious or sleeping, Piapik and Kootoo were present.

Zalapski and Villeneuve did not move, nor did they have to. Both Pudlu and Will knew their affection for the little girl; she was the only person who could put a genuine smile on Villeneuve's face and a light in his distant dark eyes.

Will took Pudlu's hand, put a hand on his shoulder, and looked him in the eye. "I am so sorry—so very sorry. We are all sorry." He accompanied Pudlu back to the Inuit cabin.

Pudlu did not have to translate Will's watery eyes and choking voice. Naudla was lying down, Piapik still in her arms, wrapped in a small blanket. One side of her tiny face was visible, darkened, and blue.

Will knelt beside the bed, took Naudla's hand, looked into her eyes, and repeated the same words he had said to Teemotee. "Sorry." It was all he could say, so little and painfully inadequate. He held her hand for a fleeting moment and felt her gentle squeeze around his fingers.

He wanted to rant about unfairness and injustice, and question how God could take this special child. *Why didn't you answer these prayers?* He looked at Pudlu's well-worn bible on the table.

Will turned to Pudlu. "How is Kootoo?" He realized that another tragedy might lurk in these cramped quarters.

"Seems a little better, not throwing up as much."

"Come with me, Pudlu. I'll help you get things ready."

They walked in silence to the storehouse.

Will picked up a pick and shovel. "You are good with woodworking tools. You should make a box and cross."

Pudlu nodded. "Maybe dig on that flat spot just above the cabin, on the east side."

Will knew the spot. It got the sun all day and was Naudla's favourite place—where she scraped and dried skins while the kids played games. Precious memories. It was the very place from where she had shot and killed the two marauding polar bears.

Pudlu knew that the spot was mostly gravel and well drained and would be the easiest place to dig in the partially frozen ground.

It took Will the entire day to dig the shallow grave. A few times, he had to use a blowtorch to thaw boulders frozen in the soil, as though set in cement. In those hours, a thousand thoughts raced through his mind. Not one could he hold or focus on for more than a few seconds, but in one way or another, Naudla appeared in all of them. Would they ever be together again? Would Teemotee and Pudlu find out? Was he any better, or worse, than Villeneuve?

Late that night, with the sun directly over their heads, six adults and one child stood over the tiny hand-hewn coffin made by a loving uncle. Will and Zalapski lowered it into the frozen ground. Naudla wept uncontrollably. Teemotee, who stayed at her side, tried to comfort her, with his chest heaving from grief and the deadly cough that had claimed his child. Kootoo stood at his mother's left, also weeping.

Pudlu read from the bible and spoke to God in Inuktitut. He picked up the fine gravel in his hand. The solemn, holy gesture translated as ashes and dust. He spoke only two words of English. "Lord's Prayer." The Mounties prayed with the Inuit. For Will, this was a gesture. Today had done nothing to restore a single fibre of faith increasingly becoming uncertain.

Will felt alone and isolated. He watched Teemotee, despite continued coughing spasms, lead his wife and son back down to their cabin. Will loved Naudla but could not offer her any comfort.

Zalapski and Villeneuve followed, still sick and weak from climbing the hill, despite their normally strong, physical stamina.

Pudlu placed a cross, with white paint that had not yet fully dried, at the head of Piapik's grave. He had carved four syllabic symbols that Will believed simply said, *Piapik*. Below it, *1921–1925*.

Pudlu picked up two shovels, passed one to Will. Together, in silence, they covered her remains with gravel and a mound of heavy stones.

CHAPTER 9

NOT IN THE PLAN

A line from the Scottish bard Robbie Burns ran through Will's mind when he assessed his situation two days after Piapik's death: *The best-laid schemes of mice and men, and Mounties, oft go awry.*

The top RCMP brass, the prime minister's best advisors, and some of the best patriotic brains in the country sat in imposing ornate offices on Parliament Hill forging policies, plans, and logistics to cement, once and forever, Canada's sovereign claim over the frozen frontier of the High Arctic. *Who among them could have predicted the death of an Inuk child, or that two Mounties, unable to control their heads, hearts, or hard-ons, would cause it to unravel?*

Will stood outside the door of the detachment in the sun's warmth. A soft wind blew from the south. For months, throughout cold, darkness, and blizzards, they all longed for a day like this, when a new season and new world emerged. Yet, in the 48 hours that followed Piapik's death, Dundas Harbour felt eerily quiet, strange, and remote.

Her tiny white cross dominated the sky, the towering cliffs, and endless ice. Will knew that any passing ship would see that cross long before they would see the cairn the Mounties had built 700 feet above her.

Villeneuve and Zalapski were recovering, eating a little, and, dividing their time between their bunks and the table—never talking, just existing in different places within the same confined physical space.

A brief encounter with Pudlu the night before told Will that Teemotee and Kootoo, like the Mounties, were slowly recovering. As much as he wanted to see Naudla, he believed that his presence in her cabin would only complicate matters.

Will was at the small creek filling buckets with fresh water when Pudlu approached. His slow walk and hesitation when he tried to speak telegraphed bad news.

"Will, tomorrow, we are leaving. We cannot stay here any longer. It is too much for Naudla. It's more than Piapik. Naudla will never feel safe here again."

Will had sensed their discomfort and apprehension ever since the New Year's fiasco. It would be senseless to try and persuade them to stay. Moreover, why would they want to? They had no stake in defending Canada.

Then, for a fleeting moment, Will turned inward. *Does she also want to leave because of me—because of our moments together? In my own way, am I just as responsible as Villeneuve?*

He wanted to blurt out, "You can't take Naudla." But all he could manage was, "I'll miss you, Pudlu. I'll miss all of you. But I understand, and I think I would do the same. Where will you go?"

"I don't know. See how the ice is. Right now, still good travel for a few weeks. I think Arctic Bay is the best place, but it depends on the ice. Maybe I should go to Craig Harbour instead. Maybe spend summer on the land. Depends on the ice."

How confident! Will had heard Villeneuve and others refer to the Inuit as snow gypsies. *But surely,* he looked at Pudlu's serene face and listened to his matter-of-fact but uncertain travel plans, *that's a compliment—go wherever the wind, ice, or water takes you, and still be at home. Above all, never worry about money.*

"What do you need in the way of provisions?"

"Not much. Tea, flour, lard, butter, two boxes of 306 cartridges, and maybe a few gallons of naphtha for the stove. Four tins of tobacco."

"We'll have all of that for you later today. And I'll ask Villeneuve or Zalapski to draw up a credit note for any amounts left owing."

"We'll leave you a qamutik and maybe 10 dogs." Pudlu picked up and carried one of Will's buckets, as they walked together back to the detachment.

For the first time since meeting Pudlu, Will felt awkward and speechless in the company of his friend. He was about to lose much more than Naudla. He would also lose his best friend, the one person whom he knew he could trust with his life. He could almost have shared his secret love for Naudla, except to do so would have caused too much pain for his friend, her protective brother.

Will delivered the news directly to the recovering infirmed.

"From tomorrow on, we'll be alone. Pudlu just told me they are leaving. The loss of Piapik, and your moves, Villeneuve, make it impossible for Naudla to remain here."

"Good Christ," said Zalapski. "We need them."

A long silence followed.

"We don't need them at all," declared Villeneuve. "They're free to go wherever. I don't give a shit, but neither will I be a scapegoat. I didn't touch her, and you both know it."

"I spoke to Pudlu. They'll need to be paid for the months worked and the 10 dogs they'll leave for us. Who's going to do that?"

Villeneuve smirked. "You bum chums took the keys to the kingdom. You want control of all of that, so I hope you get it right."

"I'll figure it out." Zalapski reached for his coat and boots. "Right away."

"I'll go with you." Will did not want to be alone with the man designated as leader—another scheme of mice, men, and Mounties gone awry.

Zalapski had an ease with the books and ledgers, calculating the days since Teemotee and Pudlu had signed on. He saw O'Halloran's payout notation to Naudla for the polar-bear skins and sewing. He calculated 50 cents a day, six days a week, offered a generous $5 for each of the dogs, deducted amounts for the supplies, including several cans of tobacco at $1.19 each, and wrote credit notes that said that the RCMP owed Teemotee and Pudlu $157 each. The credit notes could also be used to receive trade goods from other detachments, especially Craig Harbour.

Pudlu and Teemotee were sorting and packing bundles when Zalapski and Will arrived with the staples that Pudlu had requested. They had thrown in a few extra tins of beans, pears, and a box of hardtack as a bonus. Will pointed to 50 pounds of flour and gas left outside the storehouse.

No one felt like talking. Will was disappointed that he did

not see Naudla. She and Kootoo were in the cabin. Pudlu and Teemotee went directly to pick up the flour and gas.

That night, Will couldn't sleep. The uncertain future kept him tossing and turning. Could the patrol survive without Pudlu and Teemotee? Would he ever again see Naudla?

He had just fallen asleep when the sounds of excited dogs caused him to jump out of bed.

Pudlu and Teemotee were near the beach, harnessing the dogs to qamutiks loaded with everything the family owned. A skin kayak crowned the bundles, boxes, and barrels lashed to each qamutik.

The land was almost snow-free, but the Arctic ice stretched to eternity in every direction, broken only by sporadic small openings or leads, ranging from a foot to 50 feet wide. The leads gathered the runoff from the snowmelt and invited seals and walruses to nurse pups and bask lazily along with them. The mammals invited predators—polar bear and man—who were, in turn, followed by the scavenging foxes and gulls. Will was discovering the natural order of Arctic life.

"They're leaving," Will announced. "I'm going to say goodbye."

Zalapski scrambled to get his coat and boots and followed. Villeneuve watched from the doorway.

"He'll never let go of his prejudices and resentments," Zalapski offered as they approached the shoreline.

Will carried a small object, wrapped in a towel, that he had spent most of the night finishing. It was his recovery program to regain the use of his hands and relearn his craftsman's skills.

He approached Kootoo. "Something for you, my little man." He put the object in the boy's hands. "Be careful with it."

Kootoo unwrapped the towel and looked, astonished, at the small hand-crafted model airplane, a Sopwith Camel, a replica of one of the many airplanes Will had serviced and repaired during the Great War.

"It's an airplane," Will said. "Someday you'll see lots of them up here. Maybe someday you'll fly one yourself."

Pudlu was as excited as the boy, translating and trying to explain big machines that can make men fly.

Pudlu turned to Will. "Nukara, this is for you."

He handed Will a small, hand-crafted wooden box with intricate hinges and catches made from a heavy hide that Will guessed was walrus. He opened the case. It was the ivory and stone chess set that Pudlu had laboured on for so long. Each square was carved and inlaid with absolute precision in the inside top and bottom of the chest, so when opened, it formed the full board. Every pawn, rook, knight, bishop, queen, and king spoke to Arctic wildlife and people. All fit perfectly inside the box.

Tears filled Will's eyes when he looked at Pudlu. "Nakurmiik. Nakurmiik, my friend. I just hope we will meet again." Though in his heart, Will couldn't imagine how that could ever happen.

He turned to Teemotee, shook his hand, and one more time lied and deceived. "Goodbye, good luck, nakurmiik, Teemotee."

Then he turned to Naudla, unsure of what to say or do. She stepped forward, her eyes swollen from grief and lack of sleep. He tried to manage a faint smile. To his surprise, she wrapped her arms around him in a warm hug. A slight squeeze didn't ease his guilt and shame.

She turned and also hugged Zalapski but, to Will's inner joy, for not quite as long.

Without another word, they were on the qamutik, Naudla with Teemotee, Kootoo with his uncle. Will and Zalapski watched them move out onto the ice. The dogs stretched out in a sprint. He could see that Naudla looked back, her eyes fixed on that part of her that would remain here forever, marked by a white cross.

Will watched until they were no more than a small, dark dot on the white horizon, and then disappeared in the evaporating snow mist. He didn't need to wipe the tears away—thankfully, Zalapski had left him alone.

It was Dominion Day, July 1—Canada's 58th birthday. "Pleased to be of service," Will scoffed aloud and walked toward the detachment. Disrespect for the mission hit, together with feelings of self-disrespect and heartbreak.

He met Zalapski at the door of the detachment, coming from either the storehouse or the shithouse.

Villeneuve was sitting at the table inside. "Well, that's finished, but we have real work to do—and unfinished business here."

Will and Zalapski looked at him incredulously. Villeneuve considered himself above and apart from recent events.

Will was about to respond but caught himself. Several seconds of silence followed.

"The first order of business is the storehouse." Zalapski broke the silence. "I'm keeping control of the stores. Vee-Vee, most of the lemon, vanilla, and orange extracts are gone. We're prepared to follow your lead on the patrols, but not the supplies, not the rations, especially not anything that you can drink."

Villeneuve swallowed hard and stared.

This time, Will broke the silence. "Do you want to keep leading the patrol?"

"Yes. I know you two pansies aren't up to it."

Zalapski stayed firm. "I'm not a pervert or a pansy, and I'm not taking any more of your insults. I was about to build a cabin of my own. Now I'm going to move into the cabin up the hill."

"I have a better idea. I'll move out. The worst part of this posting is sitting here, night after night, with you bum chums. I'll eat here, but I don't need to live here."

He took some maps off the shelf above his bunk. "As for the patrol, be prepared to pull out tomorrow for a few days inland."

Will took it all in, surprised, convinced that another shoe was bound to fall. But for now, he was relieved that the July 1 fireworks had gone better than expected.

Villeneuve immediately dismantled his bunk and gathered belongings, documents, and the logbook. That night, he recorded: *July 1, 1925, Dominion Day. Eskimos left in the morning for good.*

At supper, Will stared at his plate of salt pork, dehydrated potatoes, and canned vegetables. *The only thing I can taste is the tension, and silence is the only sound. Will it always be thus?*

Finally, Villeneuve broke the unsettling hush. "Part of our assignment is to explore a possible overland route to Craig Harbour. We can pack enough food for a week, put packs on three or four dogs."

He laid out the map on the table. "I'm guessing that it is about 80 miles across the island." His finger was on the southeast corner of the map. "Remember we went up the big valley here, about 30 miles, but it turned into a dead end in that narrow gorge going west."

"I remember. Who can forget?" Will looked at his crippled hands.

"I'm thinking of going up this smaller valley to the east, right here." Villeneuve pointed to a spot about 5 miles east of the post. "If this brings us up to a mountain plateau, it may give us a good winter overland route with dogs. But it's one step at a time, small steps. Maybe we can explore the first 20 miles."

Zalapski looked closer at the map, putting his face only a few inches from it, eyes squinting, and then stepped back. "Okay, Skipper, that's why we're here. We'll start getting ready right away."

In the morning, Zalapski and Will were at the dog line, picking out four dogs that they deemed the strongest to be their pack horses. Will was surprised to see a pup about three months old that had been Piapik's playmate.

She and Kootoo each had a "puppy doll" from the last litter, born on the trail toward the end of the spring patrol. He remembered her carrying it like a baby in her amauti and then, last week, watching child and puppy cuddle in a peaceful sleep on a skin blanket while Will and Naudla sated their desire.

Will also remembered Pudlu's efficiency in culling the females and smaller males from the litter. He assumed that Kootoo had taken his pup with him.

This one, the survivor, was a beauty. His broad chest, mane, and front legs were snow-white. A jet-black V began just between his eyes and flowed over his forehead and down the full length of his back and sides. The piercing blue eyes made Will smile.

"You must be a Grant or a MacKay." Will untied him. "You're coming with me. Maybe I should call you Cop."

The pup's ears perked forward. His blue stare was riveting and the bushy tail swinging high over his back proclaimed, then and forever after, to both and man and beast, that he was in charge.

Will saluted. "Okay, how about Inspector?"

The men put canvas canine saddles over the backs of the chosen pack dogs, half filled with dog food, half filled with the rest of their provisions. Each dog would tote about 25 pounds. For the rest of the dogs, Will left big chunks of half-dried, half-frozen seal, walrus, or polar-bear meat. It was a feast for two days, sleep and shit for two more, then famine until the patrol returned.

It was just after noon when the patrol left, and the going was tough from the first step. The first few miles along the shore were familiar ground, but after that, as soon as they turned northward, it was all uphill, over rocks and gravel. The Mounties had 60 pounds each on their backs. Villeneuve a little more, considering that he was carrying the tent.

All three men had a pack dog on a leash. They couldn't risk one running off with provisions, but the fourth instinctively followed the pack, and so did Inspector.

Every hour trekking up the narrow valley became more arduous. They couldn't hike more than seven hours a day, without facing exhaustion. Finally, they hit the wall, or walls, when a series of steep-faced ledges confronted them. They looked skyward beyond the highest ridge and saw the edge of the Devon Ice Cap.

Villeneuve swung his pack from his shoulders, carefully placed his rifle on top of it, and sat on a boulder. They'd camp for their third sleep and would start back down tomorrow, he decided.

He got no argument from either Will or Zalapski on that point. However, both were shocked by his comments as the three sipped tea after the evening meal. "We don't need to worry about anyone coming at us from behind—from the land, or over that ice cap. We only need to protect our shorelines."

Paranoia again prevailed. A patrol to connect with other posts and establish sovereignty had become a manoeuvre to protect the rear flank from an imaginary enemy.

More troubling was the mood shift. Increasingly, it was becoming evident that Villeneuve was most engaged and communicative when he saw danger and snipers lurking behind every rock. Zalapski and Will knew that if they called him out on his growing obsession, matters would go from bad to worse. They thought it better to make him talk.

Zalapski asked, not for the first time, "So, Skipper, who do you think is out there?"

"The goddamn Krauts haven't surrendered. They won't ever give up. Why can't our generals and politicians realize that it's just as easy for them to sail around Greenland and land troops as it is for us to sail north out of St. Lawrence? We're supposed to be concerned about American activity. The Americans are our friends, not our enemies. It wasn't the Yankees that killed our boys in the trenches—your friends, Zalapski—and shot down your pilot buddies, Grant. No, it was the Germans."

It was Will's turn to probe. "But wouldn't someone have seen German ships, or a landing, or at a settlement, or something?"

"No, because we're not looking for them. We're told to watch out for the Americans and a few Norwegians who hate the Krauts more than we do." Villeneuve became more animated. "Believe me, the Germans are smart and patient. They'll start small and knock on us one by one, starting first with snipers."

Zalapski probed deeper. "So what do we do?"

"We keep our eyes open. We do our patrols. We set up and maintain our watches. We keep our rifles close by. And we remember how determined those bastards were to kill all of us."

Zalapski took a reassuring rather than challenging tone. "I think we've been doing that, don't you, Will?"

"We have, and we'll keep on."

Silence again filled the air.

Will focused his attention on Inspector, lying next to his feet. Both Zalapski and Villeneuve approved of the name and the addition.

Will scratched the pup's ears and thought about words for mental instability: lunatic, deranged, insane, madcap, crazy. Shell-shocked had been Zalapski's diagnosis. They would need to set their game plan.

The return trip was much easier, downhill, and packs lighter each day. But the weather soured; cold rain and heavy mist and fog filled the gorge.

Will, wanting to break the silence and lighten the mood, was about to say "a good day to dodge snipers," but caught himself.

They pitched the tent twice on the return trip. Villeneuve's assessment of 10 miles a day over this terrain was accepted as a compliment.

Back at the detachment, warm, dry, and fed, and missing neither Villeneuve's moods nor insults, Zalapski produced half a bottle of rye whisky that he had been hiding in his footlocker and poured a drink for himself and Will. Will confided that he still had one bottle of rum that he was keeping for a special occasion.

"Did that sniper conversation surprise or scare you?"

"What surprised me is how convinced he is that we may be under siege. If we were a dozen people here, someone would take him out of the loop and put him under watch. I know that that happened in Pond Inlet a few years ago and two of the lads were assigned asylum watch. They got extra pay for it."

Zalapski thought for a moment. "Well, I can't see the two of us spending the next 14 months guarding one guy. The thing is, and you saw, he's easy to deal with. He thinks there's someone out there. I think we take it a day at a time, go with the flow, as long as he doesn't start putting us at risk."

"Okay, a day at a time it is." Zalapski had read his mind.

The next day, Villeneuve set out plans better than either constable expected. The map was back on the table.

"Look at this cape to the east." Villeneuve pointed with his finger. "It's about 4 miles, but an easy walk. We've all been there. You can see northeast a long way up the coast, and across the Sound. We need to also be looking for ships. Surely the ice will soon shift. My idea is that we rotate three days, three nights each, right here. We'll set up the tent and bring in some provisions."

How clever, thought Will. He'd changed the game, short patrols, with baby steps. No need for Inuit.

Will and Zalapski both did the math: for six days out of nine—two-thirds of the time—neither would be in Villeneuve's company.

Will inquired, "And the rest of the time?"

"I thought about that. The rest of the time, one man will do a day patrol westward. The other will maintain the post. We have a lot of work to get done. The boats need to be readied. We need to lay up the fish and meat for the dogs for the winter, and I want to make sure that anyone out there will see the RCMP painted in big letters on that high hillside behind us."

Visible white rocks had become a trademark at Arctic police and trading posts. Will recalled that, last August, Pond Inlet had been unreachable because of the shore's fast ice, but the distant letters on the hillside confirmed their location.

"When do you want to start?" Zalapski asked.

"Right now. I'll take the first watch, but you can both help by packing a few provisions, including one of those extra mattresses and wood to build a bunk and bench. We should take advantage of the ice while we can and use dogs for the first few trips."

Will and Zalapski smiled as they lashed bedding, naphtha, grub, and a toolbox on the qamutik. That evening, the three ate tinned pork and beans at East Point.

Paranoia aside, Will noted that Villeneuve had picked a good point for observation. It was about 250 yards wide at the shoreline and tapered to the reef about half a mile out into the Sound. A flat spot 200 yards from the cliff was high enough to offer protection from breaking ocean waves in high winds and low enough to be leeward from the northerly gales. Most importantly, from Villeneuve's perspective, it provided a sweeping view of shore and ice.

Will and Zalapski enjoyed the ride home, as did Inspector, still too small to keep up with the big boys.

That night, Villeneuve recorded the establishment of the satellite post in the log. It had been exactly one year since they had sailed out of Quebec City.

They drank a toast to survival and the future from Will's dwindling stock.

The next morning, Will's first task in the new routine was converting some packing crates into Inspector's headquarters. The dog had begun following him everywhere. Will recognized and accepted that the bond with the dog was more than a distraction from routine and boredom. The dog was also Will's connection with Pudlu and Naudla, and he wanted to believe that's why Pudlu had left him behind.

Zalapski declared the doghouse next to the door of the detachment "a fine touch."

Weeks and East Point rotations rolled together. On the hillside above the main post, white rocks and letters were taking shape. It was more a labour of rearranging and painting boulders than lifting and carrying them. A 10-foot two-by-four ensured the letters' uniformity of scale.

At the detachment, Villeneuve continued to sleep and live in his cabin, carrying out westerly patrols on alternate days with more determination than either Will or Zalapski. He was also the best rock painter.

As July faded and August emerged, the ice remained fast. All three had readied the boats and wondered when or if they would get them in the water.

Westward, at the mouth of Char River, a small bay opened, more due to ice melt than wind or tide. It offered a good place to set a gillnet. Every few days, fresh Arctic char was back on the menu for men and dogs. Each Mountie shot at least one seal on the ice at East Point, and Zalapski dropped one bull muskox that had wandered near the detachment.

Will woke in the tent on the third morning of his watch. Inspector was under his bunk. All night a strong wind had been blowing, making it difficult to sleep, especially because the sun remained high in the night sky. Will stepped outside and rubbed his eyes, ensuring that what he was seeing was not an Arctic mirage but real open water. The ice had moved.

It was August 15, almost a year since they had landed. Will's excitement mounted. Maybe they would see a ship. Or maybe a ship—any ship—would see them.

Will's heart sank when he scanned the horizon with his binoculars.

There was no promise of a rendezvous because no one knew the sailing schedule from year to year, and ice conditions were even more unpredictable. All they had was a vague "if we are close next year we'll come by and see how you're faring."

The ice had moved but no more than a few miles eastward and southward. Some open water was visible to the west, but chances of a ship from the west were always slight.

Will knew that Villeneuve would relieve him that day. He made tea on the Primus but could barely focus on anything except watching the distant horizon, trying to gauge the extent of the shifting ice.

By mid-morning, he began wondering where his relief was. They usually changed watches before noon. It was well past noon when Inspector's ears raised and he began pacing and half barking. Will listened. Shortly, the unmistakable chug, chug of an Acadian motor was clear. He walked inland to a fine gravel cove to meet Villeneuve.

"The engine sounds good," Will greeted him.

"It was missing a little at first but seems to be settling down. I think it's best to keep it here to be ready if someone comes through that ice."

Will listened for some excitement in Villeneuve's voice. There was none. But at least he was not fully focused on hostile invaders either. "Get your gear and your buddy there, and we'll take a run and see if we can get a better idea where, or even if, that ice is still moving."

Villeneuve and Will spent a few hours weaving in and around ice pans and guessed that the open lead was 5 to 7 miles east and south of the post. They noted landmarks along the shore to track movement. Villeneuve brought him back to the detachment in the boat and returned to East Point.

For three weeks, the ice barely moved. When it did, it merely moved back and forth and never east or south beyond the points that Will and Villeneuve had recorded on the first day.

Will shared his anticipation and disappointment with Zalapski.

"I was so excited when that ice first moved. I was sure a ship would appear right after that."

"Me too, Will. But remember we weren't promised a ship this year. We were put here for two years and given enough supplies to keep us for three."

The nine-day East Point rotation resulted in their spending much less time together—in fact, only three days and nights in the cycle.

Neither of them, particularly Zalapski, maintained any personal contact with Villeneuve, who remained in the small cabin he had fashioned to suit his comforts. He appeared convinced that if anyone emerged from the icefields, or along the shore, it would not be friend but foe.

Will looked forward to Zalapski's company. He set up Pudlu's chess set. Teaching Zalapski to play was a welcome distraction and pastime.

"I know I shouldn't expect a ship to appear. But I can't help longing for some reassurance that the world knows we're here. I just want to see one of those foreigners or traders we're supposed to be watching for."

"I'll give you this, Will. It would be good to know what's happening in the country and the world, and to at least send a letter home."

Whatever uncertainties they faced, hunger was not one of them.

They fished for fun with rods, reels, and spoons, and landed Arctic char by the dozens. Will filleted and dried the char as he'd seen Naudla do. The work reminded him of his mother and father salting and storing codfish. The char was not only tasty and nutritious but, once dried, it was light and easy to carry.

They shot several more seals from the motorboat and watched dozens of walruses basking on rocks 5 miles east of the post. Wildlife watching was the best, maybe only, form of entertainment.

None of the men were equipped or inclined to hunt whales, but they observed and marvelled at the number of humpbacks, fins, and bowhead whales. Will favoured the smaller narwhals— that unicorn of the ocean, with its long ivory tusk extending from their heads—that often entered the harbour, or sometimes surfaced near the motorboat for a closer look.

It appeared to the Mounties that this stretch of ice-free water off eastern Devon Island was the narwhals' sanctuary.

Will and Zalapski were on the shore in front of the detachment, watching a pod of at least a half-dozen humpbacks singing their mournful songs.

"Certainly, a nice distraction from the sniper saga," Zalapski noted.

They both laughed. Zalapski added, "Thank God, he's been quiet."

Will sensed that this was the moment to ask questions that had been troubling him for months. "Why does he attack you? Why does he call you a fruit? How do you put up with it?"

"Where have you been, Will? It's convenient. It's the time we live in. It seems like everyone needs to hate someone for either the colour of their skin, their flag, or both, like happens with Orientals." He paused a moment. "Or religion. Especially Jews. When all else fails, you can just label someone a fruit. Maybe he attacks me so that he doesn't have to look at himself."

Will thought about the times he had probably said things about people without consideration or foundation.

"Society makes it very easy to hate. You heard Villeneuve. He's a policeman, and he enjoyed raiding a bathhouse and putting men in jail and probably beat them up for good measure.

It's simple, Will. He's allowed to hate. We all are."

The two fell silent.

By September 15, the ice had moved back into the bay. They expected it, even saw it coming, and hauled up the boats high and dry on shore for the winter.

The next several rotations at East Point were excruciatingly depressing and boring. Will finally accepted that no one was coming—not even snipers. He appreciated the detachment with its few comforts: a warm bunk, hot food, a place to connect with Naudla.

On a mid-October day, with overcast skies, and light snow falling, Will felt a burning need to touch their spot once more before the snow buried it for the next eight months.

Zalapski would soon head east for his watch. He passed Will the keys to the storehouse. "Thanks, I'll see you in a few days."

Will turned westward. This walk had become more than a routine. It was now his ritual. He recognized that, because it connected him with Naudla, it maintained his vulnerable sanity. Today, like many days, he continued for another hour to that awe-inspiring waterfall.

He drank some of the clear, pure, glacial water that dropped hundreds of feet from above, boiled tea, and again convinced himself that his private Arctic fountain made his tea superior to that of any king, queen, emperor, or tsar. Carrying a few bottles back to the post was now an obligation. He shared his bannock and bully beef with Inspector, now about six months old. "You're going to be a big boy." He estimated that the husky was already 50 pounds.

They began the journey toward the detachment. Snow squalls had blown up, and the northeast wind stung his face. Snow was blowing and swirling across the ground. Will noticed how quickly it either covered or erased the dog's tracks as Inspector led the way.

They crossed the final ridge and the dog stopped, whined, and barked a few times. His nose was in the wind and he was moving it lower, higher, back lower again, his nostrils expanding and contracting, honing in on something.

Suddenly, the husky ran. Will felt uneasy. He began to run after the dog. He was almost at the detachment when he heard Inspector's frenzied bark. Seconds later, he came around the building and froze.

Zalapski was on the ground, on his back, face skyward. A pool of blood framed his head.

Will felt paralyzed and then began to shake uncontrollably. The dog edged closer to Zalapski, snapping Will out of his trance.

"Get away, Inspector." Will gave him a short punt on the hind with his foot. The dog cowered by the doorway.

Will knelt by Zalapski's side. His eyes were wide open, his face badly distorted. Black marks, gunshot burns, were clear on the right side of his face, and so was the small hole at his temple. His arms were spread wide apart, and less than a foot from his right hand, Zalapski's service pistol, #267 clear on the grip plate.

Police training and common sense said that Erik Zalapski had committed suicide.

Fellow policeman Will Grant didn't believe it. Above his common sense, his sixth sense said that Zalapski had been murdered. But how could he prove that? If he was correct, there was only one suspect.

Will got a rope and tied up the dog. He checked the cabin. Nothing appeared out of place. Zalapski's footlocker, where he kept his pistol, was open. Will looked closely. Everything was in order. Personal items were still folded neatly.

His journal was between the F. Scott Fitzgerald covers, in the bookcase. Will was sure it had not been touched. The last entry was three days ago—October 12. *Good to be back from no man's land. Winter is coming fast. Looking forward to Will's company and cooking again.*

Will couldn't help but be moved. It made suicide all the more unlikely. For the past few weeks, it seemed that Villeneuve's abuse had diminished considerably.

Will thumbed back a few pages, the last turbulent year was in instant perspective. Chills ran down his spine. His stomach tightened as he read Zalapski's words. His sense was that he was in grave danger, that a deranged Villeneuve had killed Zalapski.

It is now certain to me that I made a serious mistake today, one I suspect I will continue to regret, and one I will not be able to undo.

I confronted Vee-Vee about his condition and what I observed after the accident. I told him I became worried about him because as he rescued and carried Grant, he suddenly came to believe that snipers shot Grant right there in his arms.

I said I was concerned, asked if he was OK. He flew into a violent rage, called me every kind of homosexual and twisted pervert under the sun, grabbed me by the throat, threw me on my bunk, and was choking me to death. He was so powerful, I was helpless. The only thing that saved me was that Pudlu came in the door. Villeneuve snapped out of it.

Will went outside. He walked around the cabin but could find no tracks or signs of another human being. He noted that

Zalapski was not dressed for the weather. He wasn't wearing a hat or gloves, just a sweater. He didn't like the cold. Even if he were going out for no more than a moment, he wore a coat. But not today, not on his last trip out the door.

Will looked at his watch. 3 p.m. Villeneuve would have been waiting for his relief since noon and the sun would set in two hours.

Will went to the storehouse, found a large tarp, and covered Zalapski's body. He did not move him or touch the pistol. He took the dog with him but kept him on the leash and started eastward at an aggressive clip. Halfway, he saw Villeneuve coming toward him, and waited.

"What's happened with Zalapski?" Villeneuve asked.

A straightforward question Will thought. No derogatory or snide swipes about the "pervert" or "pansy."

"He's dead. I found him dead in front of the detachment. It looks like suicide, but I can't believe it. He's shot through the head, from very close—inches."

"Are you sure it's not snipers?"

Will was watching Villeneuve for the kind of shock he had initially experienced. There was none.

"I'm sure. You'll soon see for yourself."

They were back at the detachment just as the sun went down. Will lit lamps, which each held over Zalapski's twisted and discoloured face. Villeneuve was all police business as he examined Zalapski's face, head, and the firearm. He looked for any sign of distress, for any possible footprints.

"I don't think there's any explanation except the same one you came to. He committed suicide."

Yes, that was the only logical explanation, and yet Will held on to his doubts, curious that Villeneuve did not appear to consider him a suspect. The senior constable's matter-of-fact approach was unnerving.

"Let's pick him up and take him to the storehouse for the night. We should bury him tomorrow." They wrapped him in the tarp, placed him on a qamutik, and hauled him inside.

The next day, Villeneuve built a box. He later joined Will a few feet from Piapik's grave. Together they laboured to cut through the frozen ground, thawing it with coal and kerosene until they dug down 3 feet.

Will's waning faith was evident in his words over the grave. "Lord, hear us from this distant place. Take this fine man, our friend and comrade who has served his country, take him into your kingdom, bless him and keep him forever. Amen." Neither survivor cried openly.

From this day on, Will knew that he would live in fear. *Am I in danger? Did Villeneuve kill Erik? Would he kill again?*

CHAPTER 10

WE ARE NOT ALONE

Will sat alone, wrestling with growing depression, grief, and doubt, and talking to himself as he wrote in his journal, a practice that was becoming more common.

I will never believe Zalapski did himself in—that Erik shot himself. But if he did not die by his hand, then whose finger pulled the trigger?

Will knew that there was only one possibility. But, if someday, others considered it not suicide, but murder, there were two suspects: Vincent Villeneuve and Will Grant.

The table in the detachment had had many uses over the past months: eating, drinking, baking, butchering, card playing, reading, writing, patrol planning, and surgery. Now, it was the workbench for Zalapski's epitaph.

Will wondered if he would join Zalapski and Naudla's baby in the frozen ground before the next ship sailed into Dundas Harbour—next year, the year after, the year after that?

He tried to square Villeneuve's response to Zalapski's death with his evident and frequent paranoia. How easily he accepted suicide as the only possibility. He didn't ask Will a single basic question about his actions and activities that day, not even about what time he'd returned to the post or if he had heard any shots.

After months of imagining a sniper behind almost every rock and ridge, Villeneuve didn't envision the enemy simply walking up to Zalapski and killing him at point-blank range.

Point-blank range was the only certainty. Will did not believe in snipers.

He knew then, as he scraped out small chips of wood to form the letters in Zalapski's name and the date of death, that from that day onward, he would need to be vigilant, every day and everywhere.

Fear must not override self-defence. Will was determined to plan and execute every move with apprehension, fully aware that he was living with a killer. His focus and priority: never allow Villeneuve to see, hear, or feel Will's suspicions.

He worked on the marker all day. It was slow work. The white paint he had applied the day before had dried overnight. With the small artist's brush that he had used to paint the model airplane, he filled in the lettering with black paint. He gathered a drill, a half-dozen brass screws, and a screwdriver from the storehouse, and stopped at Villeneuve's cabin.

"How about a hand putting the crosspiece on?"

Villeneuve, who had been studying maps, jumped to his feet.

They had set the post in the ground yesterday when they filled the grave and covered it with rocks. Will held the crosspiece level. Villeneuve drilled a few small pilot holes and easily twisted the screws deep into the wood.

Will stared at the size and strength of Villeneuve's hairy hand.

He could easily imagine those thick fingers wrapped around the pistol an inch from Zalapski's head.

Suddenly Will had no doubt. He could see Zalapski's eyes in the last second of his life, wide open in panic—the way they were in death. The truth was in Zalapski's eyes: the fear, the surprise, the panic. If Zalapski had killed himself, Will reasoned, he would have been at peace with himself and his decision. Surely, he wouldn't have had that look of absolute horror on his face and in his eyes.

Will knew that he too was now wide-eyed and he could feel the fear and rage in his stomach. The fear was in his stomach, but he would not let it show. He turned his head away from Villeneuve's ugly hand.

"I'm shaken by this, Vee-Vee. I need a day or two to adjust."

"Well, me too. Take your time, do what you want to. I think I'll go up the valley tomorrow morning looking for muskox."

Will did take a few days to contemplate, sometimes from the end of the table, other times high on the hill overlooking the two graves, or staring off across the distant ice, wondering if he would see a ship ever again.

Villeneuve's hunting trip paid off. He had shot two muskoxen at a fairly close range, less than half a mile from the camp. Will helped with the skinning and packing the meat back and hanging it in the storehouse.

Villeneuve paused, took the stone, and sharpened his knife.

Will watched as though he was waiting to also use the stone, wondering if Villeneuve were to make a move, would he do it now, with a razor-sharp, 6-inch blade? Will's hands were aching and cold. He felt his vulnerability. "Nice job, Vee-Vee. My father the butcher would hire you."

It brought a thin, non-threatening smile to Villeneuve's lips.

They saw little of each other for the next three days, except when Villeneuve came to the detachment for fresh stew.

Will spent days trying to put Zalapski either out of his mind or at least in context. He would never allow Villeneuve to see his doubts, suspicions, or fears—but neither would he trust him.

When he was sure that Villeneuve had retired to his cabin for the evening, Will looked at the few ounces remaining in his last bottle of stashed rum, poured himself two fingers, and re-corked the bottle.

He recalled what Zalapski had called Villeneuve's eight-month "extract exercise." Could the alcohol be tied to Zalapski's death? Will remembered passing the key over to Zalapski that morning. *Did Villeneuve return to the detachment after he had left and demand the keys to raid the storehouse? Did they quarrel? Did Villeneuve shoot Zalapski and then leave the post, only to double back later?*

Will knew that alcohol could make men desperate, and desperate men do desperate things. Desperate men, like Will, could also be strategic, tactical, and calculating.

Will began by preparing a decent meal, a rump roast from Villeneuve's most recent trophy. It was quite tender, and the gravy masked the stale, dehydrated potatoes and tinned vegetables.

Will put the last of his booze on the table and offered Villeneuve a drink as they sat down to eat.

"Is this Christmas?"

"No, Skipper, it's not Christmas, but there's no point in hoarding this any longer. We may as well enjoy it while we can. You know you were wrong nipping into the extract, but it's no good going back over that now. I just think we should enjoy what's left of this last bottle. What's in the past is in the past, but I'll hold on to the storehouse key. I still need something to bake with."

"Okay, here's to better days—our health and a ship in August."

"Good health." Will raised his arm.

They ate in the awkward silence that had become as predictable as the taste of stale food. Will found the silence unbearable. He looked for ways to gauge what was in Villeneuve's head.

"I packed up all of Zalapski's things and put them in his footlocker, including his service pistol. Is that okay?"

"Good idea, I expect O'Halloran will want to see it. Did you empty it?"

"Yes, but I didn't clean it. It didn't seem right and I want to put the whole kit in the storehouse." Will let the thought tail off, not asking permission.

Villeneuve had a bewildered look in his eye. "Okay, that makes sense. It's not like he's going to be needing it."

Will was sure that Villeneuve didn't know about Zalapski's journal. Certainly, it was only in the past few weeks that he'd told Will, adding that he wanted it kept under wraps.

It was October 31. Villeneuve had his maps out.

They congratulated themselves that they were physically prepared for winter. Ice was cut and stored. Coal bags were stacked close to the doors. The detachment and the cabin were sound. The shithouses had been relocated and strapped down.

Neither dared mention whether they were mentally prepared; as hardened Mounties, neither would confess a weakness.

Will feared his ability to face four more months of darkness with a superior whom he believed to be both paranoid and a killer. He certainly didn't know whether Villeneuve was capable of self-assessment, but he doubted it.

Villeneuve laid out a map on the table.

"How about tomorrow we hitch the dogs and put that last patrol into the books? The days are getting short. We should go here." He pointed to Cape Sherard, the most southeasterly point on Devon Island. "It's about 40 miles out."

"I'm ready." Will needed a change of scenery, if even for a few days. The past two weeks had had him on the edge of despair.

He had nightmares about having to kill Villeneuve to protect himself, and then, more frightening, Villeneuve returning to kill him, shooting Will over and over in the chest, but Will refused to die. He woke from the nightmare, a little shaken. His twisted Grant sense of humour gave him a moment of relief. *Jesus, I'll wave a white flag and roll out a red carpet for those Krauts.*

Will keep track of the rapidly diminishing light. October 16, the day Zalapski was laid to rest, had had eight hours of sunlight. Two weeks later, they enjoyed just over three and half hours of sunlight and, in a week, as of November 7, the sun would not rise for another four months.

Every night, Will stared at the northern lights, imagining Naudla staring at them too, speaking to her as though she were by his side. *If not in this life, Naudla, then the next—but I know, we'll be together.*

Will and Villeneuve made the best of the short hours of daylight as they travelled on the sea ice east of the post. Ten dogs were in harnesses; Inspector ran alongside. Will called it "shotgun," and he decided that this was the dog's last free ride and that he would soon be introduced to the harness.

The qamutik was not fully loaded. They planned to be gone for four days but carried food for a week.

The dark, overcast skies made it difficult to determine the sky from the ice. Will was careful to keep land in sight, knowing the unreliability of a compass at almost the same latitude as the magnetic pole.

About two hours past East Point, it was dark, and the dogs began running and shifting direction erratically. Ice-cold drops hit Will's cheek, as the sled runners skipped over 3 feet of open water.

One minute later, another open patch passed beneath them, then another. Fear gripped Will, as he realized that they were in a field of broken and moving ice. Last year, with Teemotee and Pudlu as their guides, they had travelled over 600 miles and hadn't encountered anything like this.

Villeneuve threw down the snow anchor, shouting stop orders to the dogs.

Through binoculars, Will detected a complex web of thin, dark lines crisscrossing the ice. Open leads. Some were narrow, the kind the dogs had already easily jumped. Some were too wide to jump and, big or small, wide or narrow, they were shifting with the wind and tide.

"We need to get ashore." Villeneuve turned the dogs straight for the closest land. Five hundred yards farther the dogs stopped dead in their tracks. A hundred yards of open water separated them from shorefast ice. Villeneuve and Will were stranded on a small ice floe only a few hundred square feet, now drifting helplessly farther east and away from land.

Of all the dangers they had encountered or tried to prepare for, this was not one of them.

Villeneuve, who always found it within himself to rise to the occasion, admitted defeat. "We're at the mercy of this wind. This ice has been breaking up. There's nothing we can do but wait and hope this pan doesn't split."

They were cold. The dogs howled. The two men, no matter their fear and loathing and disrespect for each other, struggled to get the tent up in the brisk cold wind. Now they depended on each other.

They kept watch, at half-hour intervals, scanning the ice and water, looking for movement. All they needed was a narrow ice bridge, even 3 feet wide would be enough to connect them with another floe that hopefully connected with the shore.

Will was on watch. Villeneuve sat in the tent, his down-filled sleeping bag over his shoulders. Through his binoculars, Will noted a patch of black between two white sheets closing, becoming closer and closer. "Vee-Vee," he shouted. "I see a link." The dogs stopped howling; they too could sense it.

Villeneuve bolted from the tent toward the ice edge, sleeping bag fluttering behind him like a cape.

Will had already gripped the canvas when he heard Villeneuve shout. "Grab the tent. Unhook the dogs. We have a chance."

Will kicked the tent poles down. His hands felt stronger in the face of life and death. He rolled the canvas like a rug, threw it on the sled, jumped on top, and pulled out the snow anchor and, in barely a minute, he was alongside Villeneuve, who jumped on the back, on his hands and knees. The dogs ran hard, pulling the qamutik and its load from the broken ice pan to the rougher and thicker ice. The men neither spoke nor celebrated until they were on the shoreline, beneath the big cliffs.

They set up the tent, this time properly. With a lantern lit, the dogs fed, and hot stew in their bowls, Villeneuve offered an observation. "That was an experience I didn't expect."

"Neither did I." Will agreed. "My mother has an expression: It's what you learn after you think you know it all that counts."

Neither man could sleep. Their sleeping bags were warm and the tent a good windbreak, but the blowing wind and shifting skies and clouds had all the makings of a storm.

In the morning, they packed quickly, made tea, ate a piece of hardtack, and set off toward the detachment, sticking close to the shore. Intermittent snow squalls and gusts ripped at their faces and, at times, visibility was severely limited. They estimated that the wind had carried them 8 or 10 miles. By 6 p.m., in darkness, Villeneuve pointed to East Point silhouetted against a patch of clear sky and traces of northern lights.

They knew that they could be back at the post in a few hours. The wind was shifting and the sky was closing in again. They had to keep moving.

They were well fed and comfortable in their bunks when a blizzard hit them broadside. As whiteouts go, it was a medium blow, not lasting more than 12 hours, and dropped a foot of snow, making land travel easier.

Even an ill wind blows some good. The gale and stranded ice-pan adventure focused Will's attention on the second winter of boredom and isolation ahead.

Will rationalized that his survival would take more than beating the brutal winds and cold. Survival also meant controlling and managing his mind, protecting it from being warped and manipulated by demons named monotony and seclusion. Those demons become more ruthless in the extreme cold and darkness. Will noted that he was having this discussion with himself on the last day of sunlight, 1926.

In the morning, he rearranged furniture, dismantled, and stored Zalapski's bunk in the loft, and created a small but warm workshop in its space. He would hone his meagre carpentry skills and become a boat and qamutik builder.

He and Villeneuve shared one large qamutik. Will began building one of his own, smaller and suitable for short, one-man trips. He also drew plans for a small multi-purpose dory that they could carry with them and, if needed, ferry themselves and a few dogs at a time over open leads. It was also his way of saying that the last adventure was a mistake he wouldn't repeat.

As well, mooring the boats was challenging. They were too heavy to haul up on shore, and anchoring the bow and stern in the small cove was laborious and sometimes tricky. A little dory to shuttle back and forth would be ideal.

Without one stroke of the plane or swipe of a saw blade, Will already felt more at ease with the challenges ahead.

As he surveyed the storehouse, he made a mental note to someday thank and congratulate the supply people for their foresight and planning. If he couldn't find exactly what he was looking for, there were always ways to improvise alternatives.

It only took a few minutes for Will to confirm that he had everything he needed for the qamutik and a fine 8-foot dory. He was pleased to see so much pine in 6-, 8-, and 10-inch widths and 12-foot lengths. Rolls of oakum for caulking indicated that someone expected boat repair, if not building.

It took Will a little more than a week to build the qamutik.

Using Pudlu's as a model, he copied the design, lashings, ties, and knots that held it together.

The dory took more time. He devoted a few hours to it each day, and each day he felt less handicapped. His remaining fingers were stronger and thicker. Sometimes, he imagined Naudla holding them, stroking them. The workshop was a good place to be with her, if only in his troubled mind.

Will jointed, shaved, and fitted each board, from the bottom to the keel to the gunwales. Every night, he swept up his sawdust and shavings and set them aside as fire starters.

He set aside a few outdoor hours every day for coal, ice, and storehouse chores, as well as long walks, usually westward over now familiar trails with Inspector. Will and Villeneuve each took five dogs on their short runs, and Will introduced Inspector to his team. Inspector instinctively became part of the pack. After a few minor skirmishes with a few of the older male dogs, Will was satisfied that Inspector could hold his own.

At night, Will tried reading, but he could no longer concentrate on written words. No matter the author or the story, his mind would shift to his predicament—and Villeneuve.

As the days stretched into weeks, Villeneuve said less and less. He walked daily and maintained regular entries in the log that consisted of nothing more than a record of cold and shorter days.

Will often suggested a card game, and several times offered to introduce Villeneuve to chess, but Villeneuve remained blank, or worse, became more distant. Not even Christmas changed the routine or the descent into despair.

One night, weeks after they'd buried Zalapski, Will lay awake. A vicious wind had been blowing. He needed to light the lantern.

Snow had been falling since early morning, sometimes quite heavily. It was fine granular snow, but the wind had remained calm, even deadly quiet. When Villeneuve came through the door for the evening meal, he commented that visibility was getting low. When he left 45 minutes later, he paused to ensure that he had a line on the cabin 100 or so yards up the hill, before tucking his head in the hood of his parka and making the dash.

A roaring gust rattled the detachment, making the dishes on the table and the boards on the sawhorses shake. Will jumped out of his bunk. Avalanche.

Inspector, startled by the sound, paced, then sat in front of Will, ears cocked, staring at him. Another blast brought a series of whines and half-barks. For 10 minutes, the gale continued, sporadic gusts giving way to sustained battering. Inspector barked at the door, ears cocked and frantic. A light went on in Will's head. Someone was out there—and it could only be one person.

Will opened the door carefully. Before it was halfway ajar, the dog was gone into the blinding blizzard, barking. The northeast wind rushed around Will, sucking every breath of warmth out of the cabin, leaving Will standing in the lee side. Lantern in hand, all he saw was a wall of driving snow.

For a few seconds, the howling gale subsided, as though inhaling, readying for the next cruel blow. Will thought that he heard a voice. "Over here. Over here."

Will tried shouting. "Villeneuve. Villeneuve." The wind was back and he could barely hear himself.

He stepped inside the cabin, grabbed the double-barrelled 12-gauge shotgun from the rack, took two shells off the shelf, loaded, and fired twice into the sky. Inspector's bark grew closer.

Will pushed the lantern forward. He saw the dog—or a moving form he thought was the dog—and, behind him, a dark hulk slouching downward, arm extended, gripping the dog's bushy tail. Will moved aside and the dog and Villeneuve pushed past into safety. Will slammed the door shut and bolted it.

"What in Christ's name happened?"

Villeneuve couldn't answer. He looked like a snow zombie. His face and chest were covered with driven snow. It was in his ears and eye sockets and even in his sleeves. He was gasping for breath and trembling. Finally, he focused on the chair and dropped onto it.

"That dog saved me. I was blind, and I was going in the wrong direction away from the post, maybe out on the ice."

"But what happened?"

"Half the roof of the cabin is gone, torn right off. I couldn't see a thing. Couldn't get a lamp lit, but I knew where my clothes were and was able to get them on. I thought the rest of the cabin might go, or the stove.

"I thought I could find my way down the hill from memory, and run right into the detachment, but the wind knocked me to my hands and knees. I could hardly get up and, when I did, I kept getting turned sideways. The winds got stronger, and I had no sense of direction.

"I couldn't see—blind—and most of the time couldn't breathe. That wind sucked the air right out of me! I didn't even see the dog. I could hear him and then I felt him at my legs, so I grabbed him. You are one bon chien." Villeneuve looked directly at Inspector.

Will stuffed the stoves with more coal. The tin stovepipes shook as the dampers shuddered and rattled with downdrafts that no tinsmith or chimney sweep could have imagined. The bare wooden walls did little to diminish the roar of the brutal winds, constant, loud warnings that the danger hadn't passed.

"The lull within the storm," Will offered.

"Pardon?"

"I'm just thinking out loud, Vee-Vee. If the roof came off one building, it can come off the other just as easily. You've been out there. You know better than I do the fix we're in here."

Villeneuve nodded. Will lit another lamp and checked the time. It was shortly before midnight.

He made fresh tea to warm Villeneuve. After a bit, he said, "Give me a hand." Will went into the loft and passed down Zalapski's bunk and mattress and then got extra blankets and a sleeping bag.

In the loft, the sound was even more deafening. The roof was shaking violently. He looked in the corner where Villeneuve had repaired the cave-in last year. *Probably the strongest part of the structure.*

Neither man slept that night, but the dog, having had considerable praise from both, curled up in his usual spot. Will looked at Inspector, always equipped to face the Arctic elements in a way he never would be.

He thought of Naudla and Pudlu. They were also equipped. Will remembered the lifeline, no more than 30 feet long, from the doorway of their cabin, the same cabin that just shed its roof, connecting to Pudlu's iglu.

"Vee-Vee, if we get through tonight, the first thing tomorrow I want to build an iglu next to this building. We need an emergency backup."

"Good thinking. Thank you, Will, and thank you, Inspector."

If a night ever seemed like an eternity, this was it. Hour after hour, the building trembled and rattled. Will divided his time between lying on his back on the bunk or sitting on the edge of the bunk or at the table. Frequently, he stoked the fires.

He watched Villeneuve on his partially reassembled bunk, his shoulders slouched inward, head down, staring at the floor. Will was able to study him. He shook when the wind gusts were the loudest, like explosions.

He thought of Zalapski's shell-shock theory. Will imagined Villeneuve a decade ago, huddled the same way in a trench, in a different kind of violent storm, with shells exploding all around and bodies lying close by.

Will considered this confusing contradiction. All these months he was convinced that Villeneuve had murdered Zalapski. All these months he measured every word and movement, careful never to enrage, and staying forever vigilant.

Not once did Villeneuve threaten him, with word or deed.

Will wondered if he had been wrong. Could Erik have killed himself?

Will realized that he had just had the opportunity to rid himself of all his fears, to take the ultimate act of survival. He could have let Villeneuve perish in the storm. It never crossed his mind.

Will watched Villeneuve get up only twice through the night, once to the piss-pot, the second time to throw up. But both times, he tended to the stove. He did not speak. Will concluded that it was because he was unable to. If there was a worse place in this world to spend the night than in this blizzard-battered bunker on Devon Island, he thought, that's where Villeneuve was.

Sometime, shortly after 6 a.m., nature ran out of heavy artillery.

The wind dropped, no longer exploding, just howling, the building stopped quaking and shivering. It creaked and groaned, and the stovepipes finally relaxed. The battle was over.

The dog whined and went to the door, wanting to go out for a leak. Will obliged, even stepped out to join him. Through blowing snow and darkness, he could just make out the shoreline. He longed for a few hours of daylight. The lash of the wind and snow on his bare face snapped him back to reality. They had made it. He had made it. And yet, they had such a long way to go.

Will stepped back inside and the hero followed. Will lay down on his bunk and finally slept for a few hours.

The room was still warm when he awoke. Villeneuve was not there, nor was Inspector. Will checked the stove, and the tea was hot. He drank a cup, dressed, and stepped outside into the stillness.

By the faint light of Arctic twilight, he saw Villeneuve coming down the hill toward him, carrying his footlocker. Inspector was following.

"A few things blew away. The place is half full of snow, but at least I had the log and maps in the locker. Half the roof is gone, and I don't know where in hell it is—maybe Baffin Island. My packs with the skin clothes are under the snow. I'll dig them out later."

Will and Villeneuve surveyed the main detachment building, saw heavy buildup on the roof, and immediately shovelled it off. Then they checked and fed the sled dogs, who were none the worse for the blow.

They ate a hearty meal. Then, true to pledge, that afternoon they built an iglu at the front of the detachment, connected with a rope from the doorway to a wooden packing-crate panel, which served as the doorway to the emergency iglu. They stocked it with reserves of food, blankets, skins, a Primus stove, and candles, remembering the horrors of the night before, and hoping that they would never have to use it.

Villeneuve was unusually talkative. As Will prepared the evening meal, Villeneuve opened the log.

"We have a story to tell today. *January 7, 1926, was a hurricane. The roof was torn off the cabin, and the wind knocked me down. I was blind, had trouble breathing. Grant's dog saved my life, got me to the detachment. Grant suggested we build an emergency snow house next to the detachment. Did so today!*"

Will tried to assess where the storm had left them. Will had to appear to be glad that Villeneuve was alive, but he could never forget that the senior constable was responsible for Erik Zalapski's death.

That night, he watched this man sit at the same table and recount his fortunate survival, and, within days, witnessed his mind again vanish into a dark void.

In a crisis, Villeneuve was dependable. He had shown that in the storm at sea, the avalanche, the collapsing roof, the open water, and during the hurricane. And even the misguided belief that they were being watched by snipers brought out some degree of humanity. But he wondered where Villeneuve's mind went in times of peace, and why.

The detachment had become Will's sanctuary and safe house. Could whatever demons that had sparked Villeneuve to attack Zalapski suddenly compel him to do the same here, in the detachment in the middle of the night?

Parallel routines developed. The two men said good morning to one another, but little more for the rest of the day. Each went his way, either walking or taking weekly trips with small dog teams to their respective traplines. Villeneuve attended to the dogs and maintained the coal supply. Will cooked and cleaned. Weeks crept by. Occasionally in the evening, Villeneuve asked if Will had an observation that ought to be entered in the log.

Villeneuve continued to ignore Will's subtle suggestions about reading or a game of cards. If he did anything other than stare into space in the evenings, he sat and stared at the maps instead.

On February 6, 1926, Villeneuve broke the silence. "Good entry today. *The sun rose finally. Anything you want me to put in?*"

Will was dismayed by Villeneuve's lack of enthusiasm. The sun had shown its face after more than two months, just after 11 a.m. Will had been outside with Inspector in -30°F for an hour waiting for it. When he saw the sun rise, he did a happy dance, then watched the sun for the full 45 minutes it was above the horizon. For Will, this was the biggest day of the year. Villeneuve's being so blasé led Will to wonder where the big man's mind had drifted.

"Well, you can say that the dory is finished," Will offered. "I gave it the last coat of paint this afternoon. But we have a long wait before putting it in the water."

Will was pleased with the little dory. He knew that it was tight and light, perhaps 90 pounds. He had taken his time shaving, joining, and caulking every joint and seam. The real purpose had been to keep his mind occupied until the sun appeared. It worked, and he had something to show for it.

He could see Villeneuve making the notation.

Two more weeks went by. Will's spirits grew with every day

of the increasing sunlight that deepened the beauty of the land, mountains, ice, and sky. Many nights were equally beautiful, crystal clear with spectacular displays of northern lights that provided mental tonic and stimulant. On the most dazzling nights, it was not uncommon for Will and Inspector to walk for over two hours.

He noted that Villeneuve's vocabulary had few adjectives— *beautiful* was not among them.

But Villeneuve was clear that they would record at least two significant patrols, one west in April and one east in May.

By mid-April, the weather was warming, although still below freezing for at least another month. But they could feel the sun's warmth and knew from experience the extent to which it could brown and burn the skin.

It was easy travelling: 11 dogs, including Inspector, fanned in front of them. After three days of travelling seven hours a day, they passed the easterly headland of Devon Island at Cape Sherard and continued another 40 miles up the east coast of Devon. They built cairns at both points, and left the required canisters, reminding anyone who might discover them that that land had been claimed in the name of Canada.

On the second last day of the trip, April 29, Will noted and Villeneuve recorded: *The sun did not set.*

In Will's mind, summer had arrived; the shortest of the two Arctic seasons, four months: May, June, July, and August. The other eight months were winter.

Villeneuve had planned the western trip for the last week of May and early June, just when the land and ice would begin melting. He pointed out the route on the map. Last year, they had crossed the mouth of Croker Bay about 30 miles west of the post. The briefings they had had two years earlier and the maps told them that the Devon Ice Cap, one of the world's great glaciers, connected to the tidewater in Croker Bay.

For weeks, they had been blessed with ideal weather conditions, light winds, mostly sunshine, and very little precipitation, making travelling easy.

Not far from the post, they shot a seal and cached part of it. Toward the end of the second day out, they saw the face of the glacier towering above the massive cliffs and mountains. Two monstrous arms of ice embraced a mountain spire pointing skyward. The arms transformed into huge clenched glacial fists, each about a mile wide and, in Will's view, maybe 100 to 150 feet high.

At first, he tried to think like a poet. *Such great, white, towering, silent sentinels. Pure, white cathedrals, their spires reaching heavenward.* His feeble attempts at whimsical and romantic language vanished when the great glacier spoke. At first soft groans, and as if irritated by not being heard or obeyed, it thundered, loudly and consistently. Will and Villeneuve lay bundled in sleeping bags in a tiny iglu, dwarfed in the vast shadows of ice walls. Villeneuve's arms were pressed against his face and ears.

Then a sleeping giant roared and a thunderous crack rolled across the ice. Villeneuve wasn't hearing the sounds of cracking, settling, and falling ice. He heard cannons.

In the hours ahead, he heard a thousand more, some short and sharp like a rifle shot; others, like exploding bombs, cracking and shaking the ice beneath them. Some were distant, but too many seemed so close. Will felt the ice under them shake as it would during an earthquake, as walls of the glacier peeled away, ramming the frozen ocean below.

He could see Villeneuve, pulling his blanket more tightly around his shoulders. The dogs howled. Inspector, privileged as he was and spared the indignity of being chained with the others, stuck his head in the doorway and whined.

For a fleeting moment, Will thought of Zalapski and his astute observations about shell-shock syndrome. "We will never get a half-decent sleep here, Vee-Vee. Why don't we pack up and move on? Let's just put cairns at the headlands on both points of the harbour."

Villeneuve didn't speak. He just pushed out of the sleeping bag and began getting on his boots and outer clothing. Will did the same. It was midnight when they set out, heading northwest, or diagonally, across the 8-mile stretch at the head of the harbour, both faces of the glacier shrinking with each mile. And the sounds, becoming fainter, until finally, they became the occasional rumble of distant cannon.

Will could see the panic in Villeneuve's eyes. He wanted to shout, "We're all alone here. What are we running from?" Instead, he took his cues from Villeneuve, who acted as though they were being pursued by the devil himself, stopping only briefly every few hours to rest the dogs.

They pitched camp at 8 a.m. at the west cape of Croker Bay and Lancaster Sound. Will estimated that they had travelled just over 20 miles. Villeneuve had not spoken the entire time.

Will was exhausted. He worried about Villeneuve stirring in his sleeping bag, but finally fell into a deep sleep. That evening, they put a cairn and canister on Cape Home on the west point of Croker Bay. They maintained the same campsite for a second night, and, as they ate, Will offered an alternative.

"You know, Vee-Vee, it's still a patrol if we go up that little river and try for char. It's that time of year and it's not far."

Will believed he saw a faint smile in Villeneuve's nod.

The next night, they pulled a huge char from a hole in the ice. There was laughter, giving Will a twinge of optimism.

Two nights later, they were back at the detachment with fresh, delicious char on their plates. Villeneuve spoke the last words Will wanted to hear.

"Those snipers were shooting at us. They almost got us. We need to be more careful."

CHAPTER 11

DARK SIDE OF THE MIDNIGHT SUN

I t had been a long, uneasy winter—especially since January, when Villeneuve had moved back into the cramped detachment following the big storm. Watching Villeneuve unravel in a tent to the shakes, shifts, and groans of a glacier indicated that the summer might not be much better.

Will focused on his own well-being and survival. He had become strategic, discovering payoffs by affirming Villeneuve's leadership and beliefs.

Villeneuve focused only on patrols, although no longer for Canada's sovereignty. He was at war. Will watched Villeneuve carefully as he mechanically carried out mundane chores, like heating water, bathing, and washing clothes. He was a man in a trance, silent, scowling, and paranoid.

Summer reinforced Will's sanity as the presence of migrating birds swept away his hollow feeling of isolation. *Like the geese, ships also migrate north every summer. I need to see a ship.*

It was mid-June. Even the best mariner could not navigate a ship into Dundas Harbour for another two months. Yet Will found himself looking at the horizon, as though it would arrive at any moment.

The small streams near the detachment were melting. The sun and wind were sweeping the land clear of snow. The thermometer read 40°F. For the next week, it stayed there, give or take 1 or 2 degrees.

A soft southern breeze came up, and the sun was out. Will realized that he was sweating. He shed his parka. Villeneuve did the same.

"As soon as the ground dries, probably next week, I want to set up the tent and camp at East Point again," Villeneuve said. "I know you don't like it down there, that you would rather be here. So, how about a five- and three-day rotation? I'll do five, you can do three, and keep order here and patrol west."

Will tried not to show his relief. For the summer, they would pass like ships in the night.

"That's a grand plan, Skipper."

Villeneuve picked the summer solstice for his first sortie. He took his dog team, believing that he could use them for the first few rotations.

Will left at the same time, heading westward on what he called in his heart "Naudla patrol." It had been almost a year since their encounter, and he needed to relive every moment of it. There was a spring in the long strides he took along a now-familiar path to their spot.

He picked Naudla's eggs from the ledges and ground nests. At the waterfall, he pretended that she was standing under the ice-cold spray with him.

All winter, he had waited to come back here. Not a day went

by that he did not think about her, long for her, and wonder where she was. If Will's determination and commitment prevailed, and he survived this island, he would find her and make his feelings clear. Beyond that, he had no plans. She might reject him. Teemotee might kill him at first sight.

Until then, he would live, cherish, and control the encounter with Naudla in his mind. She was now more than his lover; she was at the core of his sanity. In Will's fantasy, he was free to set scenes, write lines, recite poetry, and live dreams. He blocked out thoughts of Teemotee, as though he had drifted away, far beyond the horizon on a disappearing ice pan.

In the 24-hour sunlight, June slipped into July. Gradually days grew warmer and anticipation mounted. A dozen times a day, Will tried to gauge if the ice had shifted, even though he knew that it hadn't. If it were to move at all, it wouldn't do so until late July.

He determined to keep busy. He opened the doors and took the shutters off the storehouse to let in light and air, counted every can and box, and measured the contents of every barrel. For weeks, he tried not to think about their prospects if a ship failed to arrive. But at the same time, he had to know what provisions remained if they had to face a third winter.

He first checked the remaining bottles of extract. There were three, and they were his, either for cooking or a stiff drink. When they were gone, to use Pudlu's word, "Taima!"

About 100 pounds of flour and nearly as much sugar remained. All three Mounties had been tea drinkers. Only enough remained to last a few months, but plenty of coffee. Will could live with that.

All the seal, walrus, muskox, polar bear, and Arctic char they'd eaten had left a stock of tinned meat. There was also a supply of hardtack, tinned fruit, and juice. There had been fewer mouths to feed lately.

But on this day, and in the weeks to come, Will needed little of these rations. He would feast on fresh eggs, roast goose, duck soup, and Arctic char.

Villeneuve spent five days looking for snipers. Will spent three days staring at the ice and looking for ships.

The weather pattern for 1926 mirrored that of the previous year. In the first week of August, a brisk northeast wind cleared the ice out of Dundas Harbour, raising Will's hopes and expectations. For Villeneuve, a lack of ice put them in more danger from snipers. The open water needed to be patrolled.

Without Zalapski, it was difficult to get the 24-foot motorboat in the water. Villeneuve and Will anchored a block and tackle to the rocks and winched the boat into the water. Considerable effort was required to hand-crank the stubborn engine to life.

Will dropped his dory into the water to determine how quickly the wet wood expanded. He was pleased to see only a few leaks, which he sealed completely.

Villeneuve surprised him with a compliment. "It's a great little dory, Will. You've found your calling."

"As I once told Pudlu, I'm the son of a fisherman who is the son of a fisherman who is the son of a fisherman."

Villeneuve's mood changed. He wanted no reminders of the Inuit. Not once in the year since their departure had he acknowledged their contribution to their basic survival. The subject was off-limits.

Will also dared not speak about Zalapski and the void he had left. Conversation became difficult, haunted by old suspicions.

The motor started easily and the two began the open-water patrol in strained silence. They travelled 5 to 8 miles east and west, and 2 to 3 miles into Lancaster Sound. In every direction was heavy ice, some of it 10 feet thick, that only wind and currents would budge.

Three days later, Will climbed several hundred feet to the top of Talluruti, the big mountain behind East Point. There was no better vantage point for observation. All he could see in every direction was ice and sky. It refused to budge.

They made the last long ice patrol by boat on September 4. As far as they could see across the distant ice with the naked eye and binoculars, there was no break in the vast, white, still, ocean and nary a ship or sniper.

Villeneuve pulled back the throttle. They drifted close to the ice edge. "Okay, Will, let's accept it. We're not going to see a ship this year. Bernier, if he's still with us, or any other captain out there is now pointing his ship south."

Will stared at the infinite ice. He wanted to speak but feared that opening his mouth might reveal the depth of his depression. Fearing that he might even cry, he spoke in the silent voice he used more and more often. *Can I even survive another year of this? Villeneuve is a paranoid killer. What's my mental state going to be this time next year?* His stare remained fixed. Inspector shifted and curled at his feet. He was a constant companion and good in the boats, even the dory. Above all, he was a comfort.

It was a full hour before Will broke the edgy silence.

"I told you earlier that we're okay for provisions, but I think we should go into that cove just east of the big Cape and look for walrus. It seems that there's always a herd there. Time to start thinking about feeding the dogs all winter."

No matter how cruel nature had been with storms, ice, and darkness, the bountiful land and sea always provided. They shot two small walruses out of a herd of about 30. The others growled, snorted, and huffed their massive hulks into the water.

Each walrus easily weighed a ton. The men were confronted with a big butchering job, one that was fast, bloody, and brutal. They cut 50- to 100-pound chunks of meat and stowed them in the boat.

Time constraints dictated shortcuts for the second walrus. They hacked it into a dozen big sections that required them to work together to carry the meat across the rocks to a crevice that served as a cache. They would retrieve it later in the winter with dogs.

As they laboured, the weather turned sour. Cold rain and north winds brought misery to match disappointment. They were looking directly into the cold, cruel eyes of year three on Devon Island. Every night was now well below freezing, and most days, ice built along the shore.

It was dark when they returned to the detachment. They were too tired to do anything except eat and sleep.

The next day, with snow squalls blowing in, they unloaded and stored the walrus meat and winched the two boats out of the water. Will put his dory in the motorboat, upside down, lashed it securely, and placed a 100-pound boulder on top for insurance.

Their timing was impeccable. Two days later, a wind shift blew the ice shoreward, leaving them ice-locked.

Villeneuve insisted on maintaining his five-day patrols into October. On October 2, Villeneuve left for East Point, declaring it his last stay there for the year. Will would not relieve him. Will grappled with the year ahead. He cut ice for the winter, thinking and talking to himself silently, or out loud to Inspector.

"The first year was all adventure and excitement. Last year was routine. This year is monotonous. And this is the worst."

Only his walks eastward to his sanctuary delivered him, at least temporarily, from the tedium.

Encountering a half-dozen muskoxen was an added distraction, although it underlined the extent to which boredom had set in. Hunting was no longer a thrill. He wanted to watch them and had difficulty settling down with Inspector, who had other ideas. Will stared. The dog growled and whined. The herd shifted into its unique defensive semicircle, shuffling shoulder to shoulder, staring motionless, fearless, dominant, and appearing ready to charge.

Will knew it was a bluff, a façade. All of that magnificent posturing only presented the hunter with the easiest of targets. Will took his time picking out those he would kill. In the world of the small, medium, large, and extra large, he took one medium and one large, and only after the second one dropped did the others scatter. Will did not let Inspector give chase.

On October 7, Will took a large roast from the latest kill out of the oven, waited until an hour after dark, and then ate alone. For the second time, Villeneuve was overdue. No boats or dog teams were involved. He was on foot. It didn't make sense.

Will left for East Point as the first morning light was breaking in front of him. It was cold, -10°F overnight. The ice was fast. He could have hitched the dogs and gone along the shoreline quicker. But Villeneuve had left by foot and should be returning overland. The trail he followed was familiar to them both.

From a half-mile away, Will could see the big tent. He looked for smoke from the stove, but saw none. A few minutes later, he spread the flap back and went into the tent. Villeneuve was not there, and it appeared that he hadn't been there for some time. The stove was cold and everything was frozen solid.

He stepped outside, calling Villeneuve's name. Will's echo was the only response. Will walked shoreward toward the cliffs. Less than 2 inches of new snow had accumulated. It was still soft and revealed no signs of tracks or life.

He turned 180 degrees and walked past the tent down a slight slope to a small flat point close to the water's edge. Will stopped. His heart pounded as Inspector leaped forward, barking and standing over Villeneuve.

Villeneuve had been dead for days. Half his body was covered with a thin layer of icy spray from the rocks. Will could feel his body and hands shake. He wanted to throw up.

All these months, Will had feared this man, and never doubted his suspicion about what had happened to Zalapski. As he looked at Villeneuve's dead, frozen body at his feet, he still feared him. Slowly, Will managed to collect his courage and clear his thoughts.

"Ghastly!" He stared at the body. Villeneuve was frozen stiff, but it wasn't the cold that had killed him.

Inspector, still barking, thrust his nose toward the corpse the way dogs do when people or things don't respond to their alerts.

Will took a short rope out of his pack and tethered Inspector close by. The dog kept watch, his whine distraught.

Will knelt, facing Villeneuve's twisted body. He was lying partially on his left side. Will tried rolling him over. From the top of his head and muskrat Mountie hat, the length of his body, to his sealskin kamiks—the only part of the Inuit culture he embraced—Villeneuve was cemented by cold and ice to the ground and rocks. His legs were spread apart, his ankles also frozen to the ground. His eyes were open. His face, white from frost and cold, was void of expression.

Will bent down on his knees, twisted his head close to the ground, and peered under Villeneuve's arm, bent at the elbow. He could see most of the dead man's chest. On the left side of his row of buttons, a small red frozen patch of blood made it clear that Villeneuve had been shot clean through the heart.

Will removed his mitts, moved behind Villeneuve, and ran his hand below Villeneuve's shoulders at the back of the rib cage. Close to the ground, he was sure his index finger detected a small hole, likely an exit wound. If he could move Villeneuve a few inches, he could be more certain, but Villeneuve was immovable.

Villeneuve's 303 Lee-Enfield rifle, locked in his left hand, raised more frightening questions. The rifle bolt was partially open, with a live bullet in the breech. Villeneuve had been in the process of advancing a new round into the chamber. He was reloading when he drew his last breath.

Will brushed aside the fine snow beneath the rifle, 2 feet from the body. He knew from experience the distance that the 303 Enfield threw a spent cartridge. He uncovered four empty shells, all within a few inches of each other. It looked as though

Villeneuve was about to fire shot number five when he was hit by a fatal bullet.

Will's shock, shakes, and nausea turned to cold chills.

Villeneuve was dead. But who could have shot him?

How many times had Will and Zalapski scoffed at Villeneuve's paranoia that a sniper lurked behind every rock or ice pan? Will didn't want to believe in Villeneuve's snipers. But who could have killed him, so cleanly and swiftly?

Will walked out on the ice but found no trace of man or beast. Suddenly he stopped. "They're both dead," he proclaimed, to no one. "I'm by myself! But I'm not alone. Who is out there?"

From that moment and a hundred more times in the months ahead, Will replayed every detail of the past year since Zalapski's death. Was he wrong to believe that Villeneuve had killed Zalapski? Had whoever killed Villeneuve, here at East Point, also killed Zalapski?

Will scanned the ice, the rocks, the cliffs, the ledges, wondering who was watching.

He went back and knelt behind Villeneuve's frozen remains. Again, he tried moving his legs. Nothing budged. He needed to develop a plan to remove the body, but it would have to wait. He suddenly felt exhausted and overwhelmed.

He knocked down the canvas tent, folded it like a blanket, covered the body, and pried some rocks loose to weight it down. The heavy grub box and stove anchored everything.

It was dark when he and Inspector walked into the detachment. Will's crippled hands burned with pain as he struggled with matches to light the stove. He was numb: head, heart, and hands, chilled to the bone.

Christ. All those evening drinks and this is the first time I feel that I need one. Some planning! If the extract was good enough for Villeneuve, it would be good enough for him. He chose the lemon, found it more powerful than store-bought rum, and, once more, congratulated people in a warehouse far away for their provision.

The room was warm and his stomach full, but his hand was still shaking when he took the pen and made the nightly log entry.

October 7, 1926. Found Villeneuve dead at East Point.
The state of his frozen body indicates that he was
shot in the heart, probably two to five days earlier.
Covered the body and will return tomorrow. Cannot
fathom who could have killed him or why.

The entry described the position of the body, the site, the spent cartridges, every detail he could recall, including the weather and freezing conditions.

He did not sleep that night, but he did formulate a plan.

He knew that he couldn't jar Villeneuve free from the ice without considerable force. The only way to free an object from frozen ground is to hit it with an ax, hammer, or rock. He abhorred the thought. He also knew that he hadn't the means to melt the ground and ice. It would be 10 months before Mother Nature could offer a helping hand.

He also questioned whether, even if he could move Villeneuve and give him the kind of burial afforded Piapik and Zalapski, that would be the wisest decision. He weighed the facts. Three Mounties had come to Dundas Harbour two years and one month ago; two were now dead from gunshot wounds.

If he survived, Will would have many questions to answer.

Investigators could suspect that he had killed Villeneuve or label him insane.

Will's future and freedom might depend on ensuring that O'Halloran and any others who showed up at the detachment could see what Will had seen. He knew what he had to do. That didn't make it any easier to sleep. He lay in his bunk, wide awake. A steady stream of images of his two dead comrades flashed continuously through his mind, their twisted faces and bodies, bullet holes in head and heart.

The next morning, Will took a tarp, a saw, claw, large sledgehammers, a can of spikes, and half a dozen boards from the storehouse. At the side of the cabin rested the roof that had been blown off months ago. Villeneuve had found it on the path to East Point and dragged it back. They had intended to reattach it.

Will sawed it in half, took both 3-foot-wide panels and tied them to the qamutik with his other materials, harnessed six dogs, and set out to finish the dreaded deed.

Will approached the covered body and lifted back the tent. He would feel less nervous if he shattered the silence. "Well, Skipper, for the next few months or until we see a ship, you're going to have the world's most primitive crypt. Rest in peace."

He shielded the body with the tarp that he'd covered Zalapski with. He did not try to pry the rifle free of the frozen death grip, nor did he attempt to close the bolt or remove the half-lodged bullet. He knew that someone else needed to see this the same way he had found it.

The temporary tomb consisted of the two roof sections joined together in an A-frame structure that would cover the entire body. Will sawed planks into shorter pieces and nailed both ends tightly shut. It was solid and firm. He spent an additional two hours swinging the sledgehammer, dislodging heavy boulders, and adding weight to the structure for protection against animals and the winds.

As he worked, the same haunting questions as the day before raced through his mind. *Who killed you, Vee-Vee? Are they watching me? Am I next?* That night he recorded every detail of the site in the logbook, adding sketches of the body and the tomb. He preserved his questions in writing.

Difficult sleep was filled with horrific nightmares. In all of them, Will was in dark places, unable to see. No doubt his unconscious, or subconscious, mind knew that, in just one month, total darkness would return. Will drank half a bottle of peppermint extract. More powerful than the old Hudson's Bay black rum, but sweet like syrup.

He made porridge and fresh bannock for breakfast. He ate slowly, hoping that that might slow down his mind. He spread molasses on the warm bannock and smiled. Why didn't he think of it before? Pop MacKay's liquid fruit cake. The storehouse had dried apricots and oranges, several gallons of molasses, dried yeast, lots of brown sugar, and extract.

Before noon, a 5-gallon salt-pork barrel containing a much different stew sat behind the stove. Will was pleased. Fermenting would take days, enough time to devise a still. He smiled again. The log would not record that Grant's fine whisky had expanded from Scotland to Devon Island.

Every morning and every evening, he lifted the cheesecloth from the pail, pleased to see particles rising and falling. Even the simplest things kept his mind occupied and his boredom and emerging paranoia at bay.

He chose a simple stovetop-still method, requiring only three components: a round-bottom baking bowl that fit snugly over a 2-gallon lard pail, and a large Mason jar, suspended by wires, hanging directly under the baking bowl. The production line and science were equally simple. The bowl was filled with snow. When vapour from the boiling mash rose and hit the bottom of the cold bowl, it immediately condensed and trickled to the lowest point of the bowl. From there, it dripped steadily into the suspended jar.

Will remembered Pop's formula. He'd get about a gallon of moonshine from 5 gallons of mash. He also knew that it could be dangerous to try and extract more than that.

On November 7, he lamented the end of daylight with a stiff shot of Grant's Single Malt Devon, and a salute that turned into a ritual. *What you lack in good taste—and you lack everything— you make up for in kick. And you kick a lot. Bless you!*

Will's entire focus was on his physical and mental survival. The uncertainty surrounding the violent deaths of Zalapski and Villeneuve constantly nagged. He did not for a moment waver from his conviction that Villeneuve had killed Zalapski. But he did not have a clue about who could have shot Villeneuve, or why.

Since the deaths, Will had learned that Villeneuve's abuse of Zalapski was even more cruel and more severe than Zalapski had even let on; Zalapski had also recorded more evidence that Villeneuve was a man more deranged than Will had realized.

The day after he covered Villeneuve, Will brought Zalapski's journal and his own out of their hiding places. He was determined to keep them both with the log. They were now evidence. If anything happened to him, he wanted the journals to be part of the official record or investigation. Both provided much more detail about the troubles, lives, relationships, and interactions of the three Mounties than the sanitized daily log ever would.

Months ago, when Will had removed Zalapski's journal from its hiding place, he felt guilty and had read only a few passages. The feeling of invading Zalapski's privacy was strong. Perhaps he also feared discovering things about Zalapski that he didn't want to know.

Now Will found comfort in Zalapski's beautiful penmanship and what it revealed. Rather than exposing dark inner secrets, Zalapski's journal revealed a kinder, gentler, and more caring person than Will had recognized.

Most telling was Zalapski's account of the avalanche. Certainly, Will didn't need to read how attentive and caring Zalapski had been throughout his recovery.

There is no doubt Villeneuve may have saved Will's life, finding him the way he did, pulling him from being buried alive, and then the way he carried him over the rough snow and rocks to the sleds.

What scared and surprised me is what followed. He said, "He's dead. The bastard snipers shot him through the head in my arms." Villeneuve's mind was somewhere else and it stayed there for two days. It was clear to me he was not on Devon Island, but in France in the trenches.

I know he is suffering from the trenches, as so many of our boys are. He reminds me of dear brother Charles, who returned with his body intact, but his fine brilliant mind destroyed. Every day I wonder if he is still confined to that dreadful hospital ward.

Will turned the page and read Zalapski's touching concerns about his condition and prospects of recovery. He acknowledged that Will had chosen the right surgeon, and noted: Will was always embarrassed about needing help to take a piss.

Except for the encounters with Villeneuve, Zalapski's journal paralleled Will's own accounts, except they were better written, more concise, and descriptive. The cold, dark, boredom, land, ice, sky, and adventures were graphically recorded.

Zalapski did not ignore Villeneuve's consistent verbal abuse. Rather than resort to or retaliate with bitterness and anger, several passages expressed empathy and acceptance.

The skipper is in his dark place again today. Grant and I live and work around it. He calls us twisted fags. We just focus on trying to get through this, all of us. Including the skipper. I know I will raise it with O'Halloran when and if the time finally comes. I expect Grant will do the same.

When Will read that passage, he wondered if Villeneuve might have also read it. Could it have been a factor in Zalapski's death?

He recalled that Zalapski's footlocker had been open, and the journal was in its hiding spot. Will also reasoned that had Villeneuve known of the journal's contents, he would have destroyed it.

Will studied every page. What he did not find, and perhaps why he felt twinges of guilt for prying, was any indication or revelation regarding Zalapski's sexual tendencies. Will wondered if subconsciously he was looking for a truth that would allow him to rise above society's prejudices and bigotry and declare that it doesn't matter.

Finally, he told himself, it didn't matter. "Why should it matter?" he asked Inspector. "Perhaps someday it will not matter. All that counts is a character, and Zalapski was a man of great character."

Zalapski had become a true friend that, regrettably, Will had come to know and respect more in death than in life. They had much more in common than they ever spoke about: a faraway home, a brother, mother, and father missing them and wondering every day whether they were dead or alive.

Will made Erik Zalapski four promises:

I will survive.

I will not forget you.

I will deliver your letters to your folks.

And I won't rest until I learn how you died.

CHAPTER 12

THE ART OF SURVIVAL

Will reached for the logbook that sat on the table at all times, near the oil lamp and the inkwell that never froze, and recorded. *December 31, 1927. Temperature 34 below zero F—another day of darkness. Severe north wind blowing and blinding snow. Hard to go out to feed the dogs. So, 1927 ends with a resolution: Survival.* He scribbled his initials: WFG.

The word survival came unconsciously. Will made a New Year's resolution.

"I will survive!"

He raised the mug toward the chairs, place settings, and spirits of his once-loyal colleagues and the mysteries surrounding their deaths.

He compared their fate with that of forsaken Yukon Klondikers and recalled a line from Robert Service's gold rush tales, penned a quarter-century ago. *Dissolute, dammed, and despairful, pitied, palsied, and slain.*

Will added a word aloud. *"Determined."*

"To determination," he toasted and drained the cup.

Will tapped the logbook and thought ahead to the day that he would make the final entry: *Ship arrived today.*

He made a second resolution: protect the log against water or fire. He would keep it in the steel box provided, knowing that it would reveal the insanity and paranoia that had festered in Villeneuve's mind and Will's suspicions about who had killed Zalapski.

The vision of the CGS *Arctic* under Captain Joseph Bernier sailing south into ice-choked waters 28 months ago was buried deep in his mind. From wherever Will stood at Dundas Harbour, he could see the very point on the horizon where it had disappeared on September 10, 1924. It was nine months to September 1927, and the time—when and if the ice and Arctic gods allowed—the ship would reappear, perhaps first as a mirage, and then like a miracle, and his Canadian Eastern Arctic Patrol would end.

Will was feeling a little groggy when he awoke the next morning, January 1. More and more he was beginning to bemoan his circumstances and more and more he spoke to the dog, if not to ghosts. "Helluva way to bring in the new year, spending all night reliving two and half years past."

Back in the present, he looked at the New Year's resolution he had written hours before: *I will survive.*

Will reached for his journal. *Surely this is solitary confinement in its coldest and cruellest form. Were I at the bottom of the deepest mine, I could not be more alone and forsaken.*

He underlined his resolve. *I will survive.*

He had taken to putting more of his feelings on the record. His journal sat alongside Zalapski's and the daily log. "Live or die," he said aloud. "This is the written trilogy of the Dundas Harbour detachment."

One thought of warmth and humanity rose above the despair and disillusionment.

Naudla. He could still feel the electricity, the magic when they had locked arms and he had swung her in the grand dance of the First Annual Constables New Year's Ball.

Will knew that survival was becoming more difficult. This winter had him on the ropes.

Again today, the thermometer is showing 46 below zero.

For two weeks, the warmest it had been was -42°F and it had gone down to -50°F the week before. *I cannot go out. I cannot move except to try and feed the dogs, and that is becoming a huge chore.*

The extreme cold locked over Devon Island blocked all low-pressure systems. Any moisture in the brutal cold froze to a hazy ice fog that obliterated the few hours of midday Arctic twilight. The cold and dark of 1925 and 1926 had become darker, colder, and crueller. Frightening blizzards like those that had endangered them in the two previous years were infrequent. There was much less snow and a few hard drifts.

Will struggled to cut enough snow blocks to insulate the drafty detachment. Two years earlier, they had stacked thick snow blocks as high as the windows; this year the blocks barely reached a foot above the floorboards.

He had to carry blocks to build the emergency shelter iglu next to the detachment. He moved it an extra 20 feet from the detachment, recognizing that he needed protection against fire as well the wind. He stocked it well and fastened the lifeline.

The detachment was unbearably cold. Only 18 bags of coal remained. There was lumber, and the shithouses and the remains of the cabin up the hill could be fuel in a crisis. But only coal provided lasting heat. He kept one stove lit, used blankets and rolls of wool duffle as a partition to preserve heat. Rarely did the inside temperature rise higher than 50°F. Most times, he wore cotton gloves. His hands continually ached.

He set priorities: keep warm, or as warm as possible; keep clean; keep body and mind active. That last one, the mind, he knew was the most important. And considering the place, the loneliness, the past, and the unending and unyielding cold, it was by far the most difficult.

Last year, he became Will-the-carpenter-and-boat-builder. This winter, he would be Will-the-artist. For all the High Arctic had deprived him of, despite living in hell frozen over, the great North gave him a deep and abiding appreciation of nature's splendour and beauty. He began painting, and improvisation his necessity rather than his art form.

His canvas was cut from the heavy duck cotton that had been provided for packs, clothing, and sails, or he used foot-long sections of clear pine. The storehouse had five colours of paint—black, white, red, yellow, and green—which had all turned to sludge. But with warming and stirring, and the addition of paint thinner, the paint became reasonably pliable. He made small brushes from a larger one, adding a few clips of coarse hair from Inspector's tail and choice snippets from his own polar-bear pants.

Win or lose, good or bad, his mind and imagination were working. Northern lights were becoming his forte—sweeps of colour on a darkened background of silhouetted mountaintops and a grey frozen ocean foreground.

He painted a couple embracing under a towering waterfall, his continuing comfort dream with Naudla. He painted landscapes with cliffs, crevices, and gulls. Invisible to anyone but Will, and perhaps Naudla if she were to ever see them, were the tiniest spots of white, dotting the ledges, the gulls and eggs that had brought them together. Two weeks went by. The temperature stayed at -40°F or colder.

Will logged the full moon of January 17 and dressed for a brisk walk. Except for tending the dog lines and an occasional trip to the storehouse, it was his first walk of any length in three weeks. He had learned to measure time in increments of small victories. *If I can survive and stay sane through one day of cold isolation and deprivation, it follows that I can maintain sanity the next and the next.* He extended the rationale from days to weeks to months.

Will saw no contradiction between his commitment to maintaining sanity and his habit of pontificating from the head of a cluttered table, at the end of the evening meal, to dead men in empty chairs and bare plates with properly placed dinnerware. Perhaps a mark of pending madness or strange unconscious survival, contrivance was a way of clinging to human contact—even with the dead.

One day, Will could be profoundly philosophical; the next, bitterly personal.

"Admit it, Villeneuve. Erik was right. You are deranged. It's because he knew that, even tried to understand it, that you killed him.

"Oh no, don't deny it, you bastard. You killed him. But the brass won't believe that. They'll swallow the suicide setup. But I know the difference. His expression told me the truth.

"But who killed you, Vee-Vee? Not your snipers. There are no snipers, never was. Erik knew that. So did I. But we played your game, and yet you're dead, and there's no explanation and only one suspect—me.

"Erik knows the truth. He knows that if I had killed you, it

WHIT FRASER

wouldn't be from a distance like a sniper, but up close, so that you could see it coming. The same way you did him in."

That night, the thermometer reached bottom, -54°F. Will spread out the large map that Villeneuve had pored over for so many hours and nights. Every patrol was neatly noted with thin pencil lines and dots, indicating the dozen points and peaks where they had placed canisters in the name of Canada.

"You know, chaps, they sold us a bill of goods. This that whole patrol is all folly—pure bullshit. Who in the world believes a few half-mad cops, human frozen flagpoles, can stake a nation?

"Remember when I asked Pudlu how many Inuit camps he knew about along this coast, Baffin and Ellesmere, and westward? How many places did his finger point to? Perhaps 20. Or was it more? There's where the dots and lines should be!

"The government acts as though we are the only people here. They think this little oil lamp and a building put up almost overnight means something. What about the hundreds, perhaps thousands of seal-oil lamps, hollowed out from stone, that flicker in a thousand iglus? Why don't they mark Canada's presence?

"How can we, who were just dropped here, define and exert sovereignty? But the people who have lived here longer than our history, they could and should be our sovereignty! We steal their land but don't let them be part of our country."

Most times, in the unending mind-bending cold and boredom, the rants were repeated in Will's journal.

It was too cold to even paint. His refuge was the wooden chair almost touching the stove that gently warmed half his body, leaving the other half exposed and chilled. Often, he alternated his face and back to the stove, gazing into space and thinking about

Naudla, rescue, home, childhood, survival, and dead comrades in the Arctic and France.

He spent more of his days in his bunk, covered with blankets and muskox hides that offered the only relief. It became difficult to find the energy to tend the stove. He lay as long as he could before going for a piss. It was most often the insistent Inspector that mobilized him.

Basic hygiene, which Will and the others had set as sacrosanct, was sacrificed. It was harder to wash, shave, chop, and haul ice for water. The piss-pot was full and frozen. Every time he needed to go, it meant outside.

The dog team became a burden. A daily trudge up the hill to chop chunks of frozen walrus was now a dreaded chore. The dogs were on the feast-and-famine rotation. It was all that he could do. More than once, he thought of just letting them fend for themselves.

Inspector was different. He stayed close by, slept near Will, ate if Will ate, pissed near the porch when Will forced himself out that far. The dog was his last line of defence against total madness.

Physical breakdown locked step with his mental collapse.

Will began trembling and coughing and went through hours of persistent chills, even under the hides. He drifted into a half-sleep and woke up, soaked in perspiration. He knew that it was a burning fever. His mind flashed to the mystery that had killed Piapik and laid Zalapski, Vee-Vee, and Teemotee low.

Will woke from delirium. The room was freezing. Inspector barked and scratched the door to be let in. Will could not remember when he had let him out. He struggled to light the fire and change his clothes, wet from hot sweats. He had no idea of the time. He hadn't wound either his watch or the clocks.

The temperature had changed—only -36°F. "Seasonal," he muttered, "but still cold." He looked at the sky. No Arctic twilight for a few more hours. He waited to see some change in the morning light and then guessed the time to be 10:30 a.m.

Will was not sure what had laid him low, or even how low, but he had recovered. His mind was clearer than at any time over the past month, but his body was weak. He couldn't be sure when he had last eaten.

Finally, the water for tea and porridge boiled. The room was gradually warming and he set out to do chores. He tended the dogs, brought in more ice, checked the storehouse, gathered staples, and found a pail to replace the foul, full piss-pot.

After about two hours, Will realized that the room appeared brighter. He looked out at a faint trace of light emerging in the southern sky, growing brighter by the minute and stretching east and west across the horizon. The sun emerged—a wedge between ice and sky. The cold edge of the sun. "I have crossed hell frozen over to the cold edge of heaven," he declared.

The almanac that had been included in the detachment library told Will that it was *February 6, sunrise 11:32 a.m.* Between his illness and sporadic depression and despair, he'd lost a week. He had thought it was February 1.

For the first time in weeks, his spirits rose, back in sync with the sun and moon. It didn't change the fact that he was living in a frozen void. But physiologically, there was again order in his small, solitary world.

The next day, Will watched the sunrise with six huskies stretching out in front of him on a journey to nowhere. Just a run across the ice for a few hours for man and dog to exercise mind and body. Back among the living and free.

He steered the dogs to East Point. A dreaded chore, but he needed to see if predators had invaded Villeneuve's tomb. Everything was intact, most of it now covered with a snowdrift. In his relief, and for the first time in two months, he repeated his commitment to himself. "Yes. I will survive."

That night, Will splurged on coal, lit the second stove, heated the room and water. He bathed, shaved, cut his hair, put on a new suit of red Stanfield's woollen underwear. All three Mounties had been issued four extra suits of long johns. Will had found the last two pairs in the storehouse. He pulled them on, shouting, "Oh, the luxury! This must be how warm millionaires feel."

The mission and sovereignty patrols had been finished. From here on, he ran the dogs and himself for physical and mental exercise. Every day, as daylight extended, his mind became clearer. He wondered what had come closer to killing him: germ fever or cabin fever?

A westward trip toward the mouth of Croker Bay presented another Arctic delicacy—blue ice. A huge iceberg, freed from the glacier but locked on a rocky reef, stood out against the mountains, clear blue sky, and endless ice-covered ocean. It was magnificent: a huge castle, with sweeping, smooth columns, spires, and summits, all shaped and sculpted by wind and water.

Will peered into the centre at a deep wide cavern. "Your majesty, you have opened your heart and soul." He was smiling, savouring the resplendent blue and turquoise at the centre of the stunning grandeur. "I can hear you calling, 'Come drink from my soul.'"

In that instant, he was back with Naudla and Pudlu, remembering the excitement when they had found a similar screeched and swooped at the invasion. The commotion made Will brush off Inspector's panicked barking as a natural reaction to the birds. He turned to hush the dog. A mere 25 yards behind him, the husky was head-to-head, tooth-to-tooth with a massive polar bear.

Fifty yards farther behind them lay the double-barrel 12 gauge, fully loaded. It may just as well have been a mile away. He was helpless and petrified as Inspector stood his ground.

The bear lunged, swinging a huge left paw at the dog's head. The husky bolted back, twisted away from the swing, darted behind the bear, and in one motion, took a rip out of the bear's rear left flank. The bear turned the other way, tried another swipe, but Inspector, with the agility of a panther, spun counter-clockwise and took a rip out of the other flank.

After a few losing rounds, the bear backed away slightly. Seeing him retreat just inches was an opening for the cunning dog. He ran circles around the bear. Every few turns, he attacked from behind, tearing at one flank or the other.

Soon, Inspector had the bear on the run back out onto the sea ice. The dog was in pursuit, biting at the bear's hind flanks, then falling back, but keeping the bear moving away from Will.

Will watched them vanish beyond a rocky point. He grabbed the shotgun and ran to the shore and a hundred yards onto the ice. The bear was moving westward at full speed, with the dog charging at random, refusing to let up. Will was pleased and proud of his fierce and loyal companion. He returned to shore, gathered his goods, and waited.

An hour passed, and he worried. After the second hour, with no sign of the dog, he began to panic. Another hour, fear and heartbreak were now his companions.

Will scoured the ice with his binoculars, but nothing moved except gulls, ducks, and geese. He climbed to a high point on the rocks for a better view: across the vast ice, not a trace of the dog or the bear.

Will felt duty bound to go after Inspector. He debated the merits and put reason over emotion, recognizing dangers and possibilities. He feared that the dog might have chased the bear into a lead of open water and then jumped in for the kill. If that had happened, the bear had all the advantages.

He walked back to the cabin, did some chores, but couldn't eat or sleep. At least he was alone. No one saw a grown cop cry.

At 4 a.m., he heard a bark and scratching at the door. He opened it. The husky walked in as though nothing had happened, went directly to his dish, and looked at Will with eyes that asked, "Where's my dinner?" Three pounds of roast muskox was all Will could find. They shared it.

Mid-July came, normally when the northern-bound ship would be clearing St. Lawrence and entering the Strait of Belle Isle. A brisk wind came in from the northwest. For two days, Will walked the shoreline east and west of the post, watching ice moving steadily, east and south.

A half-dozen times he stopped to admire yet another Arctic spectacle. He caught frequent glimpses of seals and walruses with newborns, drifting by on an ice pan as though it were their royal coach. He watched whales in a dozen leads of open water frolic, twist, turn, dive, and breach.

Standing on the shore, dwarfed by the sheer cliffs and mountain behind him and the sweep of Lancaster Sound with its breadth, beauty, and marine life, he felt like an insignificant bystander as

The motor coughed again, and then quit. Will grabbed the crank, tried to restart it, knowing that every failed twist put him closer to the rocks.

He grabbed the oars and hauled for all he was worth on the port side to get the bow around. The boat was too big for one man and two oars in a stiff wind. He was inching straight westward. But for every foot forward, the wind and swell and tide pushed him 6 feet closer to the rocks.

Will was beaten. He turned the bow to the rocks, hoping to protect the prop and shaft, and rowed in reverse to soften the blow. It hit hard, knocking him to the deck. The backwash pulled the boat off the rock and the force of the next wave bashed him a second and third time, finally grounding the boat.

The dory bobbed and beat against the stern. Will untied it, and pulled it into the boat, slid it up over the bow and higher up on the rocks.

Inspector believed that if he snarled enough at the white frothing and foaming sea, it would yield. Will yelled, "Come on, boy. Here, boy," as he climbed over the bow, with one arm hooked through his pack.

Will slid the dory farther up the rocks, using it for support. Three more lunges provided solid footing on a flat rock. Will watched the boat take a few more heavy blows. He was sure the boards cracked.

He caught his breath, then slowly slid the dory across the rocks. With the wind at his back, he manoeuvred it toward the land. As predicted, the quiet cove lay 20 feet below. He eased the dory down and into the water, then slipped into it. He steadied it and coaxed Inspector in, untied his hand-hewn oars, and paddled safely to the gravel shore. Heavy rain fell.

He found shelter under an outcrop. "You stupid bastard," he berated himself. "You could be here for days. For two years, you've been watching for the ship that will be here anytime and now it will not be able to find you. How goddamned stupid can you be? You didn't even take a shotgun or rifle."

The wind blew for most of the night, subsided considerably, and switched to the northeast. Finally, the rain stopped and the sky partially cleared. Will put the dory in the water and rowed, keeping close to shore. At least he would be able to see a ship. With luck, they might also see him. It was 6 a.m., August 17.

Twelve hours later, with little to eat. Will pulled the dory up on the fine gravel and walked to the detachment. He was exhausted and starving. He fried some fish, gave half to the dog, and fell into his bunk, exhausted.

A series of nightmares haunted him: avalanches, shipwrecks, snipers, a naked Naudla, making love on the ice, barking dogs everywhere.

Suddenly, the sound of only one dog. Inspector was at the door.

"Hello, hello, anyone here? Do you want some company?"

Will opened the door. Inspector Ransom O'Halloran and two Mounties stood there. Will stared. O'Halloran and the Mounties waited. For all they knew he might be a raving lunatic; they saw no one else.

Finally, Will spoke, his reaction surprising himself. "Well, sir, don't mind my saying, it took you long enough." His eyesight blurred with tears. His throat went dry. He tried to swallow and speak but could do neither.

He turned back into the room, opened the logbook, and wrote, *August 18, 1927, 3.30 a.m.—Ship arrived today. One survivor,*

William Francis Grant. Then added his initials.

He was still holding the pen when O'Halloran approached, offered a handshake, and looked at the final entry.

"Are you alone? My God, what happened here, Will?"

O'Halloran looked at Will's hands.

"I expect you have a lot to tell me."

"Yes, sir, I do. And as you'll discover, a lot of it, for many reasons, is not here." He tapped the logbook.

"Can we begin now?" O'Halloran pulled out a chair and sat down.

"I think we'd best go for a walk. There's something you must see. The unfinished business that tells a great part of the story."

Will put some tools in a pack and put it across his shoulder.

O'Halloran introduced him to the constables, said something about replacements, but Will couldn't grasp it. There was too much on his mind.

They walked eastward. Inspector fell into step beside Will.

"Nice dog," offered O'Halloran. "What's his name?"

"With respect, sir, it's Inspector. He's always in charge and is too well mannered to be a mere corporal or staff sergeant."

O'Halloran, to Will's relief, laughed. "Well, Inspector, do you also hate paperwork?"

Will stopped and pointed to the makeshift gravesite. "Sir, the story begins up there. That's where Zalapski is buried beside Naudla's baby. We'll go there later."

As they walked, Will recounted the events of Dundas Harbour and the partially doomed patrol. O'Halloran did not interrupt. A few times, he took a small pad from a side pocket and jotted down a note. "Continue, Will, please."

The two constables walked quietly and discreetly behind.

Will doubted that they could hear.

They walked slowly. A hike that used to take an hour, stretched to two. Sometimes, Will found that he needed to stop and think or look O'Halloran directly in the eye while making his point. O'Halloran didn't rush.

By the time they reached Villeneuve's crude crypt, Will had covered in some detail the senior constable's black moods, his sniper paranoia, Zalapski's diagnosis of shell shock, and Zalapski's abuse at the hands of the man he so often respectfully called Skipper.

Will was also clear with his convictions, including his unwavering certainty that Zalapski had not taken his own life, but that Villeneuve had killed him in cold blood.

O'Halloran stopped when he saw the site. The two constables stood a few feet behind; neither of them knew what to expect.

Will reached in his pack, took out a pry bar and a hammer, and dismantled the crosspieces that tied the roof sections together at both ends.

"You'll see him exactly as I found him, although by now, I expect he's at least thawed."

O'Halloran motioned to the younger of the two constables. "You can do that. Will's done enough."

He turned to Will. "Tell me about the hands."

"I told you about the avalanche. I didn't get around to the injuries and frostbite, but at least all of that is in the book."

There were only four boards on either end of the crypt. Once one side was free, it was easy to use the planks as a lever, pull them back, and separate the roof sections. The two constables pulled back the tarp. Will was shocked. Villeneuve was white. His colour had changed dramatically, but he had not decomposed. The cold ground had helped preserve him. The ice around him had barely melted, but in Will's view, he would still be difficult to move.

O'Halloran stood between Villeneuve's spread feet, looking out to sea, and offered an observation that surprised Will. "Whatever he was shooting at was either out on the ice, or in that cluster of rocks about 50 yards out."

"Sir, my report does say not say *whatever*. It says *whoever*."

O'Halloran stared; he hadn't expected to be challenged by a constable, but considering what Will Grant had been through, he turned to face Villeneuve.

Now bending down, he called to one of the constables. "Help me." Together they rolled Villeneuve partially on his right side, his arms and head remained rigid. The exit wound was visible. The hole was considerably larger than the one at the front, proof that the bullet had gone through his body. The lower back panel of his parka showed dried bloodstains.

O'Halloran and the constable returned the body to its original position. The movement and the summer thaw caused the rifle to release from Villeneuve's left hand. O'Halloran picked it up, examined it, and placed it back beside the body. All the time, his back was turned to Will.

Then he turned to the constables. "Cover him up again. Use the boards, as well. We'll come back tomorrow with a boat, pick him up, and bury him on the hill."

"I built a box for him. It's in the storehouse."

On the return walk, O' Halloran asked Will to go over every detail of last year's East Point patrols.

"All the details are in the log and most of them are in Villeneuve's hand."

When Will had found Villeneuve dead last October—the last sortie of the year—he believed that he had been shot on the first day of the rotation, or early on the second, based on the condition of the camp. Little or no food had been touched and, as far as Will could remember, everything had been as he left it when he finished his tour.

Back at the detachment, O'Halloran asked for the logbook and personal journals.

Villeneuve hadn't kept a personal journal, at least to Will's knowledge. Will reminded the senior officer that the journals were personal property, and he was determined to deliver Zalapski's to his parents.

"Neither of us has anything to hide, sir, so you're welcome to them, but I insist that they both be returned."

"You have my word, Will. Now, why not come to the ship, have a good meal, a bath, and sleep on clean sheets. It doesn't stink anymore." They both laughed.

"We have a new captain. I miss Bernier, but this fellow also knows his stuff," O'Halloran informed Will. "I'll get some extra help tomorrow to deal with Villeneuve. I'll decide tonight, in light of what has happened, whether I should leave these young guys here for two years. What do you think?"

"If the graves of two Mounties are to remain on that hill, sir, then I would say that Canada has staked its claim at Dundas Harbour."

"You're probably right."

On board, Captain Enoch Falk was hospitable and polite, immediately offering both Will and O'Halloran a stiff drink of good scotch.

Will enjoyed the meal, the bath, and the bed. Inspector slept on deck in the dog pens. It was all so civilized, so unfamiliar.

The next morning at breakfast, O'Halloran set out the plan. He would not put men or equipment ashore at this post—at least not this year. They would take Villeneuve's remains to the post by boat, clean him as best as they could, and bury him beside Zalapski.

"Then, we're headed south. But first, we need to stop in Arctic Bay."

"Very good. I was hoping that we would stop there or at Pond Inlet. I want to find a home for my good friend, and leave a few things for Pudlu, the Inuk you hired as a guide, if he ever comes this way. My surgeon!"

Will held up both hands, minus three fingers. "He became a great friend, but you'll soon read all about it. What about the other dogs?"

"We'll take them to Arctic Bay. The post there can use them."

Will, who wanted to take his dory to Arctic Bay, suggested that O'Halloran might also want to have the ship's crew check out the detachment's motorboat on the rocks at Cape Warrenger to determine if it was worth salvaging.

They had just finished, when four more Mounties appeared at the door.

"You sent for us, sir?"

Will recognized one of them as the constable who had been posted to Craig Harbour, but he couldn't remember his name. The other three had finished their tour and were on the way home.

Two were assigned to retrieve Villeneuve, another ordered to go through the storehouse and take anything of value. The tools, lumber, and dry goods would go to the post at Arctic Bay. The fourth Mountie would join three crew members from the ship and dig a grave. "Will, you just make sure we don't miss anything."

Will gathered his belongings into a large canvas pack and placed it on the beach with Zalapski's and Villeneuve's personal effects.

He checked the storehouse. Constable Dan Roy, whose name Will finally remembered, was efficient and needed no help.

Will wanted to take one last walk. "There's a place that helped me keep my sanity, and I want to see it one last time," he told Roy. "I'll be back long before they finish the grave or, for that matter, prepare the skipper."

Will wondered how many times he had made this journey, and yet, there was no trace that anyone had ever walked here. He had had the same thought yesterday while walking with O'Halloran. The only evidence that anyone had been here was the soon-to-be abandoned buildings and dead men.

Will sat beneath Naudla's rock, looked out to sea, wiped away a tear, wondered about the unknown, and walked back.

At 8 p.m., they lowered Villeneuve into the frozen ground and covered him. Several people from the government's scientific party participated. One of them said a prayer and read from the scripture, adding the predictable words, "Defending Canada, serving, and protecting."

Will held back his cynicism. Defending, serving, and protecting who? Politicians, stuffy self-serving officials. Who? Not people like Pudlu and Naudla—or even Teemotee, whom he had almost erased from his mind.

Not the truth, just words people wanted to hear, a practice Will would soon become more familiar with.

CHAPTER 13

SOLEMNLY SWEAR TO LIE

Will stood at the stern, portside, the four-legged Inspector by his side. The whistle broke the stillness of the calm Arctic evening, snapping Will out of his reverie. The dog howled. A whiff of black smoke from the stack of the SS *Beothuk* momentarily obscured the view, like a theatre curtain dropping, setting the stage for a new act.

The last words from the Inspector with the brass buttons offered little comfort. They had just finished burying Villeneuve. "Will, in the days ahead, I'll need to talk with you more. I want to finish my investigation and report before we arrive in the south. There's more at stake than people's lives and reputations. It's also about the good order, discipline, and credibility of the Force itself. I know you have had a rough time, so please bear with me."

Will thought it a strange way to talk about an unsolved murder and a second mysterious death.

His eyes swept across the landscape for the last time, beginning with the west ridge, just beyond which he had maintained his sanity. The buildings were empty and silent. "May they stay that way forever," he said. Will looked over the hill and the graves, remembering Naudla sitting on the qamutik when they left, driven away by Villeneuve and tragedy, her eyes fixed on Piapik's grave. Dundas Harbour was shrinking, disappearing on the horizon of the great blue ocean and midnight-sun sky that grew larger and larger.

He had shed all his tears earlier in the day. Now, he stared one last time, sure that he would never see it again.

Three years and a lifetime, heaven and hell, the best and the worst.

He had survived because of Pudlu and Naudla. Now, they represented life's unpaid debts.

Will tied Inspector to his designated spot on the aft deck with the other dogs and started toward his cabin. The wrecked motorboat was lashed upside down on top of other deck cargo. He ran his hand along three cracked boards on the starboard side bow. Now fancying himself a boat builder, he guessed a reasonably skilled carpenter could return it to a seaworthy state in a day.

He passed two well-dressed gentlemen, in tweed woollen jackets, heavy corduroy pants, neckties, and highly polished shoes. They spelled money and status. They were engaged in conversation but politely nodded as he passed. A few other men also acknowledged him, but none attempted conversation.

Will was neither surprised nor offended by their indifference and, indeed, even welcomed it. He knew that by now tales of his exploits and the dead Mounties would have spread to every crew member and passenger, and if others had trouble finding the right words to say, so did he.

Right now, he found it hard to be around people. He accepted that he was no doubt afflicted with cabin fever or, in Arctic lingo, he was bushed.

He went to his cabin. He knew he wouldn't have this privacy for long and that more people, including Mounties, would be boarding in Arctic Bay.

Three letters sat on his bunk, all from his favourite niece, Louise, in St. Francis Harbour, one each from 1925, 1926, and 1927, no doubt placed there by O'Halloran. They were written in her beautiful flowing handwriting. That skill and her easy way with words made her the designated family letter writer.

Louise had a knack for turning the mundane into newsy and sometimes amusing accounts of comings and goings, joy, hardships, realities, and losses. He could imagine her at the kitchen table and her father, his brother Ed, perched at the head of the table, puffing a pipe, and like a big-shot tycoon dictating to a secretary: "Now, Wheezie, don't forget to mention the new boat and be sure and tell him we got a steel bridge across the gulch."

The 1926 letter brought bad news. *We were all so saddened when darling Pop Mackay went to his Fiddlers Green, remember how he talked about that heavenly place where old fishermen and aging sailors go—if they don't go to hell?* Will smiled, knowing that he would reply, *Sweet niece, on the matter of going to hell, the lovable old pirate and I have both been there.* He was not surprised with the words that followed: *Everybody from around the Bay was at his funeral in Guysborough.*

Brother Ed was doing well fishing and on the social scene— *some right good dances in the hall these Saturday nights.* In the 1927 letter, she confessed to seeing a young guy with a model T,

Marvin, a railroader's son living in Mulgrave, very handsome,
a great mechanic but a terrible dancer.

Will felt better, slowly becoming reconnected. He read the letters again and would soon reply. He had a lot to tell. He would send her one of the paintings he'd decided to keep.

O'Halloran joined Will at breakfast. "Do you miss your cooking?"

"Not now, sir, and not ever, but once a year I'll miss those big gull and duck eggs."

O'Halloran had more questions. "Tell me again how you found Villeneuve's rifle?"

Will explained that it was still in his arms, that he was in the process of inserting a new round into the chamber.

"What else did you see?"

"Four ejected cartridges. I left them where they were. I'm sure you saw them when we were there."

"Yes, I did. Just confirming. I picked them up and put them with the rifle. Now tell me again about his fixation with snipers."

"For the past two years, that was all the patrol was about. Americans, he said, are our allies, and we needed to be always on the lookout for the Germans. Snipers became his mission."

"It's all very troubling, Will." He paused. "How did you sleep? I can't keep that bridal suite for you forever. The captain says we'll be in Arctic Bay tomorrow night.

"Tomorrow, Dr. Livingstone would like to examine you, just to be sure everything is in order. You've had quite an ordeal. I'm sure you'll remember that he examined all of you just before you embarked three years ago."

How could Will forget? Everyone either knew or knew about

Dr. Livingstone. At first introduction, most naturally thought of the Dr. David Livingstone of Africa fame from nearly a century earlier.

"Only a few years ago, he removed a boy's appendix in an iglu, with Eskimo assistants. He's been travelling north now for close to a decade, visiting every camp or community that he can get into. Sometimes I wonder if he even has a first name."

The *Beothuk* sailed straight across Lancaster Sound, with a favourable sea and winds dead on its stern. As the vessel approached land, Will watched the magnificent snow-capped mountains and glacier-filled valleys of Baffin Island emerge and grow more captivating by the minute.

He also watched one of the two well-dressed gentlemen sketching.

It was not the first time that the size and grandeur of this big bold land brought him to a personal crossroads. He was torn. Part of him needed to be away from this place, but the rest of him, his eyes and sense of wonder, never got enough of it.

A hundred times in his isolation and loneliness, he had read Robert Service's timeless tributes to Yukon and the Arctic, many of the most memorable images and tales he had committed to memory. Looking at Baffin Island, one verse unconsciously burst out:

You come to get rich, damn good reason,
You feel like an exile at first,
you hate it like hell for a season
and then you are the worst of the worst.

From above on the bridge deck, a voice picked up the next stanza:

It grips you like some kind of sinning
It twists you from foe to a friend.

It's been that way since the beginning
it will be that way till the end.

Captain Enoch Falk laughed. "I love to read Robert Service. Someday I hope to attend one of his recitals. Drop by my quarters tomorrow night before dinner and have a drink. Till then, I have my hands full getting her close and anchored."

"I'll do that, Captain. Thank you."

Will turned back to the shore. He could now see the white-painted Arctic Bay rocks. He had expected much more than what lay before him.

There were a total of three buildings: the RCMP detachment, the Hudson's Bay post, and a rather ramshackle mission that he assumed to be Anglican.

Half an hour later, landing boats went over the side. Will was ready, and he had the dog with him. "Can I get ashore with you, sir?" he asked O'Halloran, who was standing next to him. "I've got a few things to do here."

"Absolutely."

Dr. Livingstone joined them. "Inspector, I can report to you and the constable that he's in fine health. I would see the dentist about that tooth as soon as you can, Grant, but you're remarkably fit and in good health, all things considered. As for the missing fingers, as I told you, I couldn't have done a better job of cutting and closing myself."

Will wouldn't have to search for the people he was looking for. The entire post population was on the shoreline, gawking at the second big arrival of the year. The HBC's *Nascopie* had arrived a week earlier, dropped its cargo and three passengers, and departed within 48 hours.

WHIT FRASER

Will saw Arctic Bay as two distinct communities as the motorboat glided toward the shore. On his right were about 20 Inuit, young and old, men, women, and a half-dozen children, and a few young dogs still enjoying the freedom that only puppyhood brings.

From his left, the establishment approached. Three Mounties, two Hudson's Bay clerks, and a minister, all caught the bow of the boat to soften the landing and ease it over the smooth pebbles and fine gravel until it sat secure on the beach.

The minister was the first person Will wanted to do business with, and it had nothing to do with God or salvation.

"Good day, Reverend," Will said after the minister had greeted O'Halloran, the doctor, and the other three men. "My name is Will Grant, and I expect you know Pudlu."

"I know him well. I'm James Moore and I'm pleased to meet you."

Will wondered if he had ever seen a beard that big, that round—round like the reverend himself. Beginning with the reverend's face, or at least what Will could see of it, everything was round, the head, the chest, even the hips, and the dark eyes— round, bright brown, and laughing.

Will felt instantly comfortable in his presence.

"Is it possible that he's here?" Will, eyes wide, hoped for an answer in the affirmative.

"I'm sorry to say that he's not here. When we see him, it's usually in the spring. Most of the year he's out there, somewhere!" His round hand and forearm made a sweep across the vast seascape and down the fjord. "Sometimes at Christmas, he may go to Pond Inlet."

With that big deep voice and proper high-tea English accent, the reverend must command every pulpit and steeple he spoke from and under.

"Are Naudla and Teemotee with him?"

"Yes, they're always together, and Naudla's mother is with them too."

"Pudlu was with me and my deceased colleagues in Dundas Harbour. I had hoped to see him. He is a very good friend. How is Naudla after the loss of her baby?"

"It has been a year since I have seen them, and her heart has remained broken, but she was doing as well as she could. She has great faith, thanks to her brother."

Will struggled with mixed and confusing emotions. Naudla and Pudlu had not lost their faith. What had happened to him?

There had been a time when Will would have asked the minister to share a prayer, or asked about church services. His instincts told him that there could be no easier minister to talk to. But this was a different Will Grant; the months had changed him in ways he had not yet fully realized. The Beechy Island Franklin experience, Piapik, all raised doubts about God and salvation. The exact day or place it happened, he wasn't sure. But somewhere in the cold and dark, he had simply lost or abandoned his faith—or it had rejected him.

The minister broke the silence. "Pudlu told me about you, Will. You seem to be none the worse for the wear."

"Reverend, I have a favour to ask. I built a dory and want to leave it with Pudlu. Can you see that he gets it if I take it to the mission?"

"But of course, I'd be happy to."

"And there's this fella." Inspector had been quiet, sitting by Will's side. "May I ask you to look after him for me? And then if you're not too attached to him, pass him on to Pudlu. Don't say it too loudly, but his name is Inspector. It breaks my heart, but I can't take him south with me."

"He'll be fine with me and Pudlu." He bent down to pat the handsome head. "Good name," he added with a smile, "though not as good as Deacon or Bishop." He looked again. "Interesting, you have the same eyes."

Now Will was smiling, comfortable and relieved, knowing that the dog would be well cared for.

"I'll bring him by later when I bring up the dory and I'll place something for your church on your account at the post."

Will walked the ridge behind the HBC main building, enjoying the view and feeling the soft tundra beneath his issue Wellington boots. He saw a lanky Hudson's Bay clerk, hardly more than 20, go inside. He either had a very sharp razor, Will thought, or he's not old enough to shave. The shock of thick straw-coloured hair above the fresh shiny face made him 2 inches taller than 6 feet.

"I'm W.A. Anderson. How may I be of service?"

Will laughed. "With that highland accent, I should tell you that I have two grandfathers who would say you're from fine stock."

"Aye, the Orkneys. "

Will left a generous $20 donation to the mission, in the spirit of kennel fees rather than spiritual renewal or redemption.

He walked back to the beach, picked up the dory, swung it over his shoulders, and laboured back up the hill to the Mission.

Reverend James was waiting for him.

"I have to do this quickly, Reverend. Inspector has been a great friend and companion, and he saved my life. I know you'll be good to him."

Will shook Moore's hand, put the leash in it, turned and left, his eyes in tears, his chest heaving, and ears burning with the sounds of Inspector's whining. Will did not and could not look back.

That evening, at 5 p.m., he found the captain's quarters. The door was open and a small group had gathered.

"Come in, Mr. Grant," boomed the captain, a big man with muscular wide shoulders, dark hair and eyes, dressed in uniform, and extremely friendly.

Will felt trapped. He panicked. He had been alone for months. He should have declined this invitation.

The captain didn't give him a chance to retreat.

"Gentlemen, let me introduce you to Constable Grant, who has had a remarkable experience. We've also discovered that we are mutual admirers of the great Robert Service." He finished pouring a generous portion of golden scotch, which he handed to Will.

"This is Mr. MacLeod, and he's in charge of the government party and kindly leaves the ship's business to me. One of the few to do that, I might add." Will shook hands with the government's portly balding bureaucrat. His soft hand confirmed his line of work.

The next two gentlemen, the two he had passed on deck the night before, also had fine features and soft hands. "This is Doctor Frederick Banting—yes, Dr. Banting, the discoverer of insulin—and this is his friend, A.Y. Jackson, an artist of considerable reputation. They have both become Arctic men. I am honoured to have them on my ship."

Will shook hands with both, trying to guess the odds of stepping onto a ship after three years in Dundas Harbour to share a drink with two of the country's most famous and distinguished citizens.

Will studied the famous artist: medium height, lean with an

angular, chiselled face. He knew from a magazine portrait about the Group of Seven that Jackson was a war veteran. He would have more in common with Villeneuve and Zalapski, having been injured in battle.

After Jackson's injury, the war department replaced his rifle with brushes and employed him as a war artist.

His piercing eyes looked directly into Will's.

"I know you had a remarkable adventure with more than your share of hardships. How much of Devon Island and the area were you able to see and travel?"

Will told him of the first 500-mile trip west and north. He spoke about his walks, the places he had discovered, the waterfall, and the icebergs. And, most breathtaking of all, the northern lights. Jackson's eyes and words made it clear that he was taking mental notes.

"I hope that we can observe a magnificent aurora display late in the expedition, in mid-September before we exit Arctic waters. But that shimmering river of shifting light that you describe must be spectacular. Perhaps sometime I will experience a full Arctic winter."

Suddenly and uncharacteristically, Will opened up. "I should tell you that to keep my sanity over the past year, I tried to teach myself to paint and I leave it to others to decide if I was successful on either or both accounts."

"I like your sense of humour and would like to see what you have done."

"I'll show you something before we embark in the south, but because it's a hobby that I intend to continue, may I look over your shoulder from time to time?"

"Yes, Mr. Grant, with one condition: No talking."

"Agreed, sir."

"Call me A.Y."

Banting joined them. "I'm interested in what assistance the Force provided in the way of guides?"

Will knew that O'Halloran had heard the question and would be interested even more in the answer. He wouldn't lie, but he would set out as best he could, the priorities the most essential truth among "many truths."

"Quite frankly, sir, I wouldn't have survived without them. The lessons we learned in the first year were those that saved us, saved me for the duration. I had hoped to see them here in Arctic Bay. I wanted to say thank you, show my gratitude."

O'Halloran stepped between them.

Dr. Banting touched Will's elbow. "Perhaps we can talk more later." And then gracefully turned to Dr. Livingston. "Leslie, did you have a productive day ashore?"

Will smiled. *He has a first name; he is mortal.*

Will concluded that this group probably had dinner with the captain every night and the captain had not mentioned more than a drink.

He was still a constable, a hand from below decks, but at least he had been taught good manners. More relevantly—he needed to get away.

He turned to Captain Falk.

"Sir, thank you. It was generous of you to invite me."

"You seem to have made some friends, Mr. Grant. I'm glad you joined us. We'll soon be lifting the anchor for Pangnirtung and points south."

Will joined several deckhands and four other Mounties in the crew galley and tried to share the cook's enthusiasm for the evening menu: fresh Arctic char that he had traded for sugar and tea with an Inuk hunter that morning. At least he hadn't had to catch, cook, or clean it.

Will had company. Two constables who had completed their two-year tour in Arctic Bay were planning the carousing they would do when they hit the big city. Will felt isolated. He couldn't face another day alone on Devon Island, but he had not yet prepared himself for the south. A drunk and a different whorehouse every night were not essential in his troubled mind. He would try to remain sociable and friendly with Angus and Philip to the extent required.

It was a majestic and rare day. The west coast of Davis Strait was like glass, the only ripples were the rolling wake fanning ever wider from the stem to the horizon. Everywhere else, blue, clear, still water. Pudlu had said that these were the best days for seal hunting. Will looked off the starboard rail landward. From time to time, he would see a black head pop up, survey the ship and surroundings, and with barely a ripple of its own, slip into the depths.

At the stern, in canvas deck chairs, sat A.Y. Jackson and Dr. Banting, also a fine artist, who refused to call himself anything more than an amateur painter.

Before them lay nature's stunning canvas: The tranquility of the ocean, the stately Cumberland mountains cradling the Penny Ice Cap, and the snow-capped Penny Highlands that stretched a mile or more above the water into a turquoise sky. The air, so pure and clear that one that could see for 80 miles.

Will sat on a shore boat lashed to the deck, and watched, in absolute silence, honouring Jackson's no-talking rule and watched the master artist transpose the splendour to his easel. Jackson's eyes darted back and forth between landscape and easel, brush hand poised and stroking the canvas in sync with the moving ship.

After some time, when the shapes, colours, and life of the landscape were committed to outline, Jackson spoke. "Will, it might be a good time to show me some of the things you've done."

Will retreated to his cabin and picked up two 12-by-12-inch pine boards depicting the waterfall and the iceberg.

Jackson and Banting examined them carefully. Will expected that the excitement he detected had more to do with the time and place than the quality of the work.

After several minutes of shifting his eyes from one piece to the other, Jackson commented. "I think in time, with some decent materials—which you didn't have—and with some lessons, you could be a fine painter. Certainly, with lessons and practice, you wouldn't ever embarrass yourself. I hope you stay with it."

"So do I, Mr. Grant," added Banting. "By the way, my middle name is Grant from my mother. We could be distant relatives." Will sensed kinship as well as friendship.

"Will, let me give you these." A.Y. took half a dozen partially used tubes of oil paints from his pockets and carrying case, as well as brushes and vials of linseed oil.

"Mr. Jackson, A.Y., you and the doctor have been so kind, I don't know what to say."

"Just enjoy them and use them," added the doctor. "Both of us have tremendous respect for what you and your colleagues have done and the way you've suffered. We feel that we are in your debt. You should also know that we are committed to ensuring that this great country remains a part of Canada, and in our small way, let other Canadians see and experience it."

Will looked at the water. Small ripples skimmed across the surface from the port, the northeast sky was darkening, and the wind was picking up. He had learned to read these signs when he was a boy. So had the others.

"We'd better get inside." Jackson gathered his easel and chair.

On the first deck, Will met O'Halloran, who approached him with unusual formality. "Constable Grant, I want to see you this evening after dinner, at 7:30. The captain has generously agreed to give us privacy in the ship's library for the evening. We have considerable unfinished business to attend to.

"I believe you are aware that I plan to disembark at Pangnirtung and overwinter at the detachment there. I want to finish my findings and recommendations before that so that Sergeant Joy can deliver it to headquarters."

The library was, like every facility on the ship, cramped. But it was pleasant, with several hundred stacked books in slatted shelves to guard against the rolls and pitches of the wind and waves. Four chairs and a small table with lamps left and right completed the furnishings.

O'Halloran sat at the table with several papers in front of him, along with the personal journals of Will and Zalapski.

Will had dressed in his full uniform. O'Halloran had done the same.

"Good evening, sir." Will saluted, hand to temple.

"Please sit down, Constable."

As Will settled and pulled the chair close to the table, O'Halloran pushed the two personal journals toward him. "You did say you want to visit Zalapski's family and take this to them. Is that still your plan?"

"Yes, sir, it is."

"Now, my report. From what I have concluded from the logs and your account both to me and in your journal, there are two separate deaths. First Zalapski. I can come to no other conclusion except that he died by his hand. Suicide."

"With respect, sir, I disagree."

"I know you disagree. You have made that clear. But you have not, because you cannot, provide one iota of evidence that would allow us to believe or suspect otherwise. Your personal feelings, your hunches, however you came to form them, are not enough, Will. They won't stand up to scrutiny. We are policemen, and we need evidence and facts, which point to what I have concluded—an act of suicide."

Will's temper got the better of him. "I cannot or will not believe that Erik Zalapski shot himself. I saw him and I helped bury him."

O'Halloran was also capable of showing temper.

"Grant, for Christ's sake, listen to yourself. An expression on a dead man's face does not tell us how he died. A bullet in the brain can make a million pained faces. I am trying to save your credibility. You cannot accuse someone of murder because of the look on the face of the corpse."

Will was trembling. He still believed with every fibre that Villeneuve had shot Zalapski, but he knew that O'Halloran was right. There was not a shred of evidence and no witnesses.

"In the matter of Villeneuve's death," O'Halloran frowned at his handwritten report, "I can only conclude that his death was by accident."

"Pardon? How can you say that? It's not true." Will rage rose again.

"There are many truths and the one that must guide me here and now is the Force, our mission, and the country. We are a very few Mounties charged with an enormous responsibility to establish and maintain Canada's sovereignty and jurisdiction over this grand, frozen vastness of ice, land, and mountains.

"Since the end of the war, sovereignty has become a priority for Canada. Many people have argued for it, including those you respect, such as Bernier—who by the way has retired—and Jackson and Banting.

"Why do you think they're here? They see art as a way to show Canadians what we have in the Far North, to instill the greatness of the Arctic in our national conscience."

O'Halloran paused to pour a cup of tea from the pot that had been prepared for them. "Everything we have done for the past six years, and I suspect everything we will do for the next 50 years, is either directly or indirectly focused on asserting and maintaining our Arctic sovereignty. Do you want a cup?"

"No, sir." Will's head pounded and his stomach churned.

O'Halloran turned two pages toward Will and pushed them slowly forward, an invitation to read.

Will did not pick them up, but he looked.

"I said in here that you are to be commended for leaving Villeneuve as you found him, for the imaginative and careful approach you took to protect his body and the scene. The fact is this: the best and most appropriate conclusion to come to under the circumstances is the one that I have reached. I don't think for a moment that you killed him. You are smart enough to have disposed of his body in ways and places where he would never be found. That's my view. Others may differ."

Inspector O'Halloran leaned forward, his voice both pleading and warning. "Do you not realize that for me to conclude otherwise would make you a suspect in his death? You were the only known person within 300 miles of the spot where he died. Will, your own words make you a suspect if his death were anything but accidental. We will never know what happened on those rocks or on that ice. If I were to conclude that a person or persons unknown are responsible, what would that require?

"We would need to investigate every camp on Ellesmere and Baffin Islands and beyond. And then, if we were to identify a shooter, what do we do, lay charges, and for what? Murder, manslaughter, self-defence?

"And while we do all that, what happens to the ideal, to our reputations, and overall sovereignty efforts? I believe the county, the Force, and the mission must prevail. That, Constable, is the larger truth."

Will wanted to object, but he couldn't. O'Halloran's eyes held no anger, just pleading for reason and understanding. Over four long years, leaders and generals had done the same. They had fought and reconciled losing battles, counted casualties, and buried the truth to ultimately win a great war that Villeneuve, Zalapski, O'Halloran, himself, even Banting and Jackson, were all, at one time or another, part of.

"So how are you going to explain it?"

"The rifle that I picked up, Will, the very one you so carefully preserved, had a spent cartridge in the closed chamber. I can only conclude that a bullet ricocheted off one of the rocks while the senior constable was shooting at wildlife. It is the only reasonable and logical conclusion one can come to. The two constables who attended the scene with me and helped remove the remains also examined the rifle."

"Am I expected to sign this?"

"I'm offering you the opportunity to do so. I can't force you, but I advise you to do so."

Will looked at the signatures of the two constables below the line *I agree with the above finding.*

He was cornered. Three other Mounties had signed and falsified evidence to "maintain the right" to protect the Force. Would he stand before a tribunal and accuse them of lying? Would he risk bringing the wrath of southern political justice down on the communities so that an innocent Inuk might go to jail?

Will took the pen. *Cst. William Francis Grant.*

"What will happen to me at headquarters? Should I hire a lawyer?"

"I can't comment on how they will address your physical disability. I'll recommend that you be assigned to office duties. I can't see them returning you to detachment or patrol work."

"Let me burn that bridge when I get to it, Inspector. Will that be all?"

"Yes, for now."

Will stood, took a step back, saluted, and went on deck. He leaned over the rail and threw up. For the first time in his life, he was seasick.

Two days later, O'Halloran approached Will. The ship lay anchored in Pangnirtung for one day to unload supplies and change crew at the post. O'Halloran again thanked Will for his "service, dedication, and wisdom," adding, "I do hope we meet and serve together again in the future."

He then introduced Sergeant Alfred Joy. Will recognized the name as a legend. Joy, with his rugged features and tall, lean, and powerful build, should be on every recruiting poster. He had travelled hundreds of miles solo by dog team. *This man would have made it from Devon to Craig Harbour.*

Three more Mounties embarked. One, who moved into the cabin with Will and the others, looked Irish, with a round ruddy face. *Short for a Mountie, probably had trouble meeting the 5-foot 7-inch height requirement.* He introduced himself as Paddy Gregg from Fredericton and soon made party plans with Angus and Philip.

A half-day's sail out of Pangnirtung, everyone on board lost all sight of land, sky, and water. They were locked in fog. Even at anchor in the big fjord, the low overcast skies and drizzle made it almost impossible to see the mountains or remnants of past or present whaling camps.

Will needed to get out of the crowded cabin and seek refuge in the library. There he encountered Banting and Jackson, downhearted with the sour weather which obliterated the magnificent Cumberland Sound they had come to capture.

A chessboard lay between them.

"Come, Will." Banting beckoned. "Sit down. I've been wanting to ask you more about your experience with your guides. How did you get along?"

Will was about to speak, but the doctor wasn't quite through.

"Frankly, I think it's deplorable the way that they've been taken advantage of, especially by the Hudson's Bay Company, being paid so little for their furs. And how little we—by that I mean to say, our government—are doing to improve their living and health conditions. I plan to raise those matters in my report to the department."

"Doctor, I want to answer your question by first showing you something that I believe you'll both appreciate." The puzzled look was still on their faces when he returned five minutes later with Pudlu's gift.

"I invite you to open this." Will placed the intricate box on the table.

Jackson untied the sinew straps and unfolded the set. The two men were spellbound. They picked up the ivory and soapstone sculptures. Thirty-two intricate and masterfully crafted creations.

"They were made by the best friend I will ever have. He saved my life, and he was my surgeon." Will opened his hands, showing the stumps where fingers once were, which he knew both had seen but never inquired about.

"We do worse than fail to provide properly for the Inuit—as they refer to themselves—Doctor, we fail to afford them the respect they so deserve.

"We should be looking at them as our flagpoles, our beacons of sovereignty, rather than a handful of Mounties, all of whom cannot wait to get back to their homes, families, or in the case of my cabin mates, bars and whorehouses in Montreal and Toronto. I am duty bound to observe discretion, but you must know that they did not abandon us. One of our team ran them away."

The two men nodded repeatedly.

"Gentlemen, I would be honoured if you would honour Pudlu by playing a game on his board."

"How about you and I go first, Will," said Banting, "then have A.Y. take the winner."

After 20 minutes and a dozen moves, Jackson, in the challenger's chair, set up the ivory whites, while Banting waited, his black serpentine pieces already in position.

There was little talk between the three. Will enjoyed the moment until predictably the silence was broken with a sharp "checkmate" from the smiling doctor.

The two carefully and reverently put each piece back in the beautifully made case.

"What is going to happen to you, Will?" Jackson gestured toward Will's hands. Both men had been wounded in the war, Jackson shot on a Belgian battlefield, Banting in a field hospital while he was operating.

"Like most damaged goods, I expect to be labelled unfit for service."

The artist responded. "If that happens, then read it differently. Interpret it as *steeled for greater things*. Right, Fred?"

Banting smiled. "I have learned that we all have our moment of discovery. I had mine, A.Y. has had his with the Group, and I believe, Will, that yours is yet to come."

CHAPTER 14

NO GREATER TRUTH

"This is one helluva way to earn a living, Ed, one penny at a time—and too much time between pennies."

Will, dressed in fisherman's oilskins to keep him warm and dry in the choppy waters of Chedabucto Bay, was a mile offshore in the bow of Ed's 18-foot dory, bringing up one of about 20 healthy haddock he hauled in that morning. At a penny apiece, Ed had trouble earning a dollar a day. For the Grants, it had always been like this.

Ed just smiled, pipe between his teeth, big arm bobbing up and down, the line wrapped around knarled knuckles, waiting for the next 5-pound penny to grab his hook.

Will savoured the moment. He realized, without telling his brother, that it would not happen again.

Many hours of isolation, desolation, and desperation on Devon Island had been spent pondering his future. Home had often been in his mind. Now that he was home, Will's heart was not; it was far away in another land. He just had to bring the rest of himself back here to realize that.

When he had boarded the *Beothuk* in Dundas Harbour, he didn't know that the latest Eastern Arctic Patrol vessel's home port was not Quebec City, but North Sydney, Nova Scotia.

The train from Nova Scotia to Ottawa would bring him close to his family in St. Francis Harbour. Will had arranged to get off the train in Mulgrave for a short leave.

"Nobody deserves a home break any more than you do," O'Halloran had insisted.

The fog and drizzle had stayed with the ship from Pangnirtung around south Baffin Island. They could hardly see the post and few crude dwellings at its final stop at Lake Harbour.

Will was pleased that Ed had received his telegram, sent from the ship, and Louise and her boyfriend were in Mulgrave to pick him up. In the eight years since Will had seen Louise, she had grown from a gangling preteen to a vibrant young woman with wavy jet-black hair, dark laughing eyes, and a constant smile. He adored her. She reminded him of his mother, and Will was pleased that Louise was named after her.

"Ed, I'm having a great week with you, Esther, and the kids, but on Saturday when Marvin visits, I'm going back to Mulgrave with him to catch the early morning express west."

"I don't see why you have to hurry."

The Grants had always communicated in metaphors.

"Too much unfinished business, dear brother—I've got my own fish to fry, but first I have to find and catch them."

Ed understood. Perfectly. Will wasn't coming back.

All week, Louise was excited. Marvin was coming, there was a big dance in Queensport, and which of her two dresses went best with her new white pumps?

On Saturday night, she climbed into Marvin's Model T. Wearing the form-fitting blue dress with the white collar, she snuggled close to Marvin. Will put his suitcase and the brown cotton bag that held his flat-brimmed Stetson in the back beside a violin case. He wasn't about to short-circuit this electricity.

"See you there. I'd better ride shotgun and keep your brother and father outta trouble." Louise blew him a kiss, and he climbed into the cramped truck with Ed and Francis and two more violin cases.

The hall was full, but there was much activity outside with men passing and swigging from brown-paper-wrapped bottles as there was inside on the dance floor.

Ed had been the featured fiddler at the hall for about as long as anyone could remember. His son Francis was a true second fiddle, often spelling Ed when he sampled the bootleg rum and moonshine.

The dance wasn't an hour on when Ed emerged from the outside crowd, missing the entire sleeve of his white shirt.

Will smiled, turned to Pat Meagher, an affable Irishman and old friend from before he had joined the Mounties. Pat was now friends with Marvin. "Nothing changes, Paddy." The challenger emerged minutes later in the lobby, using the shirtsleeve to nurse a bleeding nose and split lip.

Ed played on, his powerful arm bare. "Given the size and power of those arms, why would some fool challenge him?" questioned Pat.

"Bring up Louise, bring up Louise." Pat was shouting. "She's the best fiddler ever in these parts."

Three chairs were arranged on the stage, and Louise sat between her brother, on her right, and father, on her left. They began a series of jigs and reels and it seemed that Pat, Will, and Marvin were the only ones not dancing. Pat had not been exaggerating. Will was proud, but alone. He missed Naudla. Ed directed the three-piece "Scottish Symphony" with his eyes. He nodded to Francis and, with a long straight draw of the bow, they both stopped playing.

Louise stood on cue for her solo. Will recognized it as the "High Level Hornpipe." The last time he had heard it, Naudla was on his arm. *If she were only here, we'd turn some heads on the dance floor.*

He fought back tears, missing Naudla and watching his niece on stage in Queensport as though it were a grand concert hall.

Louise switched to a medley of lively reels and then, as suddenly as they had stopped, Ed and Francis, stood and joined in a trio, finishing the set to applause and whistles.

Will took his bags from Marvin's Model T, bade farewell to his family, and drove to Mulgrave with Pat, finishing the last of Pat's mickey of rum on the way.

The headline in the *Toronto Star* on September 8, 1927, took Will Grant's breath away.

He had just stepped onto the platform at Ottawa's Grand Trunk Railway Central Station beside the historic Rideau Canal, at the foot of the Parliament buildings. The newsstand was 10 feet in front of him across the platform. It propelled him back to Devon Island.

Banting Regrets Hudson's Bay Use of Eskimo.

Three paragraphs down he read: *For $100,000 in fox skins, the Eskimo receives not $5,000 in goods.*

"You kept your word," Will said aloud.

Government is investigating. Will responded to no one, "About time."

He tucked the paper under his arm, expecting that the matter would come up in his meetings with Sergeant Joy and the rest of the brass. He was comfortable knowing that he and Zalapski had paid Teemotee and Pudlu fair wages for their time and market value for the dogs.

That afternoon, Will walked between the carved stone horse-heads at the entrance to the headquarters building, about a mile east of Parliament Hill. He found Joy in a small office in the back.

"Welcome back to the civilized world. I have been told you are well settled in the transient barracks." The smiling sergeant extended his hand, noticing the newspaper under Will's arm.

"Well, you've read the paper. The shit is hitting the fan over in the Department of the Interior. But here, Banting is a hero— he's called them out and he recognizes what we're trying to do. He's been very good to us and our work. You must have impressed him on the ship."

"I don't think I had anything to do with it, Sergeant, but your patrols no doubt did."

"Thanks, Will. Sit down, please. I want to get right to the point. Your injuries are such that you would not pass the medical requirement, which means that the division manpower group is looking at a medical discharge. O'Halloran has recommended very strongly that you be retained and assigned office duties. I'm prepared to fight like hell for that. But first, I need to know what you want."

Will was prepared for this. He was determined to find Naudla. Sergeant Joy was trying to do the right thing. It was decision time.

He stood, walked around the small office, went behind Joy's desk, and looked out the window to the Gatineau Hills in the northward background, and a farther 2,000 miles beyond them.

He had changed. His mind had become his compass and whatever direction he turned his body, his mind pointed northward. One thing was certain, somewhere, in frozen living quarters, on a ship, or on a train, he had ceased being a Mountie.

"Will they give me a travel warrant back to Regina?"

"I'm sure that can be part of the deal."

"Then that's that—and I won't regret this or what comes next."

Two days later, in a grey flannel suit, a $7 a month disability pension, and three years' wages in the bank, Will Grant, a financially comfortable civilian, rolled westward in a big train with a name. *The Imperial.* Will loved the sound of the rail beneath him, the fine-tuned steam whistle, even the Pullman car rocking. He reached into his leather grip suitcase and took out his going-away present from O'Halloran. The cherished photo from Dundas Harbour, the one he had wondered if he would ever see. He stared at it. Naudla was beside him. He held it on his lap as mile after mile of Canada slipped by his window.

In his last moment as a Mountie, Will had shaken hands with Commissioner Hamilton. Hamilton was genuinely sincere when he thanked Will for his remarkable contribution and commitment to the patrol "in the face of unfortunate circumstances."

"Someday," Hamilton said, "I hope to visit the posts."

"I hope you can, sir. It would be important to those who are there to see you."

The sound of his own words, speaking his mind to the commissioner, told him that he had set himself free.

Three days later, Will placed a framed print of the same photograph in the calloused hands of a sobbing mother grieving a son. She and Will were in the tidy parlour of the Zalapski home in Saskatchewan near Lumsden, an hour's train ride northwest of Regina.

Olive Zalapski's husband, Charles, sat on the chesterfield beside her. He had also been weeping, though he tried not to. Will had kept his promise. He told them of his friendship with Erik, seeing the beauty of Greenland together, the storm, the scenery, the stillness, and the rich beauty of Dundas Harbour and Devon Island. He promised that over the winter after he had settled, he would paint a landscape of Erik's final resting place and send it to them.

He did not mention Villeneuve, the tension, or the abuse. He knew that they would read it in his diaries. In fact, for many miles on the train, Will wondered if he should take a razor blade and slice out pages that might be hurtful. Watching the parents in their tidy home, looking at the photos on the mantle, and knowing Erik's character, he was glad that he had not. They knew their son and what he stood for.

There was more in the journal that pointed to compassion and understanding of the deranged Villeneuve than there was anger and resentment. Will had concluded that Zalapski knew that someday others would likely read it. Surely, what Zalapski was comfortable writing should not be Will's place to censor.

His visit lasted two hours. The driver that he had hired in Regina waited for him in the driveway.

The Zalapskis wanted him to spend the night or a week, but he could not. The short visit was all that he could handle then, without the risk of descending into his own shell shock. "Perhaps later," he murmured, to understanding eyes.

Charles shook his hand at the door. He was a big strong farmer with a thick Polish accent, a large round face, and wide-set eyes. Olive hugged him as only a mother could hug a son. On the way to the car, Will swallowed hard. "You're becoming a goddamned baby in your old age, Grant."

That evening in Regina's train station, just before midnight, he bought a one-way ticket to Winnipeg.

When Will had first seen Winnipeg in the early 1920s when he was an RCMP recruit, he had sensed that the city was on the move, full of excitement, and growing. Everything was new now, beginning with the grand railway station, and a fine hotel, the Fort Garry, only a five-minute walk away.

Will knew that the legacy of the Hudson's Bay Company had been personified in a massive new six-storey building that matched the nearby legislative buildings in size and scope. After checking into the Fort Garry, he had his suit pressed, shirt laundered, and shoes polished. It did not take him long after that to locate the chief clerk in the HBC's northern fur division, Geoffrey MacKinnon.

"Mr. MacKinnon, I'm here to offer my services. I have experience in the Arctic. I think I can be an asset in one of your posts."

The portly, calculating senior clerk listened as Will outlined his time in the Arctic, his ability to handle the cold and isolation and manage dogs. Being a former policeman with a citation signed by the Commissioner for the exemplary dedication was impressive.

"Do I understand that you are ready to return, already?"

"We both know that now really means next year, and I'm planning to do so."

"Give me a few days, Mr. Grant, to make some inquiries. I cannot see that we would let someone with your credentials slip away. Can you come back next week, say at the same time?"

Will spent the week enjoying the city, checking out rooming houses, taking in movies, and attending evening art classes at the rapidly expanding University of Manitoba.

MacKinnon's offer was acceptable to Will. He would work in the security division, overseeing four inspectors and floorwalkers in the fur and liquor divisions, where pilferage and theft was a costly challenge. Discussion about recruitment for northern posts would not begin until the new year, but it was promised. He would be paid $10.80 a week.

Will found a two-room flat on the third floor of a 30-year-old Victorian house. A large dormer window faced west, with an unobstructed view of the endless prairies. The light was critical for the painting that now occupied his free time. Naudla, who rarely left his thoughts, frequently appeared in his sketches and on his canvas.

In early March, MacKinnon had a firm proposal. "Mr. Grant, you said that you were interested in Arctic Bay and Pond Inlet and I can inform you that the Pond Inlet clerk wants to come out for a year. Would you like to replace him for that time and then see what and where comes up after that?"

Will extended his hand. "Deal."

"We will give you training on accounts and fur grading and handling and post duties."

Will continued to keep a journal. *July 9, 1928, Cast off from Montreal on the 25,000-ton 285-foot SS Nascopie. Decks and holds laden for outposts on Baffin and Ellesmere Islands.*

Will was familiar with the ship's drill. He and half a dozen other clerks whiled away days and night in cramped quarters, playing cards, and working at fever pitch to off-load stores in now-familiar outposts, like Killinik, Lake Harbour, and Pangnirtung. Between stops, he spent time on deck painting and sketching. Though the lessons had paid off, he was painting for his enjoyment and self-satisfaction. He knew that he would never be a great painter, nor did he want to be, but A.Y. Jackson was right: Will wasn't embarrassed by his work. He sympathized with the master artist's frustration trying to capture an image from the deck of a ship moving at 10 knots in one direction, while the subject matter propelled by wind and tide drifted at a greater speed in the opposite direction.

Ice conditions were favourable. Sailing from Craig Harbour across Lancaster Sound, Will spent most of the time at the rail gazing westward. He could see the high peaks of Devon Island but felt no urge to go there. He had a mission and purpose, and he knew that Pond Inlet, on northern Baffin Island, was the best place to begin filling it.

Will was surprised that it was the young Scot, W.A. Anderson, who met them on the beach with the first boatload of supplies. They had three days to get the supplies off the ship, up the beach, into the warehouses and checked, counted, and secured.

It had been a long year for the young clerk. A letter from home last year had brought the sad news of his mother's passing and he naturally wanted to go home.

Will empathized with the young man's pain. In this land, for all matters relating to the south—even life and death—there is no tomorrow, no next week or next month. There is only next year, and sometimes the year after that or the year after that. That reality dictated that the young man had to wait a full year for a replacement. To complicate matters, poor sales and fur returns at the small Arctic Bay trading post forced HBC to temporarily close it. Everything had been moved to Pond Inlet, including Reverend Moore. Two Mounties stayed in Arctic Bay to maintain the sovereignty claim.

The unforgettable Reverend Moore bounded toward Will excitedly. "You've returned, Will. I expected you would. Our learned friend Inspector is on patrol with Pudlu. I have no idea when we will see them again. But I did pass on all your messages. He thanked God that you were okay. He was surprised that you had survived the ordeal."

"Surprised, in what way, Reverend?"

"Nothing specific. Just his reaction and a comment that he thought you may have been the first to die."

"Did he know that the others were dead? How could he have known that?"

"I don't know, but that's my point, and he was very closed about the matter, except for his relief, joy, and gratitude to the almighty that you are alive."

"When did you see him?"

"Last year, at Easter, but he was alone and only stayed one night, Easter Sunday. His mother was with him and two children."

"You say children. There was more than one?"

"Yes, the boy Kootoo and his little brother, about two years old."

The reverend seemed uneasy. "I'd better pitch in here and

get this stuff off the beach," Will said, walking away.

The sporadic peace and serenity Will had found on Devon Island, either under northern lights or an icy waterfall, came easily and almost daily at Pond Inlet.

This is a peaceful place, so magnificent in its beauty if only my feeble painting could do it justice, he wrote in his journal.

Pond Inlet is at the north coast of Baffin Island, sheltered in Eclipse Sound with snow-capped mountains and glacier valleys on three sides, Lancaster Sound to the north, and down the Sound, rising like a huge pulpit out of the ocean, the cliffs of Bylot Island.

Will knew from Pudlu, Bernier, and a dozen other people and books that few places in the Arctic were as bountiful in terms of seals, whales, caribou, fish, muskox, and seabirds.

As a shopkeeper and trader, Will found life in Pond Inlet easy and enjoyable. His Inuit language skills improved almost every day. Regular store hours did not exist; people arrived and departed sporadically to their camps, which were scattered in both directions around the bay. The ledger and accounting work was much less onerous than it had been with the RCMP—that organization was obsessive, recording the number of meals eaten, the description of every dog, and their name.

He had help from an Inuk, William Edmunds, who had been the post's hand for a decade. He could work inside, behind the counter, and also drive dogs, hunt, and do all the maintenance. Will had noted from first introductions and a quick study of the log for the past year that William was always referred to as Mr. Edmunds. He thought it fitting. Will respected Mr. Edmunds, who knew everything about the operation, including the management and transport of bags of coal from the small mine that the post operated about 1 mile inland.

There was an understood social structure in the tiny outpost. Most of the Inuit, including Mr. Edmunds, kept to themselves.

Almost every day, Will and Moore had a chat. They kept track of each other's aches and pains, teased and joked with one another about their human frailties or attributes.

"It's a crime the number of people you swindle, using seven fingers to count to 10."

"Just how many lemmings live in that beard? And do they come out at night?" Will referred to him as *The Right Round Reverend*.

Put another way, they were friends.

Once a week, Moore and the two Mounties had dinner, usually on Saturday, and most predictably, about 20 Inuit and the two policemen attended the reverend's Sunday service. The only person who did not attend was Will Grant.

The only exception was the Christmas Eve service. Will went so that he would not be alone. And he enjoyed the carols, the warmth, and the handshakes all around. He sketched the scene as the service was ongoing. Someday he would render it to canvas.

Will's growing distance from God didn't strain their friendship. Moore had learned from Pudlu that Will had begun losing his faith while at the detachment. It troubled both of them.

Not long after the Christmas Eve service, perhaps because of it, Moore confronted Will.

"My friend, tell me what happened to shake your faith. I'm here to listen."

"It's not that I lost God, James. I just came to believe that he was never there in the first place. I have read the passages about doubting Thomas, and I have read and remembered a verse in Matthew 22: *Love the Lord with all thy mind.* My mind cannot grapple with or reconcile the pain and suffering I've seen with the concept of the loving father."

"Perhaps in time, Will. God is patient and so am I."

Frequently, Will joined dogsled hunting parties for seals, caribou, and muskox. To everyone, at the post or in the camps, he said, "If you see Pudlu, please tell him that I'm here."

At Pond Inlet, he learned to accept, even adjust to, the dark months. Dundas Harbour had had 10 more days of darkness; at Pond Inlet, the sun set for the last time five days later, on November 7, and rose five days earlier, on January 29. The cold and storms were familiar; many nights he wondered if the roof would come off in the teeth of gale-force winds. A lifeline linked the three main dwellings together.

He did not fight the isolation. He embraced it. He longed for Naudla and thought of her every day. He was alone, but he was not lonely. He too was patient.

Will was balancing an account when a new arrival stepped up to the counter. Before he could finish his entry, he heard familiar words.

"Ullaakuut, nukara. Hello, Will."

Will looked up. "Pudlu! What a sight for sore eyes. I knew sooner or later you would come." Will rushed around the counter. The men shook hands, hugged, laughed, and slapped each other's shoulders. And then stood silently looking each other straight in the eye.

Will was the first to speak. "There is so much to talk about. I have a thousand questions."

"William, Mr. Edmunds, I'm going to leave you to close for the day. Tell the others to come back tomorrow."

"Let's go to the house, Pudlu."

The small 16-by-24-foot manager's house was next to the trading post. A kitchen and sitting room with a stove and two tiny bedrooms.

Will stoked the fire and filled the kettle. "We will have a drink later before supper. How far away are you camped? Where is the family? Where is ...?"

"One question at a time, Will. I have much to tell you."

Will sat down. Pudlu looked straight at him.

"The news is not good. Teemotee is dead. Naudla is far away in the south. She was very sick when they took her last year. I don't know if she is alive but I want to send a letter." He took a small envelope out of his parka and set it on the table beside him.

Will could see that it was addressed simply to Naudla. He immediately suspected that she could be in a TB sanitorium in Hamilton or Edmonton. For the one-pelt price the Bay charged for sending a letter, the Bay should damn well find out which institution.

"What kind of sickness? What happened?"

"Remember Teemotee often coughed hard. It got worse, and he had trouble breathing. Maybe TB. Naudla got the same way. I pray that she is okay now."

"Where are you camped? Who is there?"

"Not far from Arctic Bay, in Admiralty Inlet, about 100 miles away. My mother and my new wife are looking after Kootoo and little Amaujaq." Will sensed that Pudlu was becoming uncomfortable. Pudlu paused, filled, and slowly lit his pipe, the way he often did to buy time in order to reflect and choose his words.

Will filled his pipe. He rarely smoked now, but when he did, only a pipe rather than hand-rolled cigarettes.

"Congratulations, Pudlu, you should have a wife and life mate. Why didn't you bring them? I would like to meet them and see Kootoo."

"Would you like to see Naudla's new son?"

"Of course. Why wouldn't I?"

"Will, he has your eyes and hair."

Will was speechless. James Moore's words a few months ago now made sense.

"I want to see him, Pudlu. I could never tell anyone, but I loved, and still love, Naudla more than any person in this world. I came back because I have to see her."

Pudlu was fidgeting with his matches in one hand and the pipe in the other.

Will picked up the teapot and filled two mugs.

"I'm sorry about Teemotee. I liked him, and I know that he was good to Naudla. But I couldn't help my feelings for Naudla. How did he react?"

"He also loved my sister very much. He accepted and loved Amaujaq too because he was part of her. You know by now that we are more open with these things than you Qallunaat."

"And you and I, Pudlu? Are we still the same?"

"Yes. Naudla would not have been with you if she did not want to."

"Pudlu. I'm here because I want to find her. I don't know if she'll have me. But I promise this, I won't abandon them."

Will opened cans of the best potatoes, vegetables, and a smoked ham that he knew was Pudlu's favourite Qallunaat food. He added the bread that he had baked that morning and cheddar cheese.

"By the way, Will, your friend is tied outside with my dog team."

"Bring him in now. Is he looking after you?"

"Eee. Very good dog."

Will knew that Pudlu would be shaking his head when he went to get the big dog. "Nobody but Qallunaat would bring a dog into the house," he likely would be telling himself.

Inspector hesitated at the door when Pudlu untied him. He stooped. Stared and sniffed toward Will for a few seconds, and then barked and bounded forward. It was a joyous reunion, leaving Pudlu roaring with laughter at the spectacle.

"Old friend, what you don't understand is that I wouldn't have survived without that dog, in more ways than one. And I never forgot you're the guy who left him behind."

Pudlu was still smiling, shaking his head. "Eee. Eee."

Will filled three plates and put one in the corner near the stove. Inspector gulped it down, then lay quietly. He had not forgotten the house rules.

Will poured each of them a rum drink and put the bottle in the cupboard. He had adopted a ritual. One drink with dinner, no more, and some nights, none at all.

Will picked up a fork, held it, and then set it down.

"I had hoped that you would come back to Dundas Harbour, even if only for supplies."

"We did come back. Twice. Both times were very bad. We thought you were dead. We never saw you."

"When—when did you come?"

"First time, one year after we left, going west to summer camp at Cape Leopold."

"We see Zalapski and he waves, we turn to come in, and see Villeneuve come out of the building with a rifle and shoot at us. We turn away fast. Zalapski tried to take the rifle, Villeneuve knocked him down, then went inside and came out with the pistol. Push it to Zalapski's head and kill him.

"Next time, early October, we're going to Craig and look at the camp from the ice with scope for an hour and no sign of life. But we are also scared Villeneuve may be hiding.

"Then we move east and have to get closer to land at the big point because of open water, and we hear gunshots. One bullet killed a dog. Another went through runner where Kootoo was sitting. We needed to shoot back and we did."

"And someone shot the bastard?" Pudlu nodded. It was clear that he was nervous talking about it.

Will regretted the question the instant he asked it. "Who shot him?"

Pudlu stared silently. He couldn't lie and, at the same time, he couldn't tell the truth and incriminate a family member.

Will broke the tension with three words that were meant more as a statement than a question. "The best shot?"

Pudlu looked away. He could not speak.

Will tried to imagine the fear and anguish the family must have gone through.

A Mountie was dead. Who would believe them? Everyone knew how the full wrath of the law had come down on the Inuit of the Pond Inlet area a half-dozen years ago when hunters killed a crazed white man named Janes, who was threatening to kill everyone. One of their great leaders was taken away thousands of miles and died of TB, even though he was protecting the village.

Will tried to imagine the fear they must have lived with since then and the courage it took for Pudlu to come here and tell him.

"Why are you telling me now?"

"I have to. You'll find Naudla and learn then. Better if everything comes out now."

That unwavering trust almost brought Will to tears.

"Listen to me, Pudlu. Listen carefully. Don't tell the story again to anyone else. The big boss O'Halloran did not want to know the truth. He made it look like Villeneuve was killed by a ricochet, right in the heart. O'Halloran told a big lie so that there would be no investigation. He did not want the truth because he was afraid that it would make the Mounties look bad. He did not want to investigate because he did not want the world to know that Villeneuve, who was in charge of the patrol, was crazy. Crazy, same as Janes."

Will knew there were limits to Pudlu's knowledge of English, and he knew that the three dozen words he had recently heard would never serve to explain these complexities in Inuktitut.

"Tell me, do you understand? What did I say?"

"You said big boss Mountie lied, made it look like an accident like Villeneuve shot himself."

"Yes, and there's more. O'Halloran also wrote in his big book that Zalapski killed himself, because there was no way to prove otherwise, or that anyone else could have done it. What you saw happen should stay buried in Dundas Harbour.

"If you ever tell that you saw Villeneuve shoot Zalapski, then they'll ask if you know what happened to Villeneuve." Will allowed a half-minute of silence. He knew that Pudlu was thinking.

"Do you understand?"

"Eee. They think it's better to live with a big lie."

"Let me help you bring in whatever stuff you need, and you can have that spare bedroom for as long as you want to stay."

Will went to the Easter service with Pudlu. Being with him helped him feel closer to Naudla.

That evening after a meal, and over Pudlu's beautiful, carved chess set that the two were playing for the first time, Will was caught off guard.

"Do you still think God has abandoned you?"

Will was careful not to offend Pudlu. "I am sorry, my brother, but I cannot believe it any longer. Too much has happened."

"Will, you try too hard not to believe. Look at the things that have happened that could only come from God. Like being able to come back here and find the truth."

Will looked him in the eye and heard the wisdom.

Pudlu smiled. "Taima. Checkmate."

The next morning, Will watched the qamutik fade into the sunrise, along the sea ice, Bylot Island in the background. Inspector was with Pudlu, where he belonged, at least until Will and Pudlu carried out their newly formed plan and pact.

The reverend had been watching the departure too. Pudlu was barely out of sight when he opened Will's door and was greeted with a usual backhanded compliment.

"It was a nice service, James. Pudlu and I each understood five words: 'the third day he rose again.'" They both laughed. The rest of the service had been in laboured Inuktitut. Everyone teased the reverend for the way he butchered the language, but he was miles ahead of every other white man.

"You know, I'm still ready to talk."

"Thanks, James. I'm working things out. Perhaps, as you say, in time. But I have a question. Why didn't you tell me that Teemotee was dead?"

"I needed it to come from Pudlu. I trust that you and he had a long talk about Naudla and Amaujaq?"

"We have, James. I can't tell you how it will end, or even where it begins, but we're determined to make things right for everyone."

Will's mind went back to the smile and satisfaction on Pudlu's weathered face, just an hour ago, when Will held up the letter addressed Naudla.

"I won't be mailing this, Pudlu. I'll deliver it. I'll find out where she is and I'll bring it to her. I won't lose hope that she's alive."

CHAPTER 15

IN GOD'S POCKET

Will checked the scribbled map the nurse had drawn for him at the reception desk at the Hamilton Sanitorium for Tuberculosis.

The sprawling several hundred acres on the city's west mountain were impressive—clear air, wide views of the countryside, far away from the smoke and grime of the city. Hamilton, Canada's fifth-largest city—where the poorest lived in cramped, poverty conditions—suffered the worst of the TB pandemic in the nation.

The sanitorium complex contained more than half a dozen barracks-style buildings, many of them housing soldiers who had returned from the deplorable conditions of the trenches, infected with the highly contagious and dreaded disease. For too many, if it wasn't shell shock, it was TB, and for God knows how many, it was both. Doctors looked for a location with plenty of fresh air in a tranquil setting to try to help TB victims breathe—because there was no cure.

The map said building 5, southwestward.

Will walked down a long corridor, passing rows of beds and curtained-off wards, to a room at the end. It was just after 2 p.m., and he was in line with the strict visiting hours.

He could hear a familiar sound, an accordion playing a soft jig, a kind of private concert. Will didn't know the tune, but when he turned into the sunny room, he knew the performer, even from behind. He recalled hearing her play once, in the cabin for the children.

His heart stopped. He stood speechless, watching and listening, mesmerized by the shiny black hair flowing down her back, dancing back and forth across her shoulders in rhythm, her slender waist hidden behind the wooden chair back. He could see her long legs and one foot tapping out the time of her gentle tune.

Others in the room, about eight, were watching him. He raised a finger to his lips, for silence.

He stepped closer as her tune finished, and from directly above her came the words "Takuvagit naliaivagit. My love, I found you."

For five full seconds, Naudla did not move. Will placed his hand on her shoulders. "I found you, my love. Takuvagit naliaivagit. I found you."

He was now in front of her, her hands in his and the accordion on the floor. He lifted her to her feet, her eyes filling with tears of joy and her fragile chest heaving. They embraced. Everyone left the room, including an elderly nurse who seemed puzzled at the tender moment between a white man and an Inuit patient.

Will and Naudla held on to one another, afraid to break the embrace, afraid they might wake and find that it was a dream.

Will opened his eyes. He saw a worn sofa near the window and led Naudla toward it, never letting go, as though they were waltzing.

"Will ... I missed you ... every day I missed you, but I knew you would come someday."

"You are speaking English—very good."

"They teach us ... we have to learn ... no one knows our language."

They fell back into silence, staring into each other's eyes. Will touched her cheek, then took her face in his hands and kissed her lips long and softly.

Still holding her face, it was his turn to speak.

"Naudla, I'm sorry about Teemotee." She nodded. It was her turn to hug and hold him.

"Pudlu told me about Amaujaq. I want us to be together, you, me, Amaujaq, Kootoo, and Pudlu."

"Yes, Will, I want to be with you too."

They looked into each other's eyes with smiles to seal life's grand commitments and promises.

The rules said that Will could stay only until 4 p.m. The reunited couple spent more time holding one another and realizing that their dream had come true than talking.

Will passed Naudla an envelope. Inside she found two letters from Pudlu; the one he had written before finding Will and the one he had written after their visit.

Pudlu confirmed that her family was being looked after and always would be and that, when she recovered, they would all be reunited. Pudlu also noted that Will had promised that no police-ee would ask questions about how Villeneuve had died. That they ruled that he had killed himself. Will watched relief and smiles on Naudla's face as she read the words from home.

Looking out the big window, Will was surprised by how many

big wards had been constructed and the extent to which TB was sweeping across the country. It was much worse now than when he had gone to Devon Island four years ago.

Naudla had been very ill when she arrived. She could have died—as many did. TB was often too far advanced by the time patients arrived at the sanatorium. There were 10 other Inuit in the ward and that many more Indians. Another part of the building was for Blacks. All other buildings were for whites. All in all, 700 patients were housed at the sanatorium.

Will hugged Naudla one last time and promised to be back tomorrow. On the way out, he spoke to the nurse, who he recognized was probably not stern, but overworked. He asked if she could arrange for him to meet with Naudla's doctor. Will made it clear that he was Naudla's family. He would return the next day and as often as he could after that.

It was a warm, sunny day in late September. Will stepped out of the sanitorium ward, grasping the irony that, one year ago, he was northbound on the Nascopie for Pond Inlet, hoping to find her—while that same ship had picked her up a week later, 300 miles away, and brought her to this place.

Will walked the 3 miles down the mountain to the city centre and his room at the Royal Connaught. He was elated that he had found Naudla and was ecstatic that he had a son, He was also guilt-ridden and despondent because he had never seen Amaujaq.

He thought about the five months since he had watched Pudlu disappear down Eclipse Sound, Inspector in harness. Will had committed to finding Naudla, and when she was better, bring her home.

In the meantime, Pudlu committed to looking after the family—

his mother, Kootoo, Amaujaq, and his new wife, Kenojuak. Come hell or high water, Will had promised Pudlu that there would be a letter waiting for him in Pond Inlet when the *Nascopie* arrived the next August, 1930.

Finding Naudla had not been difficult. The captain of the *Nascopie* was quick to fill him in. As soon the ship arrived in Pangnirtung, a doctor determined that Naudla and two others had to be taken south, and he had accompanied them.

There's a lot to be thankful for, Will thought.

A few days later, Will met with Dr. Peter Preston, a short balding man, probably in his 50s, with wire-rimmed glasses and tired eyes. Preston agreed that Naudla could have short one-hour visits, but no more than once a week on average.

"There is no cure for this, only rest and more rest. I am very optimistic about Naudla's recovery so far, but that makes me cautious not to overdo or rush the process. Seeing you occasionally, knowing that you're close, will help, but we cannot allow any exertion or excitement."

Will explained to Preston, as he had to Naudla, that he would be travelling to Winnipeg for a few weeks, but would soon return. The doctor agreed that Will could visit again, perhaps within 72 hours before his departure west.

"I have presents for you, my love." Will and Naudla sat in the screened outdoor sitting room at the end of the ward.

Will opened shopping bags and passed her gift-wrapped packages that the department-store clerk had helped him select. First, a white and gold brush, comb, and mirror set. Naudla immediately stroked the brush through her long hair.

Next, a red blouse, blue skirt, chocolates, nylon stockings, and—especially luxurious—a bottle of red nail polish. Naudla smiled. Susan Howat and a few other nurses had red nails and she liked the look.

He could tell from his first visit that all the Inuit and Indian patients, and no doubt the soldiers too, lacked the comforts of any small luxuries. He knew that, for the first time in her life, Naudla felt pampered. Her smile indicated that she enjoyed it.

He passed her the last package. Her face lit up at the sight of two children and a puppy asleep on a blanket, in the red and yellow tundra lichen of Devon Island. Above the children, on the left, a woman with raven hair reaches to the ledges of the mountainside, white birds over her head, and, on the right, the spectacular blue sky and sweeping ice of Lancaster Sound cast light across the canvas. This was the first painting that Will was pleased with. He had tried painting the scene at least 10 times before he was satisfied that it was the best he could do.

That evening, he took the train to Toronto's Union Station and connected with the CPR Imperial going west.

He was well rested three days later when he walked into Geoffrey MacKinnon's office at HBC Winnipeg, and the exuberant Scot was excited with his ledger and log results. Will showed a good profit, and he knew that the Inuit made him look good with the number of furs they had brought in.

"I hope we can convince ye to go back, Will."

"Geoffrey, I want to go back and I plan to, but my priorities are elsewhere, actually in Hamilton in the TB sanitorium." Will recounted part of the story of Dundas Harbour but not intimate details. He was clear about his priority and focus and recounted his story and love for Naudla. "Geoffrey, I'll go back when I can take her with me. Could that be next year or the year after? No one knows, not even the doctor. I can't stay here. I'll look for a job in Hamilton or Toronto to be close."

"What about Montreal, Will? We have a big operation there. Let me write to my connection. I bet he can use you." He wrote down the address for Dougal Gordon, another Scot. "Try and contact him in about 10 days."

A week later, Will was back at the sanitorium, devastated. He was told that no visitor could enter without first speaking to the doctor. He waited in the corridor for over an hour when, finally, the harried doctor called him into a small office.

"Naudla has had a setback. These things happen. Too damn often." The doctor explained that the medical team might collapse one of her lungs, or both alternately, for several days to rest them and then inflate. It was a highly unpleasant and risky procedure, but the only treatment that they knew.

"You know, Doctor, only a few days ago I was speaking with the Hudson's Bay Company about both of us returning north next summer."

"I won't say that's impossible, Mr. Grant. I don't know where we will be in nine or 10 months or even in two years. But Naudla has had a setback, although it is the first one she has had. Until now, her recovery had been quite remarkable."

The doctor could read the confusion and panic on Will's face. "You can see her for five minutes just to let her know you are here and how much you care."

She was in a ward with eight other patients. Will could see that she was having difficulty breathing. He stroked her hair with her new brush. "They'll let me stay only for a few minutes, my love. Don't talk, just rest."

She smiled, squeezed his hand in hers, and held it for the entire time he was there.

He kissed her gently. "I'll check on you every day and see you when you are feeling better. Nalligivagit. I love you."

Geoffrey MacKinnon's contact paid off wonderfully.

Will Grant was back on the HBC payroll, this time in Montreal as a fur buyer, and well positioned to carry out the plan he and Pudlu had put in place a few months ago.

He had been given a ticket to the annual Montreal fur auction. Although the worst stock-market crash in history had happened just a few weeks previous, the ballroom of the stately Windsor Hotel held more than 60 linen-covered tables, set for almost 500 guests. Wine and whisky were being poured at four large bars, one in each corner, surrounded by elegant marble columns, all under the magnificent dome.

The financial world might be crumbling, but the fur trade was a gold rush in its own right, and discoveries were opening across the Arctic, especially in the west.

Decanters of fine red wine sat on each table. Will nodded greetings to people, although he knew no one, and looked for his assigned seat at table 48.

A hand tapped his shoulder. "Will Grant, it's a small world, isn't it?"

Will turned to see the smiling face of Inspector Ransom O'Halloran—but in a tuxedo, not the familiar uniform.

"Inspector! What a surprise."

"I am no longer an inspector, Will, but a good civilian just like you." O'Halloran watched as someone checked a name tag and quickly interjected, easily persuading the fellow to swap for a seat at table 16, "much closer to the front and easier access to the bars."

"When I came out of Pangnirtung last year, I received news that my father had died suddenly. He owned a fur brokerage in Winnipeg. It was in the family for 60 years, and it fell to me to take over."

Will was glad for the company. His new boss, Dougal Gordon, would be pleased to see him mixing as well.

"Will, how about we enjoy the evening? Want to meet me here tomorrow night and you and I go for dinner? Word got around that you went back last year to Pond Inlet. There's a lot to talk about. But this is not the place."

"Tomorrow night is ideal. How about 6 p.m., after I finish for the day?"

Will and O'Halloran enjoyed each other's company, laughed at the comic, enjoyed the music and the food, and drank a little too much.

Will was more than a little hungover as he sat at his desk in a shared office with two letters, one from Naudla's nurse, Susan Howat, and the other from Geoffrey MacKinnon.

Susan's letter was concerning. Naudla was still confined to her bed, but Dr. Preston had decided not to collapse her lungs. He was afraid that it would make matters worse. Will was determined to leave on Friday night and head back to the sanitorium.

The letter from MacKinnon informed Will that HBC was going to open a new post at Gjoa Haven in the Central Arctic, endeavouring to tap into the lucrative possibilities in that region. "Mr. Grant," he urged, "you would be the ideal post manager."

The possibility of realizing his plan with Pudlu was improving. That evening at dinner, O'Halloran wasted no time coming to the point. "I've just returned from the Western Arctic, Aklavik actually, and I've bought a schooner. I'm going to invest there, with the white fox trade. It's a gold mine and I'm looking for a partner that I can trust."

Will was dumbfounded. "Naudla is my priority, Ransom. I'm going to be with her, come hell or high water. But as she needs to recover, I can't make any decisions right now."

"Don't decide anything right now. Just think about it for the winter. I can wait a bit, I can also find others, but you bring the most to the table with your stability and good judgment."

"Tell me about the schooner."

"It's a great boat, 58 feet long, 15 tons. Modern, with a gas engine, and draws less than a fathom. The idea is to bring the trade to the trappers, by visiting them along the coast of Victoria Island, which is crawling with foxes. We would also build a small post. It's a great country, Will, with a longer summer too."

O'Halloran grew more excited and persuasive. "I'm putting up the money for the boat and its operation and will take 75 per cent of the profits. I'm offering you 25 per cent."

Will did the arithmetic. With current prices, he could earn three times more than his current $1,500 a year.

O'Halloran correctly anticipated Will's hesitancy related to Naudla and Dundas Harbour. He leaned forward. "You don't need to respond to what I'm going to tell you. I know you're still troubled by Villeneuve, but remember, that case will never be reopened. You need to know that the Round Little Reverend likes to talk, especially when he's had more than one belt of rum. He told me, even before I got to Devon, that the Eskimos around Pond Inlet were talking about a group being shot at out on the ice, near the detachment, even spoke of a bullet through the qamutik runner. It seems that one of them was a far better shot than our highly trained Mountie. Imagine that! The Force would never risk that story ever being told. And besides, Will, self-defence is justice, and frontier justice is also justice."

O'Halloran cut into his steak. Will sat speechless until the former inspector issued the last word. "It's closed. Let's never raise it again. Just take your time thinking about the offer. You have my address in Winnipeg."

Will gave O'Halloran the same response that he had sent to MacKinnon. "I need to wait at least for the new year to decide anything." Both men accepted.

Since the days when Naudla had been confined to the bed and the dismal ward, everything had gone their way. By early 1930, she was again able to move around, and month by month her breathing improved, as did her strength.

Will lay awake in a berth as the train rumbled westward through the autumn northern Ontario night. The north does move in cycles—everything seems to take a year or a year and a half, but it tends to work out.

Each time the sleeper car pitched from side to side, he felt Naudla move closer to him. He never wanted to spend another night away from her. Five days ago, November 7, 1930, they were married by the Anglican minister in the sanitorium chapel, the day she was released. Dr. Preston and Susan Howat were the witnesses.

The newlyweds had spent time in Toronto at the King Edward and were moving temporarily to Edmonton. As vice-president of Irish & Scots Trading Company, Will had to get ready for the next season, with his partner O'Halloran.

O'Halloran accepted Will's counter-offer to join him in Aklavik, become familiar with the schooner and the country, and trade at camps along the coast west of Tuktoyaktuk and north along the south coast of Victoria Island. They hired an Inuk guide, Allen Okpik, who had travelled eastward 20 years earlier from Alaska. Allen reminded Will of Pudlu, with his knowledge of and comfort and confidence in the surroundings.

They laid out some fuel and lumber caches. At the end of October, their small post at Holman Point was no more than a tent, but they had laid the foundation and floor of the new post, strategically 125 miles or halfway between the larger posts at Coppermine and Cambridge Bay.

The train rumbled and swayed westward. Will felt Naudla move closer. "Everything okay?"

"Couldn't be better, my love."

Will looked at the letter he had received from Geoffrey MacKinnon two weeks earlier.

The plan was unfolding. Pudlu received letters from Will and Naudla, and Geoffrey arranged passage for Pudlu, the family, and three others on the *Nascopie* to Gjoa Haven in the summer of 1930. Pudlu agreed to work to build the post over the winter and, in the spring, travel 250 miles overland across King

William Island and traverse the ice-covered Alexandra Strait to Cambridge Bay on Victoria Island.

Naudla loved the train ride, sitting for hours looking out the window. Every cow, horse, or herd of sheep made her laugh.

Dr. Preston had warned Will that she was still recovering and needed a great deal of rest. Will promised that seven more months waiting in Edmonton for the next journey north would provide that.

They both underwent medical checkups and were declared in good health. The doctor said that Naudla's lungs sounded strong, exactly the way she felt and acted. As promised, Will wrote a note to Susan and Dr. Preston with the good news.

The couple spent the winter in a small rented house overlooking the North Saskatchewan River, close to the city centre. They attended evening classes at the university, painting lessons for Will, English lessons for Naudla. Twice a week, they went to the movies, ate ice cream sundaes, and talked about and longed for their children.

By mid-June, they had travelled 500 miles on the Great Northern Railway and 200 more miles on the Athabasca River system aboard the sternwheeler SS *Distributor*.

Will, Naudla, and O'Halloran sat in a horse-drawn mud-caked carriage near the Northwest Territories and Alberta border. Days were sunny and warm and the mosquitoes swarmed. Yet spirits were good. They had been told about the 16-mile portage from Fort Fitzgerald around four runs of vicious whitewater rapids on the Slave River to Fort Smith, where the second sternwheeler, *Mackenzie*, awaited.

WHIT FRASER

Behind them, a series of tractors and skids and more horses worked day and night hauling 200 tons of freight over the well-worn path, loading it for the communities along the big river and beyond to the Arctic coast.

Will considered and compared the 16-mile portage, with horses and heavy machinery, with Pudlu's journey. He had studied the maps and marvelled at his take-it-for-granted attitude toward Pudlu's undertaking.

He turned to O'Halloran. "Ransom, do you find it incredible that Pudlu, his elderly mother, his wife, and two kids are conquering the Northwest Passage the hard way, with a 250-mile portage across King William Island? I bet they'll never get their name in the newspapers or history books."

"We are worlds apart, Will, worlds apart." O'Halloran asked Naudla if she was worried about her family.

Will watched, listened, welcomed the exchange, and tried to anticipate the answer. He was pleased that Naudla had come to trust O'Halloran and accepted her husband's pledge that no one, especially O'Halloran, would ever ask about what had happened out on the ice nearly four years ago.

"I know they'll all be okay," she said. "Days all sun now and getting warm, big flat land, caribou, muskox. Pudlu knows lots of people, the Netsilingmiut who live on Qikiqtaq Island and where they camp."

That evening they were on board the *Mackenzie* to begin the 1,600-mile journey down the Slave River, across southwestern Great Slave Lake, and into the big river itself. The ship was comfortable and the small cabin and bed warm and clean. The food was also good and generally fresh, a far cry from the old *Nascopie*.

Brief stops were made at half a dozen villages to deliver supplies. What struck Will and his travelling companies was that Canada had two great Norths—the barren but beautiful Eastern Arctic, and the Northwest, with its rich vegetation, mountains, and magical rivers, like this one, the MacKenzie.

Fort Good Hope, a small settlement high on the east bank of the big river, impressed them the most.

"So many fish drying, so many furs to trade," Naudla remarked. A church bell rang, the most beautiful sound either of them had ever heard. "I want to go there."

The sound had come from a tiny white church, 25 feet wide, less than 50 feet long, with a big steeple with a cross on top, signifying that it was Catholic, overlooking the magnificent river. A French priest welcomed them. The interior and altar were beautifully carved by local parishioners. The altar had exquisite bright colours, blues that reminded him of pictures he had seen of the Sistine Chapel at the Vatican. The church had been built by Oblate priests almost 60 years earlier.

Father Emile Petitot was responsible for the artwork. Will and Naudla were astounded that something so mesmerizing existed this deep in the wilderness; Will, even more so, by the art lesson he received from the priest. The oils had been extracted from fish caught in the river. All of the colours and pigments were extracted from local plants and wildflowers in the area, or the blood of animals hunted in the daily search for food.

Will remembered Pudlu's first linguistic lesson. "We know these people as Indians, but what do they call themselves?"

The answer was emphatic. "Dene."

They sat silently in the magnificent handcrafted pews in

front of the ornate altar. Will watched Naudla kneel and pray, and he knelt beside her.

Something came over him, a feeling long ago lost, a sense of spirit and serenity. Will did not speak. Something long lost inside him had been found, even discovered. He took Naudla's hand and they knelt for several more minutes side by side.

The bell rang again. From inside the church it was even more magnificent.

Four days later, the *Mackenzie* tied up at Aklavik, the hub of the Mackenzie delta, a rip-roaring trader's town that served as the post and main transportation network for Yukon, Alaska, and the vast western and high Arctic.

It was hard to tell who was a permanent resident and who had pitched a tent for trading days and supplies. Of the few hundred people milling around, half were Dene. About an equal number of Inuit were present and even though Naudla knew that they spoke a different dialect, she was glad to try and talk with anyone in her language. She had also heard this western dialect at the sanatorium and was prepared.

Naudla made the first official trade for the Irish & Scots Trading Company.

She was most impressed by the thousands of muskrat furs tied in bales from all over the rich Mackenzie and Yukon deltas. She loved the soft silky fur, perfect for mitts, caps, or boots, inside or out. She traded cloth, needles, threads and scissors, tea, and sugar with several women for a dozen prime pelts. Her activity attracted other Inuit, and soon Will and O'Halloran were doing a booming trade, selling about 205 of their trade goods.

Naudla was comfortable walking the muddy streets talking

with people as best she could. Will, O'Halloran, Allen Okpik, and a Catholic priest looking for a passage to Cambridge Bay loaded the schooner and got her ready to sail as soon as possible.

O'Halloran had recruited the priest on the SS *Mackenzie* during the voyage. Father Rene Lemur confessed that he wasn't a sailor but he could tie knots, pull on a rope, and obey orders. He could not have been more than 25 years old, quite handsome with dark hair and complexion. Two months earlier he had left his home in France to answer God's call.

Will was glad to have one more hand on deck. His own hands were wrapped around the wheel of the schooner as they crossed Mackenzie Bay and he felt quite at home. With good weather, they estimated that they could travel the 1,000 miles to Cambridge Bay in seven to 10 days. They worked in shifts at the wheel: Will, Okpik, and O'Halloran.

Will was pleased that the sails were set and a good breeze was bringing them along at 12 knots. What he lacked in skills he knew Okpik could take up in slack. Pudlu would be first mate once they arrived at Cambridge Bay.

He set a course westward along the Arctic coast to Paulatuk and the smoking hills, a great natural phenomenon where deposits of underground oil shale, sulfur, and brown coal spontaneously ignite. They marvelled at miles of smoke columns belching skyward.

Coal deposits along the shoreline were plentiful and free for the taking and they bagged more than 2 tons to drop at the new Holman Point post with more stores and building supplies.

In a month, they had covered 3,000 miles from Edmonton to Cambridge Bay. About two dozen people were on the shoreline when Will inched against the little dock, using the motor, the sails tied and furled.

He scanned every face, as did Naudla. Not one was familiar.

Panic set in. Onshore, people were politely waving, but couldn't comprehend this vessel where no one waved back, but just stared.

O'Halloran was the first onshore and sought out the lone Mountie.

"We're looking for our party from the east," he said. "They should have been here by now."

He was quickly informed that it had been an unusual year— no one had been able to cross either the Alexandra or Victoria Straits that separate Victoria Island from King William Island. The broken ice shifted all winter, with vicious open leads making travel impossible.

Fear set in. Could Pudlu and the children have been swallowed up in the open leads? Were they stranded and adrift 1,000 miles away, or sitting in a sheltered cove waiting to be rescued?

Will and O'Halloran agreed on a plan. They off-loaded more than half the trade stores on the beach. O'Halloran would remain in Cambridge, carry out the trade, and return to Aklavik on the next freighter or tug, with Okpik. Separating was a tough decision, but O'Halloran had no choice. He could not risk being stranded for a full year.

Will, Naudla, and a guide from the community would continue westward in the schooner *Christine* toward King William Island. They suspected that Pudlu may have found a camp to wait it out.

Naudla could not speak. Being this close to her children and brother, wondering if she would ever see them again, was unbearable.

Father Rene wanted to go with Will, and he was welcomed. The Mountie, Corporal Steve Campbell, also a Nova Scotian, would go with him as well. He had considerable seafaring skills. The five set out on the high tide after only 30 hours in Cambridge.

The Inuk guide, Sala, was quieter than most northern men. But he was capable, and his eyes never left the shorelines. He directed Will toward a large island, off the southeast tip of Victoria Island, 15 miles into the Strait. They circled the island twice. Seeing no signs of life, Will steered toward King William. Sala suggested that they also check out two smaller islands 20 miles ahead, closer to King William.

On the evening of the third day out of Cambridge Bay, they were using the motor, and came around the south end of the second small island. Will, steering and scanning the shoreline, saw something move.

His first instinct was that it was a polar bear or a wolf, but when two smaller figures emerged, Will had a hunch. He could now identify a big dog running along the shoreline and hear faint barking. The two other figures were small boys.

Will pulled hard on the horn. The dog and figures stopped and looked westward. The figures then ran northward and disappeared around a point.

In minutes, Will had passed the same point. Naudla was beside him. She had seen the tail end of the little figures and was crying. Will knew it was from joy.

Finally, they saw them: three tents, dogs, half a dozen people on the shoreline waving, and this time, those on the schooner waved back.

Will could see Pudlu's smiling face as he motioned him closer to the shore, indicating deep water. He pulled in close enough to lay down the gangplank. Sala dropped the anchor, and Campbell threw Pudlu a rope to tie the stern.

Naudla ran down the plank, grabbing and hugging Kootoo and Amaujaq. The little boy was shy. He hadn't seen his mother for three years, since he was two years old. He knew her from his grandmother's and uncle's stories, but now he felt her warmth, her tears, and her love.

Will stepped forward. Kootoo smiled and ran to him. He was 11, a big boy with a strong and steady look. He put his arms around Will's waist and hugged him.

Naudla carried Amaujaq over to Will, who broke into uncontrollable tears. How he loved this little boy that he had never set eyes on but had seen in his mind and heart. How unmistakeable he was, with piercing blue Grant eyes. Knowing that it takes two sets to make blue eyes, Will considered the reality. *Naudla's Viking connection.* Naudla said "Attata, father," and as naturally as Will and Naudla had been drawn together all those years ago, Amaujaq went to Will, who embraced him tightly. The little boy laid his small head on a big shoulder and smiled at his mother. Kootoo wedged between them.

Now Pudlu was hugging, laughing, and gesturing. The celebration had been a long time coming.

Introductions were made: Naudla's mother, Meeka; Pudlu's wife, Kenojuak. Standing off to the side, a man with a familiar round hairy face. The Right Round Reverend James Moore, devoted missionary to the core, spreading the Word.

That night they had a feast with fresh bannock, fish, tinned potatoes, and fruit and chocolate for the boys. Will, Naudla, and Amaujaq slept together on the *Christine.*

As Pudlu explained, they were never in danger. They encountered the open water a mile off the island and knew that there was no way around, and simply turned back. "I knew you would find us."

Early in the morning, the group set sail for Cambridge Bay. As they rounded the southwest cape, they could see in the distance that the barge and tug were still anchored.

They spent the night in Cambridge Bay, the two vessels tied together, and had a second celebration dinner on the deck of the *Christine* with fresh Arctic char, bread, pies, and a tiny rum ration that Reverend Moore particularly savoured. Will was glad to see that the reverend and Father Rene got along well. "Same boss," he thought and then turned to Corporal Campbell while pointing to the Cambridge clergy.

"Steve, you'll have your work cut out for you with these two."

"How's that?"

"They'll be fighting for converts with duelling pistols at 10 paces."

The two ministers and the Mountie enjoyed a great laugh.

Naudla, Pudlu, and the other Inuit looked puzzled.

The next morning *Christine* was under full sail, a gentle wind off the stern. The aft was packed with dogs, half of them howling. Inspector was close to Naudla, Amaujaq, and Kootoo, sitting near the bow. Kootoo was holding the 30-30 rifle that Will had just given him. They were looking out for seals. Will guessed that he was already a good shot; but if not, from here on he'd have a good teacher.

Pudlu was close by, sitting on a box. It was Sunday and he was reading his bible.

The tug and barge had left an hour earlier, but with the wind in his sails, Will overtook them. He could see O'Halloran by the wheelhouse of the little tug, watching.

Will smiled, knowing that last night had changed everyone.

After the second celebration and farewell party, Will, Pudlu, and O'Halloran had been sitting on the deck. Suddenly Pudlu spoke.

"Tell him the truth, Will. Set us all free. Tell him the truth."

O'Halloran was confused.

Will spoke softly. "Ransom, it's simple. He wants you to know that when Villeneuve was shot, he was trying to kill four people who had witnessed the cold-blooded murder of Constable Erik Zalapski. The same four people Villeneuve tried to shoot in 1925 when they approached Dundas Harbour from the sea ice.

"When Zalapski tried to stop him, Villeneuve shot him through the head at point-blank range. Four people, one of them a child, saw it. The next year, Villeneuve tried to kill these witnesses when open water forced them close to the post, at East Point."

Will paused for several seconds. O'Halloran could not speak.

Will continued. "We know the Force and the country will never admit to what happened there. Zalapski has been forced to take one for the team. We know he would have been willing to do that for eternity because that was his character."

Slowly, O'Halloran stood and walked to Pudlu.

"Pudlu, I'm sorry. I apologize. I chose Villeneuve. I don't know if the Force will change the record but they too will know the truth, and so will Zalapski's parents. I give you my word. Pudlu, you have set me free as well. Nakurmiik."

Pudlu had accepted the apology. Pudlu had also set himself free, not from the lies but from that ancient Ilira, that inherited fear of Qallunaat.

Will looked to the port side, his old boss, new friend, and partner gave one final long wave.

He studied the wise and serene Pudlu again and thought of where they had been, and all that had happened to bring them together on this little boat. What guided them? What protected them? What had guided and protected Naudla and Will and brought them together?

He had never in his life felt better than in that moment, never more secure, more serene.

His left hand was on the wheel. His right hand slipped into his jacket pocket and his three fingers caressed the well-worn edges of the little leather-bound black bible that he had carried for so long, that throughout most of the ordeal lay discarded in the bottom of his footlocker.

Safe and home at last.

Safe as in God's pocket.

Taima.

ACKNOWLEDGEMENTS

Thank you to Arctic historian and author Season Osborne for keeping me on course and off the shoals on historic timelines and events. To my wife, Mary Simon, for translations and Inuktitut spelling assistance. To Doug Ward for his many years of encouragement to write about my Arctic experiences and for his review of the original manuscript.

Additional thanks to old CBC friends Dick Gordon, Alan Holman, Reg Sherren, and Marie Wilson for their suggestions and confirmation that *Cold Edge of Heaven* is indeed a "good story."

ABOUT THE AUTHOR

Whit Fraser was inspired to write *Cold Edge of Heaven* after visiting an abandoned Royal Canadian Mounted Police detachment at Dundas Harbour on Devon Island, which includes three hilltop graves.

Few Canadians have seen as much of the north as Fraser. Over more than 50 years, he has travelled to every corner and most communities of the north, from Labrador to Alaska, and throughout the circumpolar world, even to the North Pole itself. Fraser is a journalist, author, and vice-regal consort of Canadian Governor General Mary Simon. He is winner of the 2019 NorthWords Book Prize for *True North Rising*, a memoir of his work in Arctic communities.

He is a former chair of the Canadian Polar Commission and was executive director of Inuit Tapiriit Kanatami, the national Inuit organization.